The Red Room

M S MORRIS

This novel is a work of fiction and any resemblance to actual persons, living or dead, places, names or events, is purely coincidental.

M S Morris asserts the moral right to be identified as the author of this work.

Published by Landmark Media, a division of Landmark Internet Ltd.

msmorrisbooks.com

For Josie and John

CHAPTER 1

The letter lands on the doormat with a gentle thud, as if it is of little consequence.

I'm upstairs stacking a pile of neatly ironed tea-towels in the airing cupboard when I hear the sound of the letterbox opening and closing. Confused, I hurry downstairs to see what it is. It's Sunday today, so it can't be the postman because he only delivers Monday to Saturday.

A white envelope is lying on the doormat, face down. I pick it up and turn it over. I am startled to see that my name is written on the front in a flowing, cursive script. An old-fashioned style of handwriting, I think. An educated, thoughtful hand.

Mrs Jane Harvey.

That's my name. I stare at the words written in blue ink with a fountain pen with an italic nib, not fully comprehending them. No one has ever written to me before. Not to me, in my own name. But someone just has, and they've taken the trouble to deliver it by hand instead of putting it in the post. A personal touch.

I look out of the window to see who left it, but there is no one there, just the cold, damp winter landscape. The pearl grey sky is already growing dim in the late afternoon.

Adam's office door bangs open, making me jump, and in a moment he's at my side. 'What is it?' he asks. 'What have you got there?'

I suppress an urge to hide it from him, to conceal it under my clothing. It is my letter, addressed to me. But that is foolish. He has already heard the opening and closing of the letterbox. The thud of the letter landing in the hallway brought him here. Besides, there is no reason to hide the letter. I have no secrets to keep from my husband.

'It's a letter,' I say. 'Someone dropped it through the letterbox just now. It's addressed to me.'

'To you?' he says, going to the window. 'Who delivered it?'

'I don't know. They'd already gone when I arrived.'

He stares out of the window, as if hoping to catch the mysterious deliverer of letters still lurking there. 'Well, are you going to open it?' he asks. He looks mildly irritated, as if I have somehow let him down by receiving this strange letter addressed to me personally.

I wonder if I have, if I have failed him in some way. Now I am scared to open it.

As soon as he senses my uncertainty, he softens his voice. 'Go on,' he says. 'It's only a letter. It won't bite.'

I hold the letter a little longer, savouring the feel of it. My first letter. It might be anything. It might be nothing. Until I open it, I am caught in a delightful state of not knowing.

My hand trembles slightly as I slide a finger under the flap of the envelope and open it. Inside lies a folded sheet of good-quality writing paper. It offers a little resistance as I draw it out, paper sliding over crisp paper. I unfold it and read it to myself while Adam looks over my shoulder.

Dear Jane,
This is just a quick note to let you know that we're having a

little get-together at our house in the village on New Year's Eve and we'd be delighted if you and your husband (sorry we don't know his name) would like to come. Please let us know. We look forward to seeing you both there.

Best wishes,
Diana and Michael Potts (The Corner House)

An invitation to a party. I'm touched that someone has tramped all the way to our cottage, a mile outside the village, to deliver this invitation to me on a wet Sunday afternoon in late December. But I don't know how to respond to it. I have never been to a party before.

Adam gently takes the letter out of my hand and re-reads it properly himself.

'Do you know this Diana and Michael Potts?' he asks. 'You've never mentioned them.'

'Only vaguely,' I say, trying to remember who they are. 'I think I might have met her in the village shop once. Yes, that's it.' It comes back to me now. An older woman, with a face that was somehow both kind and stern, lively and ancient. 'She's a retired schoolteacher. I think her husband might have been a headmaster once. Cath introduced us. I haven't met her husband though.'

Adam walks through to the lounge, still holding the invitation. I follow him, waiting to hear what he has to say. I draw the curtains against the dark outside. It's only three o'clock but the light is already dwindling, being nearly the shortest day of the year.

'What do you think?' I prompt him. 'About the invitation, I mean.'

Adam scratches at the dark Sunday-afternoon stubble under his chin. 'It's very kind of them to invite us,' he says at last. 'I'm sure they mean well. But we'll have to decline.'

I thought he would say that, and I know he has good reason, but still I feel unaccountably disappointed. This was my invitation. My party.

'It wouldn't hurt to go, would it?' I ask. 'Just this once?

3

We wouldn't have to stay long.' We've been living in the village for years now, perhaps it's time. Perhaps it's time we got out a little. 'It seems rude to say no,' I add, searching for a reason to say yes.

'I'm only thinking of you,' he says gently, caressing the side of my face with his hand. 'You know you don't like crowds. I wouldn't want you to become stressed.'

He's right, of course. Adam's always right. And yet I'm sure I could handle a small gathering if he was there with me. 'The invitation says it's just a little get-together,' I say.

Adam chuckles. 'That could mean anything. They've probably invited the whole village and all the farmers and their families from miles around.'

I realise that's true. If they've invited me and Adam, they will have invited everyone. The whole village, and the farmers too. It sounds a lot, the way he says it, but how many people is that really? The village isn't that big. It's tiny in fact. But more people than I've ever faced at any one time. Adam's right. I don't like crowds. Or at least, I don't think I do.

Adam has already made his decision. He re-folds the invitation, puts it neatly back into its envelope and drops it into the waste paper basket.

'Don't worry about it,' he says. 'I'm sure there'll be plenty of other people there. They won't miss us if we don't show up. In fact, we barely even know them. We'll spend New Year's Eve together, just you and me like we always do.' He pulls me into his arms and kisses me on my forehead, hugging me tight. 'I love you, Jane,' he whispers into my ear.

'I love you too,' I say back to him.

CHAPTER 2

On Monday morning the alarm clock goes off early. Five o'clock. It's still pitch black outside and will be for hours yet.

'Don't get up,' says Adam. 'Go back to sleep.' He kisses me gently on the nape of my neck and climbs out of bed.

I roll over and try to sleep, but I can hear him moving about and getting into the shower. He leaves the cottage early on Mondays to drive to Leeds Bradford Airport where he catches the first flight to London. He works in the City, and during the week he lives in a house in Putney in West London.

There's no need for me to get up yet, of course. I have nowhere to go.

By five forty-five he's ready to leave. I put the bedside light on so I can see him better. The yellow light casts a warm glow over his face. His weekend stubble is all gone now, and he looks smart and handsome in a dark business suit and tie. 'I'll phone you at nine tonight as usual,' he says, bending down to plant a kiss on my lips.

'I'll be here,' I say, smiling up at him. I won't see him again until Friday evening. But he phones me every evening when he's away just to make sure I'm all right and to ask me about my day. I don't own a mobile phone. Adam says I don't need one. But I'm always here for him, waiting for his call.

After he's gone I turn off the light and stay in bed, dozing, until half past seven when the first cool light of the winter dawn starts to penetrate the room. I put on a dressing gown and pull back the bedroom curtains. Today the view of the Yorkshire countryside is grey and bleak. The treeless moorland is crisscrossed with dry stone walls and dotted with sheep standing motionless like woolly statues against the cold, northerly wind. The fields are coated with a thin layer of frost. On a fine summer day you can see for miles, but today the clouds have closed in tight, making the world feel small.

I go downstairs, put the kettle on and make myself some toast. After breakfast I shower and dress and then start on my list of jobs for the day. I put the laundry on, vacuum the downstairs and dust the lounge. Adam likes the place to be spotless when he returns at the end of the week. I'm about to empty the waste paper basket when I notice the letter from yesterday: the invitation from Diana and Michael Potts to their party on New Year's Eve. A sharp white envelope with that elegant blue handwriting. *Mrs Jane Harvey,* it says. I retrieve the letter and re-read it.

I like the handwriting. It's a flowing script which makes me think the person who wrote it must be intelligent and warm-hearted. Of course I don't know that for sure. I only met Diana Potts once very briefly, and Adam is always warning me about speaking to strangers. But she seemed nice, and it was kind of her to invite us. I realise that I would like to go to the party after all, despite what Adam said. But I don't want to go against his wishes. And he's probably right when he says it wouldn't agree with me. Still, I put the letter on the sideboard. I'll have another think about it later.

We're running low on milk and bread so I decide to

walk to the village shop. I wrap up warm against the cold December weather and set off down the lane.

Our cottage is a mile outside the village, which is itself tiny. Just a shop, a pub, a church and a cluster of houses, all built out of the local grey stone. There is no pavement down the country road so I stay close to the grass verge, but there are no cars anyway. The only sound is the gusting of the wind across the moor. In the springtime there is birdsong, but at this time of year the birds have fled to warmer places or have fallen silent.

On my way I see the postman's red van parked by the entrance to one of the farms. There's a small post box here and the postman is opening it to see if there are any letters for him to collect. The bright red van jars against the green fields tinged with white frost. It assaults my senses and I flinch from it. I never wear red.

'Morning,' calls the postman in a cheery voice as I walk past. 'Bit nippy today.'

'Yes, it is,' I say, hurrying on past the red van. Red for danger, red for blood. Soon I hear it drive away down the road again and I realise I have been holding my breath, waiting for it to leave. I exhale and my breath mists the air in front of me.

Ten minutes later I cross a small humpback bridge over the stream and find myself in the village. I pass the church with its ancient graveyard and the village pub which is closed at this time of day. There's no one about. The postman's van reappears, tooting its horn as it overtakes me on the narrow road, and by the time I arrive at the village shop it's parked outside.

I push open the door of the shop and an overhead bell jangles to announce my arrival. The shop, which doubles as a post office, is tiny but it sells milk, sliced bread and a selection of tinned soups. I decide I might as well buy a tin of mushroom soup for lunch whilst I'm here.

The postman is chatting to Cath who runs the shop with her husband. She is the only person I really know in

7

the village because she introduced herself to me years ago when we first moved here from Oxford. She was thrilled that some new people had moved to the village because, as she told me at the time, most of the young people couldn't wait to leave, finding it too isolated.

'I'll be glad when Christmas is over,' the postman is telling Cath in his thick Yorkshire accent. 'Folks with nowt to say to each other all year round suddenly feel the urge to send each other cards and letters. You wouldn't believe the mounds of post waiting for me back at the sorting office.'

He must mean the sorting office in the nearby town. I browse the shelves whilst I wait for him to leave.

'I love receiving Christmas cards though,' says Cath. 'Don't you? How's your wife by the way?'

Cath likes to chat to everyone. The postman tells her about his wife's operation, then picks up the sack of letters and leaves.

'Sorry to keep you, Jane,' says Cath as I hand over my small collection of items for her to put through the till. 'How are you?'

'I'm fine,' I say.

'Looks like we might have snow soon.' She glances out of the window. 'Are you doing anything special for Christmas? Visiting relatives or anything?'

'No,' I say. 'Adam and I don't really have any relatives. We'll just have a quiet Christmas at home.'

'That's nice,' says Cath. 'Our Christmases are never quiet.' She and her husband have two teenage boys. 'Still, it's nice to be with family, isn't it?'

I put the items into my shopping bag and pass her a ten pound note.

'Are you coming to the New Year's Eve party at the Potts's house?' she asks. 'I saw Diana yesterday and she said she was going to drop an invitation through your door.' She hands me my change.

I'm not sure what to tell her. 'I don't know,' I say, even though Adam was very clear about it. 'We don't normally go to parties.' I can feel the confusion rising in my chest and I'm sure I'm turning pink.

'Oh, go on,' she says, patting me gently on the arm. 'It'll do you both good to come and meet some people. Me and Ken will be there. There's no need to be shy.'

'I'm not shy,' I say quickly. 'Not really. It's just that…' I'm not sure what I'm trying to say to her. I can't tell her that I have never been to a party before. I can't tell her that Adam said no. 'I'll think about it,' I say finally.

Back outside I take a deep breath to steady my nerves. Maybe Cath is right. It might be a good idea to go to the party. Other people go to parties. I could too. I like Cath, and part of me thinks why not? Adam and I have lived here for more than seven years now. Perhaps it's time that we met a few more people.

When I arrive home I put the milk in the fridge, then I fetch the invitation from the sideboard. Adam won't like it if I disobey him, but I'm sure that he will understand if I explain to him why I want to go to the party after all. I feel that if I do this quickly, I will have the courage to see it through. Before I can change my mind I hastily write a reply on a spare piece of paper I find in Adam's office, seal it in an envelope, affix a stamp, and then walk down to the post box outside the farm to post it. The white envelope slips into the red box with a thud.

There, I've done it, I think as I go back to the cottage. We'll just go to the party for a short time. We don't have to stay long. If there are too many people, we can leave. And besides, Adam will look after me and make sure I don't come to any harm.

I spend the rest of the day doing jobs around the cottage. It's an old, stone building with three bedrooms upstairs. It's been modernised, but still retains its period charm. The rooms are all painted in neutral shades: cream, beige and magnolia. I dust around the upstairs windows and look out over the small plot of land that extends behind the cottage. In the summer I grow vegetables and flowers in the garden but at this time of year the ground is rock hard and bare. The frost has gone, but the grey clouds still press down heavily on the landscape. The light fades quickly under the leaden winter sky and I pull the curtains closed to keep in the warmth.

At nine o'clock I'm curled up on the sofa reading a novel when the phone rings. It's Adam of course. His evening phone call is never late.

I hear his deep, reassuringly familiar voice over the line. 'How are you?' he asks. 'Have you had a nice day?' He always starts with the same questions.

'I'm fine,' I say. 'How about you?'

'Oh, you know,' he says. 'Busy at work as always' – he has a senior position with the insurance market, Lloyd's of London – 'What have you been up to today then?'

'Just the usual,' I say. 'I did the housework. Mostly laundry and cleaning.'

'Did you go out at all?'

'I just popped into the village to buy some milk.' My days don't vary much. I wonder sometimes if Adam finds my daily reports dull, but he always seems to be intensely interested in every little detail. I ought to tell him about my decision to reply to the party invitation, but the words stick in my throat. It would be easier to tell him face to face when I see him again on Friday. I hope he won't be angry, but Adam never gets angry with me.

'What are you up to now?' he asks.

'Just reading a book. Then I thought I'd have an early night.'

'That sounds like a good idea.'

We chat for a couple of minutes about inconsequential things and then he wishes me a good night and says he'll speak to me again tomorrow evening at the same time.

I put the phone down.

For some reason I suddenly find myself thinking about Diana and Michael Potts. What are they doing right now? Are they both curled up on a sofa at the Corner House, reading books together? Are they busy making plans and preparations for the forthcoming party? Or are they doing something else entirely? It's hard for me to imagine what. My own life follows such a regular routine, with hardly any difference from one day to the next.

Then I think of Adam two hundred miles away in London and try to imagine what he's doing right now. I know that he has an important job, but how does he spend his evenings after speaking to me on the phone? I wonder if he has any secrets. Has he ever met another woman? I wonder briefly if he might even have a mistress. If he did, I would never find out. But what am I thinking? This is a ridiculous flight of fancy. I'm letting my thoughts runs away with themselves. Adam would never cheat on me. He loves me too much.

I return to my book. After a couple of hours I can't keep my eyes open any longer so I go to bed and fall asleep within seconds.

CHAPTER 3

The next day I'm in the kitchen ironing Adam's shirts when I hear the sound of the letterbox opening and closing. It's Tuesday morning, so I know that it must be the postman this time, not someone from the village. I peer out of the window to make certain. Sure enough, the postman's bright red van is disappearing down the road.

I check in the hallway and find a single brown envelope waiting for me on the mat. It's obviously not a party invitation, and I feel a slight disappointment at the sight of it. It's almost as if part of me wanted to see something slightly dangerous, something that would upset the balance of my daily life.

Now that I have received my first letter, I am hungry for more. I am conscious of a desire for my clockwork existence to be thrown into a new pattern. I wonder how it would feel to do something completely unplanned and unexpected. I feel giddy with possibility, and frightened too. Frightened by my own desires.

I don't really understand the mix of emotions that this simple letter has stirred, and I wonder again if I've done the right thing in accepting the party invitation. It's not too late to cancel it. I could write to Mr and Mrs Potts, or

Diana and Michael, as I've already begun to think of them, and cancel. I'm sure they would understand. That way, Adam wouldn't even have to know that I'd gone against his wishes. That would be the safe thing to do.

I'm so distracted by my thoughts that I tear open the brown envelope and pull out its contents without thinking. A single letter, neatly printed. No signature, no handwriting of any kind. All too soon I realise my mistake. The letter is addressed to Adam and I shouldn't have opened it. But it's too late now. My eyes have already scanned its contents. It's from the bank and it's entitled ADVICE OF CREDIT.

> *Dear Mr Harvey,*
> *We advise you that your account has been credited with the following:*
> *Amount Credit: GBP 250,000*

I stare at the words, not understanding. Two hundred and fifty thousand pounds has been deposited into my husband's bank account. That's an enormous sum of money. Where could it have possibly come from?

I try to think if he mentioned anything but I don't think he did. I would have remembered. I know that Adam has investments, but I can't imagine where such a large sum might have come from and the letter from the bank doesn't say. I re-fold the letter and slide it back into its envelope. The envelope is torn, so there's no possibility that I might reseal it. I'll just have to tell him that I opened it by mistake and hope that he believes me. I leave the letter on the desk in his office and return to the ironing as if there is nothing wrong.

I don't need to visit the shop today, and it's too cold to do anything in the garden, and so I stay indoors, getting on with some of my jobs. But the letter from the bank plays on my mind all day. There's nothing that I can do about that now, but I could still write to Diana and Michael and tell them that we are unable to come to the party after all. That would be one thing less that I have to explain to Adam. It's the sensible thing to do, but I just can't bring myself to do it. Even if I do eventually decide not to go to the party, I still have until Friday when Adam returns to imagine the possibility that I might actually go.

I wonder whether I will tell Adam about the letter from the bank when he phones me at nine o'clock. I'm still not sure what I will do when the phone rings at nine.

'How are you?' he asks, as usual. 'Have you had a nice day?'

I hesitate ever so slightly before giving my usual answer. 'I'm fine,' I say. 'How about you?'

Adam has noticed my hesitation. 'I'm well,' he says cautiously. 'Are you really all right?'

'Yes, of course.'

'It's just that you sound… different.' He stops, waiting for me to answer.

I can't avoid telling him about my mistake. 'I'm sorry,' I say, when I've explained about opening the letter. 'I think I was distracted after the party invitation at the weekend.' As soon as I have said it, I wish that I hadn't mentioned the party. I know that Adam will be unhappy.

'Oh, that,' he says. 'I'd hoped you would have forgotten about that by now. We did the right thing by deciding not to go. You know that don't you, darling?'

'Yes,' I say. I can't possibly tell him now that I changed my mind. I try to switch the subject by asking him about the letter from the bank. 'Where did all that money come from?'

There's a pause on the end of the line before he eventually replies. His answer surprises me. 'It's money from a will,' he says. 'I would have mentioned it but I wasn't expecting it to come through so soon.'

'Oh,' I say. 'Who died?' I can't think of anyone who might have left money to Adam.

'A cousin of mine. On my father's side. We weren't

close, but she didn't have any other family so I suppose that's why she left her estate to me.'

'Did I ever meet her?'

'No, you didn't.' There's another pause. 'She was called Victoria.'

The name means nothing to me. I don't think I've ever met any of Adam's family. His mother died before we met and his father is living abroad. They haven't spoken for years. He doesn't have any brothers or sisters. So it doesn't surprise me that I've never heard of this cousin.

'She lived in London,' he adds. 'I went to her funeral. I would have taken you too, but you know how you dislike London so much.'

'That's all right,' I say. 'I never even knew her.'

'No.'

I think he can sense that there's something else on my mind, but I don't want to tell him about the party, so I say nothing. 'Are you sure nothing's wrong, dear?' he asks. 'You haven't remembered anything have you?' He hesitates, and I will him not to say it, but he presses on regardless. 'About the... the red room?'

There's a long silence after he's asked the question. It seems to hang in the air between us. At last I find the courage to answer him. 'No,' I say truthfully. 'Nothing.'

'That's good,' he says. 'Very good.'

We hang up after wishing each other a good night. I wish he hadn't asked me about the red room. He knows I hate to be reminded of that part of my life. But at least I avoided telling him that I'd accepted the invitation to Diana and Michael's party. I'm still a little puzzled about the money though. She must have been well off, this cousin, to have left him such a large sum of money. I can't understand why he didn't mention it sooner.

The rest of the week passes quietly with no more letters. On Thursday I go back to the village shop to buy more bread and milk. Cath is delighted to hear that I've accepted the party invitation. 'Diana will be pleased,' she says. She gives me a warm smile. 'I'm pleased too,' she adds.

I try to return her smile, but a lump forms in my throat. I'm still worried that I've made the wrong decision. But now I would be letting Cath down if I didn't go. I will have to stick with my decision and tell Adam about it when he gets home.

On Friday evening I hear Adam's car pull up outside at nine o'clock. He phoned me before he got on the plane to let me know when he'd be arriving. I lay aside the book I'm reading – a historical novel – and go to the door to meet him.

He greets me with a hug and a kiss. I tell him there's some shepherd's pie keeping warm in the oven.

'That's marvellous,' he says. 'I'm so lucky to have a wife who's such a good cook.'

I fetch him his supper and pour him a glass of red wine. He sits beside me on the sofa and tucks in to his food. I think now might be a good time to tell him that I've accepted the invitation to the New Year's Eve party in the village. I've been preparing to tell him all day. At lunchtime my nerves failed me and I wrote another letter apologising to Diana and Michael explaining that we couldn't make it after all. But then I tore the letter into pieces and threw them onto the fire.

At first he doesn't say anything. He swallows his food and takes a large mouthful of the wine. He puts the wine glass down carefully on the coffee table.

'Are you sure that's a good idea?' he asks quietly.

I've already rehearsed my answer to his question, so I know just what to say. 'It's just that I was chatting to Cath in the shop – you know, the shopkeeper,' I say lightly, '– and she rather persuaded me. But if you think it's a bad idea I suppose we could always come up with an excuse. Say I've got the flu or something.'

'We could do that,' he agrees.

'But I do think I'd quite like to go,' I add. 'Just this

once.'

    'If you're sure,' he says. 'But we won't stay too late.'

    'No,' I agree. 'We don't need to stay late.'

CHAPTER 4

Adam has the week between Christmas and the New Year off work. It's just as well because a thick blanket of snow falls on Christmas Eve and he wouldn't have been able to drive to the airport with the roads blocked. Flights all across the country are cancelled. We spend Christmas quietly at home together, just as I told Cath we would. We go for invigorating walks across the white landscape and warm ourselves with mugs of hot chocolate when we return home. Adam lights the log fire and we spend the evenings reading before climbing into bed and making love.

By New Year's Eve the snow has turned to ice. It's too treacherous to drive into the village. I think Adam will use this as an excuse to say we should just stay at home. But I haven't spoken to anyone except Adam all week and I feel as if I would like to see some people. Besides, I don't want to let Cath down. If we don't go to the party she's sure to ask me about it the next time I'm in the shop. I feel that I owe it to Diana and Michael as well – even though I barely know her and have never met him. I need to prove something to myself too.

'We'll just stay for an hour or so,' says Adam.

'Yes,' I say. 'No more than an hour.' Part of me wonders if it would be rude to leave early, but I keep this thought to myself. I know he's only thinking about my welfare, and I'm sure he knows what's best.

We wrap up against the cold and arm ourselves with flashlights. There are no streetlights down the country lanes and our beams of light illuminate no more than a few yards ahead. There are no cars on the road, and no animals or sounds of any kind. The ground is frozen and lifeless. Even the wind is still tonight. It's slow-going trudging in single file along the side of the road where the snow has piled up. By the time we reach the humpback bridge it's already ten o'clock and the party started an hour ago.

'We'll be late,' says Adam. He doesn't like arriving late to anything. It makes him anxious.

'Perhaps it's best if we don't arrive too early,' I suggest. 'It's awkward if you arrive too early at a party.' That's what I've heard, at any rate. But what do I really know? I've never been to a party before. I'm feeling a mix of fear and excitement. I rather like it.

'The sooner we get there, the sooner we'll be able to leave,' says Adam.

A wicked thought occurs to me then. What if we stayed long enough to see in the New Year? A tingle runs down my spine at the prospect, but I say nothing.

The Corner House is the largest house in the village, which isn't saying much. None of the houses here are very big, most of them being former farm labourers' cottages. The Corner House, Cath told me once, used to be the village school but that shut down years ago. The handful of children who live in the village now take a school bus to the nearest town. Cath said she thought it was nice that a couple of retired schoolteachers should live in the old village school.

Lights are blazing out of the downstairs windows and the party seems to be in full swing when we arrive. I feel a tinge of nerves at the prospect of meeting so many people, but it's too late now. I couldn't possibly turn away after coming so far. Adam rings the doorbell and we're greeted at the door by Diana herself. She is just as I remember her from the one time I met her before, and I find myself liking her immediately. Despite her age – she must be well into her sixties – she exudes the energy of a woman twenty years her junior. She is wearing a flowing purple dress and a necklace made out of big, colourful beads. In one hand she holds a glass of red wine. She opens her arms wide to welcome us in. The wine in the glass tilts, and I can sense Adam's eyes on it nervously. He hates mess or spills, or anything out of its place. Fortunately, Diana doesn't spill a drop, even as she gives me a welcoming kiss on each cheek. My face flushes pink, and not just because the house is so warm after the long trek along the frozen road. I give her a smile. I am determined not to be overwhelmed by all the people here.

'Jane, how lovely to see you,' she says. 'I'm so glad you could come. I was worried the snow might put you off. Do come in, you must be frozen.' She ushers me into her lovely home which smells of cinnamon and spicy mulled wine. 'And you must be Jane's husband,' she says, holding out a hand to Adam. 'I'm sorry, I don't think we've met before?'

Adam introduces himself to her, giving her one of his charming smiles.

'Well you're both very welcome. Did you walk all that way?' She takes our coats and hats and scarves and then leads us into the lounge, a large room which must once have been the main schoolroom. There are more people here than I thought there would be and the room is noisy with the chatter of voices. I hesitate for a moment on the threshold, but Adam puts his hand against the small of my back and guides me gently into the room.

The schoolroom is still festooned with Christmas decorations. In the corner is a real Christmas tree lavishly decorated in silver tinsel and sparkly baubles. They must have hundreds of friends, I think, because Christmas cards are strung along all four walls. I can't imagine having so many friends. At home we only have three cards – one from me to Adam, one from him to me, and one from Cath to both of us. Adam told me that some of his work colleagues sent him cards, but he left them in the house in London.

'Michael' – Diana beckons to a man I assume is her husband – 'this is Jane and Adam. They live in the cottage just outside the village.'

An amiable-looking man with white hair ambles over and shakes our hands. 'Of course,' he says. 'Pleased to meet you.' His voice is rich and resonant. I can imagine he must have once been an inspiring headmaster. 'What can I get you to drink? Beer? Mulled wine?'

'I'll have a beer please,' says Adam.

'Do you have white wine?' I ask.

'Coming right up.' Michael disappears and returns a moment later with our drinks. 'I hear you work in London?' he says to Adam. I don't know where he can have heard that, and then I guess that he probably got it from Cath in the village shop. You have to be careful what you say in a village this size.

'That's right,' says Adam. 'I'm down there Monday to Friday. I catch a flight from Leeds Bradford Airport.'

'And what is it you do exactly? It must be something very important for you to travel all the way down to London each week.'

Adam laughs. 'Not really. It's more a case of having someone very important to travel back to here at the weekends,' he says, smiling at me.

Michael looks at us indulgently. 'I can tell that you two are the perfect couple,' he says. 'Do you often visit your husband in London?' he asks me.

I shake my head. 'I've never been to London. It's so big, so many people, so noisy. I never want to go to London.' My voice has risen and I'm taken aback by my passion. Michael raises one eyebrow and I wonder if I've committed some dreadful *faux pas*. 'I like it here in the village,' I conclude.

Michael nods as if he knows exactly what I mean, but I can tell that he doesn't really. I'm not even sure that I do myself.

Adam continues to talk to him, telling him about his work in insurance at Lloyd's of London. I tune out and look around the room. I recognise one or two faces by sight, but most people here are unfamiliar to me. I decide to stay close to Adam's side for the moment. Then I feel a hand on my shoulder and turn around, startled. It's Cath from the shop.

'You made it then,' she says, beaming. 'Brave of you to traipse through the snow.'

'Yes. We've just arrived.' I'm not sure what else to say, so I take a sip of my wine. I have to be careful though, because alcohol goes to my head quickly. I never drink more than one glass of wine. I reach for a dainty vol-au-vent from the buffet.

'Do you know many people here?' asks Cath.

'Not really,' I admit. 'In fact I don't really know anyone.'

'Let me introduce you then.'

I glance across at Adam but he's deep in conversation with Michael. Cath takes me by the arm and starts to guide me across the room. She taps a woman on the shoulder and the woman turns round, smiling. She looks to be a few years younger than me – perhaps about thirty – and has short dark hair cut into a bob. She's not exactly pretty, but there's an intensity to her expression that is quite captivating.

'Jane, this is Bridget, the vicar's wife.'

Bridget holds out her hand. 'Lovely to meet you, Jane. I don't think we've met before. Have you lived here long?'

'Seven years,' I say.

Bridget nods enthusiastically. 'That's a long time. I

expect you know everyone here already. It's such a friendly place. We're new to the village. That's my husband over there.' She waves her hand towards a good-looking young man in a dog collar, V-neck sweater and jeans who is chatting with a group of other men. 'Which house do you live in?'

'It's the one outside the village, beyond the humpback bridge.'

Bridget looks surprised. 'All the way out there? Gosh, isn't it terribly lonely for you?'

'I'm used to it,' I tell her. 'In fact, I quite like it.'

Bridget seems to understand. 'You have your own space,' she says. 'And it must be very peaceful living there. But you're welcome to pop round to the vicarage any time you want company.'

'Thank you,' I say. To my surprise, I find myself thinking that it might be nice to do that. Perhaps I'll call in one day next week when Adam is back in London.

Diana appears in our group. 'Is everyone all right for drinks? Can I get anyone a top up?' She seems to adore playing her role as hostess.

We all tell her we're fine.

She turns to go, but Cath touches her on the arm. 'Diana, while you're here why don't you tell Bridget and Jane about your idea for a book group?'

'Oh yes,' says Diana. 'I just thought it would be a nice idea to set up a ladies' book group in the New Year. What do you both think?'

'That sounds like a wonderful idea,' says Bridget. 'I love reading and it's such a good way to get to know people.'

'What about you, Jane?' prompts Cath.

'Well,' I say, 'I do enjoy reading, although I'm not sure…'

'Oh, go on,' says Cath. 'It will do you good. I'm definitely joining because it will force me to read more. I never seem to find the time these days.'

'I'd be happy to host it here,' says Diana. 'Or we could

take it in turns to visit each other's houses.'

'Oh, I love that idea,' says Cath. 'Although if you come to me you'll have to excuse the mess. What with two teenage boys around, you know what it's like.'

Everyone laughs, but I'm uneasy. We've never had visitors to our cottage outside the village. It's just not something we do. And this is the first time I've really been to someone else's house. Adam is always warning me to be wary of strangers.

'What's the joke, ladies?' Adam has appeared at my side. He's smiling, but there's an edge to his voice that means he's concerned about me. I'm a little relieved because it means I don't have to offer to host the book group which I haven't even agreed to join yet. I need more time to think.

'We're just discussing plans for a book group in the New Year,' says Cath. 'You must be Jane's husband. I don't think we've met properly?' She holds out a hand and Adam introduces himself. 'And this is Bridget, the vicar's wife.'

'Hello,' says Bridget, smiling up at him. She shakes Adam's hand and, despite the fact that she's married to the vicar, I can see in her eyes that she's taken a shine to him. He has that effect on women when they first meet him. He can't help it. He's tall and dark, with a mesmerising gaze. He looks like the sort of man who would rescue you from a burning building.

The circle starts to shift as new people are introduced to me and Adam. I smile and shake hands but I start to forget names, or I don't hear them properly over the chatter of voices.

Adam leans close to whisper into my ear. 'We should go soon.'

I see from the clock on the wall that it's already half past eleven. The time has flown by without me noticing.

I nod. 'In a little while.' I don't want to leave just yet. I'm starting to relax and enjoy myself. I take another sip of wine. I've been sipping it all evening but my glass doesn't seem to be getting any emptier. Perhaps Michael has been topping it up without my noticing. He walks past holding a bottle of red wine and a bottle of white wine, one bottle in each hand, searching for anyone whose glass isn't entirely full. I wonder how much I've had to drink.

I find myself separated from Adam again. A group of men have drawn him into a friendly argument about the chances of England winning the world cup, something which I know Adam has no interest in whatsoever. Cath introduces me to her husband, Ken, a man of few words who soon disappears to take refuge in the food that's been laid out buffet-style on the big wooden dining table. Then Bridget introduces me to her husband Ben, the vicar. He's relaxed and easy to talk to and I take to him straightaway. If the Church of England had more vicars like him, then maybe congregation numbers wouldn't be in such sharp decline.

Before I know it, it's five minutes to midnight. Adam has found me again and makes a point of reclaiming me from Ben. He tries to steer me towards the door, saying we've stayed far longer than we intended to. But we're in the middle of the room and there's such a crush of people. We should thank our hosts, Diana and Michael, before we leave, but there isn't time to do that before the clock strikes midnight.

I assure Adam that we'll go as soon as we've seen in the New Year. He nods, but he's frowning and his mouth is drawn in a tight line. In the corner of the room, someone has switched on the television. It's showing the crowds of New Year's Eve revellers at the London Eye.

The sight of London makes me feel strange. All those people out having a good time. Something flashes in my mind's eye. I see a room packed full of people. Men are wearing suits; women dresses and heels. Sounds rush in. So many people, so many voices, all talking at once. It's a memory from a long time ago, from before I came to

Yorkshire, when Adam and I lived in Oxford. I'm wearing a dress just like the other women, but I'm turning my face away from the crowd and looking out into the still night.

I don't know what the vision means. I don't know where it has come from, and then, just as quickly as it came to me, it's gone.

Thirty seconds to go.

The television image switches to the River Thames and Big Ben. I catch my breath at the sight of the great bell tower illuminated against the night sky.

Bright red flashes through my mind. I start to feel lightheaded. I should have drunk less and eaten more. There are too many people all pressing in on me and I start to panic.

Twenty seconds. Ten. Everyone starts to count down to midnight.

'*You can't do that!*' a voice shouts. I look around bewildered but no one here is shouting. Did I hear that or just imagine it?

Nine. Eight.

I smell blood and I think I'm going to be sick.

Seven. Six.

I reach down to touch my dress and my hand comes away smeared with bright red blood.

Five. Four.

The room starts to spin.

Three. Two. One.

Big Ben chimes midnight. Fireworks explode across the Thames in London. A loud cheer erupts around me.

The cheer turns to a scream. I'm falling. I reach out and clutch at a chair, and it crashes down on top of me. Everything has turned red. I'm back in the red room again, and a wave of fear washes over me.

I see Adam coming towards me, pushing through the crowd, and a sudden feeling of anger boils through my veins. Everything is red again, then suddenly it turns black and I fall to the floor.

CHAPTER 5

When I wake up I'm lying on a couch in another room. My head hurts. The house is quiet and I guess the party must have finished now. It must be well past midnight. I try to sit up but the room lurches. Gentle hands push me back.

'Take it easy now.' Cath is sitting next to me. 'Don't get up too quickly.'

'What happened?' I ask.

Adam steps forward from the other side of the room and I am relieved to see his familiar, reassuring face. 'You fainted,' he says. 'That's all.'

I remember crashing to the floor, and I reach out to inspect myself, to see what caused the bleeding. But strangely there is no blood anywhere. My hands are perfectly clean. It must all have been some kind of hallucination. 'I'm so sorry,' I say.

'Oh, don't apologise,' says Cath cheerfully. 'It can happen to any of us.'

'Yes, but...' I don't know what to say. Adam was right. We should never have stayed at the party so late. I shouldn't have drunk the wine and spoken to so many people. We should never have come to the party at all.

The door opens and Diana and Bridget come in with a

mug of tea and a plate of biscuits.

'I've made you a strong, sweet tea,' says Diana. 'Just the thing to perk you up. How are you feeling?'

'A bit better,' I say. At least the room seems to have stopped spinning.

'Have a couple of these,' says Bridget, passing me the plate of biscuits. I choose a chocolate digestive and nibble at the edges.

Adam withdraws a little, looking awkward in this all-female crowd. I have probably embarrassed him. The women are tending to me as if I'm a Victorian invalid. Cath pats my shoulder and Diana and Bridget look on with concerned faces. I feel incredibly grateful to them. They are so accepting, they make me feel as if I didn't do anything wrong after all. I eat the biscuit and sip the tea to try to please them. They are all so kind that in that moment I decide that I will join their book group after all. It would be nice to have some female company.

I eat another biscuit and drink my tea, just as I was told. I'm definitely starting to feel better now.

'That's put the colour back into your cheeks,' says Diana, patting my hand.

Adam says, 'We really ought to be going. It's nearly one o'clock.'

'But Jane can't possibly walk all that way now,' protests Diana. 'Not after fainting like that.'

There's no question of calling a taxi, not this far out in the countryside at New Year.

'Ben can drive you both,' says Bridget. 'Don't worry, he hardly touches alcohol. He'll only have had one drink all evening.'

I notice Adam stiffen at the mention of the young, good-looking vicar.

'We don't want to put you to any trouble,' I say quickly.

'Nonsense,' says Bridget. 'It's no trouble at all. And we'd never forgive ourselves if you fainted again on the long walk home in the dark.' She's already at the door, calling her husband.

Adam helps me to my feet and then Diana is there helping me put my coat on. I can see that most people have already left the party. A few stragglers are still drinking beer in the lounge. Michael is clearing away the glasses and plates. Ben stands by the front door, car keys in hand. He smiles when he sees me.

'Take care,' says Cath, giving me a hug.

We thank Diana and Michael for their hospitality and I apologise once again for having caused so much trouble.

'You were no trouble at all,' says Diana, and from the warmth of her tone I can tell that she really means it.

Bridget and Ben guide us to their car which is parked outside the vicarage, just a hundred yards down the road. Bridget gives me a hug and says she hopes we'll see each other again soon.

'Thank you,' I say. 'I would like that.'

Adam and I sit in the back of the car on the way home and he holds my hand tightly. Ben drives carefully down the dark country lane with his headlamps on full beam. Halfway home, a hare appears suddenly in the middle of the road, its eyes shining brightly in the glare of the headlamps. Ben slows the car to a crawl. The hare stands still for a few seconds before darting safely to the side of the road.

When we reach the cottage, Adam thanks Ben for giving us a lift.

'No worries,' says Ben. 'I hope Jane feels better in the morning.'

When we're safely back inside the cottage, Adam wraps his arms around me.

'I'm sorry,' I say. 'You were right. We shouldn't have stayed so late.'

'You're home now,' says Adam. 'And you're safe. That's all that matters.'

CHAPTER 6

For the few days following the party we stay at home and don't see anyone. Outside, the weather is cold and grey, a mixture of snow and sleet that soon turns to slush and then freezes overnight. I'm glad Adam doesn't have to drive to the airport in these conditions. I'm glad he doesn't have to return to London and leave me on my own.

Ever since my fainting fit at the party, Adam has been extra solicitous towards me, bringing me cups of tea in bed and even cooking dinner a couple of times. He is actually a very good chef. It comes from having to fend for himself when he's alone in the house in London. In fact, before we moved here, when we lived together in Oxford, I didn't really know how to cook. Adam used to prepare most of our meals.

He seems very concerned to find out what happened at the party. Why did I faint? Had I been feeling ill before that moment? Was the party too loud? Did I talk to too many people?

'No,' I say, remembering how much I enjoyed being with Cath, Diana and Bridget. 'No, I *liked* talking to them.'

He frowns. 'What then? Did you drink too much wine?'

'Perhaps,' I admit, although I don't really know. 'Maybe it was the wine. I think Michael kept topping my glass up when I wasn't looking.'

'I'm sorry, I should have taken better care of you,' he says. 'I kept getting dragged into conversations with complete strangers. I thought Yorkshire folk were supposed to be a taciturn bunch, but that lot wouldn't stop talking.'

I smile, remembering the way the three women bustled around me all evening, asking questions, making sure I was all right. Usually I rely on Adam to look after me. 'It wasn't your fault,' I say, taking hold of his hand across the dining table. 'I'm glad you found someone to talk to.'

'I didn't really want to talk to them. I'd rather have spent the evening with you.' He sighs, then asks me again, 'What do you remember?' He's asked the same question a dozen times already. 'Tell me everything, exactly as it happened.'

I think back. I still don't understand the memory I had of being in a crowded room with so many people. I don't think that it can be significant. It was probably just triggered by the crowds in the party and by watching all those people celebrating the New Year in London. And then there was the smell of the blood, and the sensation of being covered in blood. Was that a memory or some kind of olfactory hallucination? Again, I think it's best not to mention it.

'Did you perhaps remember something?' suggests Adam.

I remember hearing a loud voice. *You can't do that!* But for some reason I don't feel comfortable telling Adam about that now. Instead I say, 'I was probably just overtired. I think that the crowded party and the countdown to midnight was just too much excitement.' I don't really believe that, but I have to tell Adam something, and I know that's the kind of thing he wants to hear.

'Maybe,' he says, although he looks distracted, as if he's thinking of something else.

~~~

Adam returns to work on January the sixth. The alarm goes off at five o'clock. It's still pitch black, even though the days have very slowly begun to lengthen. I hear him getting up and moving around in the dark. He comes to kiss me goodbye, then I roll over and go back to sleep.

I finally get up just after eight. I pull back the curtains and peer outside. It's another grey day, but at least it's not sleeting. That's good because I'll have to take the bus into town this morning and go to the market.

I go downstairs and find that Adam's left a note for me in the kitchen telling me to phone him if I feel ill again. The note says to take it easy and not to overdo anything. He'll call me this evening at the usual time.

I make some tea and toast and eat it standing up in the kitchen. The cottage feels empty without Adam. I'd got used to having him around for over a week, and now the place seems too big for just me. I feel an emptiness inside too. It might be loneliness, but I can't be sure. This is how I feel most of the time. It's how I've always felt.

After breakfast I wash the dishes and put everything back in its place. Then I wrap up warm and set off for the bus stop in the village. I don't own a car. In fact I can't drive, so when Adam is away I depend on the bus to get around. In these parts, buses are few and far between. There's only one bus a day that will take me to the nearest town, which is five miles away. I mustn't miss it, so I make sure I'm waiting at the bus stop in good time.

The bus arrives and I climb on board, paying for my ticket. I'm the only passenger on the bus today. I sit near the back and stare out of the window as it makes its laborious way along the narrow country lanes. There are few cars about, and no one on foot. Even the fields are cleared of sheep. They've probably been shepherded into barns to keep warm. The earth is hard as iron.

The town isn't very big, but it's a lot larger than the village and hosts a weekly market in the town square. In the summer, people linger in the market square and sit outside the nearby café drinking coffee, but today there are few shoppers, and the weather-beaten stallholders are all muffled up in woolly hats and scarves. I go from stall to stall, buying small quantities of meat, vegetables and bread. I don't eat a lot when I'm on my own at home.

The bus back to the village doesn't leave for another hour so I take my shopping inside the café and order a cup of tea. I find a seat by the window and sit watching the townsfolk going about their business. I see a woman of my own age, wrapped up with a winter coat and hat, crossing the square towards the café. She is carrying two large bags of shopping and I wonder if she has a family, perhaps two teenage boys with healthy appetites. She bumps into another woman and stops to chat. I watch them through the window as their breath condenses in the cold air. It occurs to me that I never meet anyone I know when I come to do the weekly shop in the town. I hardly even talk to anyone in the village. I am a stranger to everyone, despite having lived here for years. Sometimes I feel I am a stranger to myself.

I find myself wondering about the mysterious cousin who left Adam all her money. He has never spoken to me about her before. Would he have told me about the two hundred and fifty thousand pounds if I hadn't accidentally opened the letter from the bank? I wonder if there are other things that he doesn't reveal to me.

When I asked him about the money I was unsure whether to believe his explanation or not. I wasn't expecting him to say it was an inheritance. But it was unfair of me to doubt him. If he wanted to hide the truth, he could just have said that the money was from one of his investments. There was no reason to make up a story about a dead cousin.

Besides, I have no reason to mistrust him. On the contrary, he always has my best interests at heart. I couldn't ask for a more considerate husband.

He was right about not staying too late at the party. If I'd listened to his advice and left early I would never have fainted. But if I'd done what he wanted we would never have gone to the party at all, and I would have missed meeting Diana and Bridget.

I'm jolted out of my reverie by a rap on the window pane. I focus my eyes and see Bridget standing outside the café waving at me. She comes inside.

She seems pleased to see me. 'Hello, Jane,' she says. 'Are you on your own? Do you mind if I join you?' She's laden with shopping bags full of produce from the market.

'Not at all,' I say, indicating the empty chair opposite.

She buys a cup of tea at the counter and sits down, unbuttoning her coat. 'I love the outdoor market,' she says. 'Such a civilised way to shop and so much nicer than the supermarket.'

I nod. I never go to the supermarket to shop. It's much too big and crowded, and it isn't easy to reach by bus.

'I've been stocking up for the week,' she says, indicating her overflowing bags.

'Same here,' I say.

She glances at my one shopping bag that has hardly anything in it but doesn't comment on it. 'How are you feeling?' she asks instead. 'You're looking so much better than the last time I saw you.'

'A few days' rest has done me good.' That's true enough, but I'm also feeling better for seeing Bridget. I remember the woman in the market square stopping to chat to her friend, and I think, now I have a friend too.

'Listen,' she says, 'if you're still interested in that book group we were talking about, we're having the first meeting in two days' time at Diana's house. Do you want to come?'

I don't need to think about my reply. I had already decided the night of the party, when the three women showed me so much kindness after I fainted. 'I would love to come,' I say. 'I'm looking forward to it.' And I really mean it. I glance at my watch. 'I'm awfully sorry,' I say, 'but I must dash now. I have to catch the bus in five minutes.'

'Oh, don't be silly,' says Bridget. 'I'll give you a lift back in my car. I didn't realise you don't drive. I could have brought you here if I'd known.'

I smile faintly. I don't really mind travelling on the bus, even if it is a bit inconvenient. I don't want to be a burden to Bridget, but I don't want to appear rude either, so I thank her for her offer and wait while she finishes her tea. She drives me back to the village, passing the bus on the way. I expect her to drop me in the centre of the village, but instead she insists on driving me to my cottage.

'It's a long way from the other houses, isn't it?' she says as we drive over the humpback bridge that crosses the stream. 'You must really enjoy the solitude.'

'Yes,' I say. 'Yes, that's it exactly.'

~~~

In the evening I make a meal using the food I bought at the market and then wait for Adam to call. When he phones I will tell him about the book group, and how I plan to go. I am ashamed now that I didn't tell him before.

The phone rings at nine o'clock exactly. It's good to hear Adam's voice again. 'How are you?' he asks. 'Have you had a nice day?'

'I'm fine,' I say. 'How about you?'

'Oh, you know,' he says. 'Busy after the Christmas holiday. What have you been up to today?'

'Just the usual. It was market day so I took the bus into town and did some shopping.'

'That's nice,' he says. 'I hope it wasn't too tiring for

you, taking the bus.'

'Not at all,' I say. 'In fact, I met Bridget at the market and she gave me a lift home in her car.'

The line is suddenly silent.

'Adam?' I say. 'Are you still there?'

'I'm here,' he says.

I sense that he is angry, that I have done something wrong. It must be because I mentioned Bridget. Is he worried that I might have seen Ben too? 'She was on her own,' I say, trying to reassure him. 'Her husband wasn't there.'

'No, of course not,' says Adam, but his voice is still frosty.

'It was kind of her to bring me home,' I say. I want Adam to like Bridget. It would be cruel if he forbade me to see her. 'She has been very kind to me. Remember how sweet she was after I fainted at the party?'

As soon as I've said it, I realise I've made a mistake. I shouldn't have reminded him again about the party, and my fainting.

He pauses a long while before answering.

'I'm sure she's very nice,' he says at last. 'But be careful what you say to her. In small villages, women like to gossip. We don't want the whole village knowing all about us, do we?'

'No,' I say quickly. 'No, of course not.' Although what there is for them to find out, I can't imagine.

'Did anything else happen?' he asks. I can still hear the suspicion in his voice.

I was going to tell him all about the book group, and how I'd agreed to go. Now I decide not to tell him.

'No,' I say. 'Nothing else happened today.'

'That's good,' he says. 'I'll speak to you again the same time tomorrow.'

CHAPTER 7

The first meeting of the book group is on Thursday evening at seven o'clock. I still haven't told Adam about it. I fear that if he found out he'd be bound to try to stop me from going. He'd say that I shouldn't go to meet my new friends. He'd say that it would be too much excitement for me, that I might have another fainting fit. And so I say nothing.

I feel awkward about lying to Adam. I have never lied to him before, and there is a growing tightness in my stomach. I hope I am not going to be ill again.

It is not really a lie though, just an omission, like him not telling me about the two hundred and fifty thousand pounds. It's no different to the cousin he never mentioned. In any case, I can tell him later, when he phones me this evening at nine o'clock. I must make sure that I am back home in good time for his phone call.

Or perhaps I will tell him at the weekend, when I can speak to him face to face. That would be better. But the idea of telling him makes the knot in my stomach tighten further. Perhaps I won't tell him about the book group at all.

I wonder if it would be better simply not to go. I could

make an excuse and cancel, just like I ought to have cancelled my acceptance of the party invitation. The others would surely understand. They know that I am easily agitated.

But I want to go. I have promised Bridget and the others that I will come. I can't change my mind now and let them down. And so I get myself ready, and decide to worry about what I am going to say to Adam later.

By half past six I am waiting by the window for Bridget to arrive. She has insisted on coming to fetch me in her car. She said I shouldn't even consider walking down the country lane on my own after dark. She said you don't know who might be about. I wanted to tell her that no one is ever about on the road from the village after dark, so there's really nothing to be afraid of, but I'm glad she's coming to fetch me. It will be nice to be driven in a warm car, and even nicer to see Bridget again.

I check my watch. I have been waiting by the window for ten minutes already. It is too early to expect her. I am ready too soon. I wonder again about Adam, and what I will say to him when he phones this evening. I hope the book club does not go on too long. If it does, I will have to make my excuses and leave. I cannot afford to be late home and miss his call. Another five minutes passes. Bridget is still not here, but that is because I am ready too soon. The book club does not start until seven and it is only a short drive from my cottage to the Corner House. I sit patiently looking out of the window, but the wait does not help to ease my nerves.

At five minutes to seven I see the lights of Bridget's car approaching from the road, and I hurry outside to meet her. As soon as I see her face I feel sure that I've made the right decision in agreeing to go with her.

But the knot in my stomach hasn't gone away.

When we arrive at the Corner House, Diana already has the kettle on and Cath is putting out a plate of biscuits. We make ourselves comfortable in the small sitting room, the room I woke up in after my fainting fit.

Diana brings tea and coffee to where we are sitting. 'Jane, it's good to see you looking recovered,' she says to me. 'I was so worried about you.'

'I feel fine now,' I tell her. 'I do hope I didn't spoil the party.'

'Of course not,' says Diana.

Cath says, 'I remember when I was expecting my two, I used to feel awfully woozy and faint at times, especially if I hadn't had enough to eat.'

They all smile and look at me expectantly and I realise with a jolt that they think I might be pregnant.

'Oh no,' I say, feeling the colour rush into my cheeks. 'It's not that.'

Cath raises an eyebrow. 'Are you sure?'

'Positive,' I say, then add, 'I can't have children.'

Cath looks embarrassed. 'I'm sorry, I shouldn't have pried. It was none of my business.'

'It's all right,' I tell her. 'Adam and I did want to have children, we wanted it very much, but it just isn't possible. Don't worry, I've got over it now.'

I remember when I first heard the news. I felt as if a great void had opened up inside me, a space that could never be filled. I cried for a long, long time. The emptiness is still in me, but I suppose I have grown used to it as the years have passed. I do not cry so often now. I am so lucky to have Adam, and suddenly I feel guilty again that I haven't told him the truth about the book group. I will tell him when I speak to him next. I have no secrets to keep from my husband. It was silly of me to worry about telling him. As soon as I decide that, I start to feel better again, and the knot in my stomach unravels a little.

'Would anyone like a biscuit?' asks Diana brightly, passing the plate around. She is trying to smooth over this awkward moment like the good hostess she is. I take a biscuit and put it on my plate to please her.

When everyone has taken one, Diana says, 'So, about

this book group. I suppose the first thing we have to do is decide what we're going to read. I've got a few ideas in mind, but perhaps it would be better just to ask what kind of books everyone enjoys?'

I'm relieved that Diana is taking charge of the meeting and steering the conversation away from my medical history. I can imagine her as a schoolteacher, standing up and addressing her class with her brisk no-nonsense way of speaking. I wonder how long she has been retired from teaching. She is so lively and energetic that she hardly seems old enough to be retired.

'I like a good story, you know,' says Cath. 'Something with a bit of mystery and romance. But I don't like books with too much sex or violence.'

The other two nod in agreement.

'Maybe I shouldn't say this,' says Bridget with a sideways glance at Diana, 'but the last book I read had won a big literary prize, but I found it a real struggle to read. It had no plot so in the end I just got bored. I had to force myself to read the last few chapters.'

'Oh yes,' says Cath, 'I know the kind of book you mean. The critics love it, but nothing happens.'

I smile inwardly to myself. Many of the books I read myself probably fall into that category. But I don't want to say anything that might sound critical of the others.

'What do you like to read, Jane?' asks Diana.

'I like all kinds of books,' I say. 'I really don't mind.'

'Maybe we should begin with a classic,' suggests Diana.

'That sounds like a good idea,' I say.

'I've always wanted to read something by the Brontë sisters,' says Cath. 'Seeing as how they lived not so far from here. You can visit the parsonage where they grew up.'

'Yes,' says Bridget eagerly. 'You can just imagine them tramping across the wild moors in the wind and the rain, can't you?'

An image of Bridget striding across the moors in her

waterproofs springs to my mind then, and I have to suppress a giggle.

'Then why don't we start with *Jane Eyre*?' suggests Diana. 'It's been years since I've read it.'

'Sounds good to me,' says Bridget.

'What about you, Jane? Are you happy to go with *Jane Eyre*?'

'Of course,' I say. 'That sounds good.'

'Remind me,' says Cath, 'which sister wrote *Jane Eyre*? It wasn't Emily was it?'

'It was Charlotte,' says Diana. 'She was the eldest of the three sisters who published books. Two other sisters died in childhood, and of course there was the brother. He was the black sheep of the family.'

'Yes,' says Cath. 'I saw a documentary. They all died so young. Such a tragedy.'

With the choice of book decided, the conversation turns to the everyday. Diana asks Bridget how she and Ben are settling into the vicarage.

'Oh, we're not doing too badly,' says Bridget. 'It's a lovely old house, probably too big for just the two of us. The heating and hot water system are ancient though.' She laughs. 'The radiators rattle and bang like a haunted house.'

'I wish we had as much space as you,' says Cath wistfully. 'I wouldn't mind a bit of rattling and banging if we had a couple more rooms. We're so cramped in the flat above the shop, I'll be glad when the kids have left home.' She bites her lip and gives me an apologetic look for bringing up the subject of children again.

I try to give her a reassuring smile, but her earlier comments have unsettled me somewhat. I wish now that Adam and I had tried harder to have children. When I first found out that we couldn't, I asked Adam if we could try fertility treatment, but he refused. I even suggested adopting a child, but Adam said that the paperwork would be too intrusive, and that social services would pry into our personal lives too much.

'Jane?'

'Sorry, I was miles away.' I realise that Diana has just asked me a question but I have no idea what it was.

'I was just wondering how you manage at home all day on your own, with Adam working in London from Monday to Friday.'

'Oh, I'm fine,' I say. 'I have lots of jobs to keep me busy around the cottage, and I like to read and go for long walks. In the summer I grow vegetables in the garden. I'm happy with my own company.' Then I add hastily, 'Of course, it's nice to get out and meet people too.' I don't want them to think that I'm stand-offish.

'Did you and Adam meet in London?' asks Cath. I look at her blankly. She ploughs on. 'I was just wondering where the two of you first met? Have you been married long? Sorry, I'm being nosey again, aren't I? Do tell me to shut up if you'd rather not tell us.'

'No, it's all right,' I say. 'I don't mind you asking. We met at Oxford. We were both students there. I was an undergraduate and he was completing his post-graduate degree. We got married as soon as I graduated. Then we lived in Oxford together for a while before he took the job in London.'

'So what made you decide to come and live all the way up here?' asks Bridget. 'It's such a long way from where Adam works.' She asks the question lightly, but she's watching me closely.

I stare at my empty cup. 'Adam thought it would suit me better here. Away from the bustle of the city.'

That is only half the truth, however.

I can't tell them the real reason we came here. I can't tell them about what happened to me before. I mustn't say anything about the red room.

Cath doesn't seem to notice my discomfort. 'I know exactly what you mean,' she says. 'I enjoy going to London occasionally, but I'm always glad to get back to the peace and quiet of the countryside. You can't beat the moors for good, clean air.' She takes a deep breath as if to illustrate her point.

Diana picks up the tea pot. 'Shall I make a fresh pot?'

I look at my watch nervously. It's already gone eight-thirty. I mustn't risk getting back late and not being home when Adam phones at nine. 'If you don't mind,' I say, 'I really ought to be getting back.'

'So soon?' asks Cath.

'Me too,' says Bridget. 'I told Ben I wouldn't be late home. But thank you for your hospitality.' I think Bridget has sensed my discomfort and I'm grateful to her for bringing the gathering to a close.

We agree to meet at the vicarage in a couple of weeks, by which time we'll have had a chance to read *Jane Eyre*. Then we say goodbye and Bridget drives me back to the cottage.

'Thank you for giving me a lift,' I say. 'That's the second time you've driven me home now.'

'It's no trouble at all,' she says. 'Really, it isn't. If you ever need a lift anywhere, just ask.'

'Thanks. Good night.'

I go inside, take off my winter coat and boots and sit by the telephone waiting for Adam. It is time for me to unburden myself of my secret and tell him all about the book group. It was silly of me not to tell him sooner. After all, there is no reason for him to be angry. After seven years in the village it is time that I started to make friends. I will tell him that Bridget gave me a lift in her car, so there is no need for him to worry about me going out after dark.

Then I remember how badly he reacted when I told him that Bridget had driven me home from the market. I remember what Cath said about me being pregnant, and how I told them that Adam and I weren't able to have children. Adam warned me to be careful what I said to people. He warned me how gossip spreads in a small village like this. He would be furious if he found out what

I have done.

I wonder if Bridget is telling Ben right now about how we are unable to have a family. Or if Diana is telling Michael how Adam and I first met at Oxford. I feel certain that Cath has already told her husband everything. I remember how she chats incessantly to her customers all day at the shop. Soon the whole village will know all about us.

My stomach clenches again and I feel sick.

The phone rings at nine o'clock exactly. It rings three times before I feel composed enough to pick it up.

'How are you?' asks Adam. 'Have you had a nice day?'

'I'm fine,' I say. My voice quavers slightly, and I worry that he will hear it. 'Absolutely fine. How about you?'

'Oh, just the usual,' he says. 'Still catching up at work after the holiday. Have you been anywhere today?'

'No,' I say. 'No, I haven't been out at all. It's been much too cold.'

~~~

After speaking to Adam, I go into his office and switch on the computer. I would like to get my hands on a copy of *Jane Eyre* as soon as possible, and if I place an order online the book will be delivered tomorrow, before Adam returns from London in the evening.

There are several different editions of the book, and I choose a paperback edition with a portrait of Charlotte Brontë on the cover.

I complete the purchase and switch off the computer. Then I notice the letter from the bank lying on the top of the in-tray on Adam's desk.

I pick up the letter and read it again.

Dear Mr Harvey,
We advise you that your account has been credited with the following:

Amount Credit: GBP 250,000

Such a large sum of money. Suddenly I'm filled with doubt. How can it be that I'd never heard of this cousin of Adam's until now? A cousin isn't such a distant relation, after all. *Victoria*, he said her name was. He has never mentioned anyone with that name before. It's a mystery, but one that I can't explain. I cannot think of an alternative explanation, so I have no choice but to trust my husband. I put the letter back on top of the in-tray and go upstairs to get ready for bed.

CHAPTER 8

Next morning there's a knock at the door. I hurry to open it and find the postman standing there with a parcel. His red van is parked on the roadside behind him.

The parcel won't fit through the letterbox. It's addressed to Adam, but I know that it must be my copy of *Jane Eyre*. It's addressed to him because I used his computer to order it.

'Morning,' he says cheerfully, handing me the delivery. 'Keen frost we had last night.' The garden and the moorland beyond the road are carpeted in white, and his breath mists in the air.

'Thank you,' I say, taking the parcel from him and starting to close the door. I hope he doesn't think me rude, but I have no wish to stand around chatting, letting the cold air inside. He turns and trudges back to his van, his boots crunching loudly on the frozen path. I wait until his van drives away and all is silent once more, then I go into the lounge where a log fire is blazing, tear open the cardboard, and take out my new paperback. *Jane Eyre* by Charlotte Brontë. It is perfect in its crisp newness and I curl up on the sofa to read it, ignoring the dishes that still need washing after breakfast. I turn to chapter one.

There was no possibility of taking a walk that day.

I glance at the window. Outside the sky is dark and lowering. It's bitterly cold. As my namesake remarks at the end of the first paragraph: *outdoor exercise was now out of the question.*

I settle down to read, acclimatising myself to Charlotte Brontë's richly layered prose. The story quickly draws me in. I sympathise with the orphaned Jane's unhappiness in the home of her uncaring Aunt, Mrs Reed, and I feel her pain and humiliation at the cruel treatment she receives from her cousin, Master John Reed. When John Reed hurls her beloved book at her and she falls and cuts her head against the door, I'm furious on her behalf. I find myself cheering her along every step of the way when she physically attacks him. After what she has endured, her actions strike me as fully justified. I would do the same myself if I was treated in that way, and the realisation of this makes me feel strong. Then Jane's aunt appears and, like the mean old battle-axe she is, issues an order to the servants:

Take her away to the red room and lock her in there.

'No!' I shout out aloud.

Suddenly I'm trembling so violently that the book is shaking in my hands. I can no longer focus on the words. Tears stream down my face and land on the page, spoiling the new paper. I utter a cry and the book falls to the floor, the pages fanning out and crumpling under its weight.

The red room.

I curl up on the sofa with my head in my hands, sobbing uncontrollably.

Lock her in there.

The red room. That's where it all happened. Something so traumatic that I have spent the past seven years hiding from it. The red room is what brought me here to this tiny village in Yorkshire. It's what still makes me so afraid of other people. It's why I cannot trust anyone but Adam.

The red room was a study in our house in Oxford, its

walls painted a deep Moroccan red. The previous owners had chosen the colour, and we had never got around to changing it.

Don't ask me what happened in there. I don't know. The event itself was so traumatic that my mind wiped all traces of it. Adam doesn't know either. All he knows is that he found me there, in a blood-stained dress, dumb with fear. He took me away and brought me here to safety.

But the events of the red room itself? They are a complete mystery. Whatever happened in there, it left me broken.

Reading *Jane Eyre* has sent me back to that place. It is almost as if I never escaped.

The feeling I have right now is close to terror. Suddenly my own home feels like an alien environment. What am I doing here, all alone, so many miles from anywhere? Where is Adam? I can hardly think clearly. I am breathing so hard that I might faint. Blood rushes through my temples, and I feel an urge to flee. I scrabble to my feet and turn around, as if searching for a way to escape.

But there is nothing to escape from. I left the red room a long, long time ago. I am here in my own home, and nothing can harm me. I stand still in the middle of the room, watching the flames dance in the fireplace, and gradually my heart rate slows and my breathing returns to normal.

Apart from Adam, I have never spoken to anyone about the red room. Just seeing the colour red can cause me to become upset. Speaking about it to a stranger is unthinkable. Even telling Bridget or one of the other women in the book group is out of the question. I do not know them well enough. I have no idea how they might react. In any case, after what happened I resolved to build my life afresh, and with Adam's help that's what I have done. Disturbing the past could upset everything. I don't want to go back and risk re-opening that emotional and mental wound. I must keep it in the past where it cannot hurt me again.

I pick up the book from the floor and smooth the pages flat again. I glance nervously at the portrait of Charlotte Brontë on the cover as if she might suddenly spring to life and say something, as if the book is a living thing with some strange power over me. But it is just a book, nothing more. The portrait does not move. I lay the book carefully on the arm of the sofa.

I go into the kitchen and make myself a cup of tea. That's what Diana did after I fainted at the party, and the memory of her kindness helps me to relax now. I wonder if I should telephone her and say that I have changed my mind, that I cannot continue with the book group. But what reason could I give? I cannot tell her about the red room. I cannot tell her the painful truth about my past.

In any case, I don't want to leave the book group. I have only just made new friends, and I don't want to stop seeing them now. I have had a shock, that is all, and some hot tea will make me feel better. I sip the tea and tell myself that I must be brave.

After I've drunk my tea I feel more like myself. I go back into the lounge and gingerly pick up the book again. It is just a book, I tell myself. Just sheets of paper, bound together with glue. I will find nothing more dangerous between its covers than words, printed in ink. Just words. They have no power over me.

Yet I know that they do. These words have stirred up memories and emotions that I do not want to touch. I have spent so long avoiding them. I am scared of my reaction to the book.

And yet I must continue to read it. I cannot give up so easily. I do not want to leave the book group, or give up my new friends. Maybe if I just take it slowly, one chapter at a time I will be all right. It's only a story. It didn't really happen. It's the story of another Jane, not me.

I turn to chapter two and, with some trepidation, read on. My heart beats faster and I start to take quick, shallow breaths as I read Jane's description of the chill, stately room in which her uncle had died. *The red room.* But it is Jane's red room, not mine. Even though I share her name, I do not share her past. Locked in there as darkness begins to fall, she starts to panic and her imagination runs away with her. I close the book briefly and try to still my nervous breaths. After a few minutes I feel strong enough to read the next few lines. Jane, having worked herself up into a state of high tension, suffers a fit and collapses into unconsciousness.

It is too much. I close the book, unable to read any more. I'm shivering despite the roaring fire in the hearth. I shut my eyes and concentrate on trying to bring my breath back under control. I don't want to faint without Adam or anyone else here to help me. With my eyes closed all I can see is red, but gradually my breathing returns to normal. I do not faint. When I open my eyes, everything is just as it was before I began to read.

And yet I am changing. After years of living quietly, avoiding anything that might disturb me or remind me of the past, emotions are beginning to bubble to the surface. Reading the story of *Jane Eyre* is not going to be easy for me. It has already affected me deeply, dislodging feelings that were perhaps best left undisturbed. Something is awakening inside me, something is struggling to break free. I do not know if I am ready to allow it.

Yet deep down I understand that I have to read this book. I have to allow these feelings and memories to surface. I do not have the strength to read the book alone, but with the support of my new-found friends in the book group, I might just discover the source of these strange and disquieting sensations. I might discover myself.

CHAPTER 9

Adam arrives home later than usual on Friday evening. He says his plane was delayed due to fog at Heathrow. I tell him I am relieved he arrived back safely. I say that I'm glad to have him home with me, and I mean it. I am afraid to be alone right now, but I am careful not to show him my fear. I do not want him to worry. He hugs me tight and the feeling of being wrapped in his strong arms makes me feel safe again.

Over dinner Adam asks me about my week. As usual he wants to know exactly what I've been doing each day. This time he's concerned to know how well I have recovered after fainting at the New Year's Eve party.

The party already seems like a long time ago. I tell him that I feel fine now, that I have not fainted again. I tell him that I have started reading *Jane Eyre*, but I don't say anything about the emotions the book has stirred up. He asks me what the story is about and I tell him a little about Jane, but I don't mention the red room.

I don't tell him anything about the book group either.

'What made you decide to read *Jane Eyre*?' he asks suddenly, and I am caught off guard.

'It's a classic,' I say. 'And the Brontë sisters lived

nearby, of course.' I turn away so that he cannot see my face. I don't think I am very good at deception. I have never been able to tell a lie. I have never wanted to before. Now I have secrets, although really they are trivial secrets. *I have joined a ladies' book group and my friend gave me a lift in her car.* These are not real secrets. They are not the kinds of secrets that Cath reads about in her mystery stories.

It's money from a will, from a distant cousin on my father's side. Now that's a real secret, the kind of secret that would make Cath's ears prick up, but I say nothing to Adam about secrets, real or imagined.

After dinner we go upstairs and make love. I curl up against his warm body and feel secure. Adam didn't ever lie to me, I realise. He would have told me about the money, he just hadn't expected it to arrive so soon. When I asked him about the bank letter, he told me everything.

Adam keeps no secrets from me. He has none to keep.

~~~

On Saturday morning we have a leisurely breakfast together in the kitchen. When Adam's in London during the week, he tells me, he only has time to grab a quick coffee and a croissant. He likes a cooked English breakfast when he's at home. I enjoy preparing it for him, scrambling the eggs just the way he likes them, with a dash of butter and a twist of black pepper. A local farmer supplies eggs to the village shop. They are always fresh.

I see a flash of red through the window and the postman parks his van by the roadside. His boots crunch as he comes up the garden path and then I hear the sound of a letter being dropped through the letterbox.

'I'll get it,' I say, but Adam beats me to it, jumping to his feet and abandoning his eggs and bacon to go into the hallway.

I hear him pick up the post and put it in his office. When he returns empty-handed I ask him if there was anything important.

He shakes his head and says it was just a bill. 'I'll deal with it later,' he says smiling. 'Let's enjoy this delicious breakfast together.'

Although bitterly cold, it's a bright day, so after lunch Adam suggests that we go for a walk. We wrap up against the cold and set off down the country lane. The fields are still sparkling with frost. A wild holly bush growing in the hedgerow is dotted with bright red berries. *Like drops of blood*, I think, and then push the thought from my mind.

We don't cross over the humpback bridge that leads into the village, but descend down to the path alongside the stream. We tramp across the frozen ground at the foot of the valley for half an hour before turning around and heading home.

Adam lights the log fire in the front room and cooks his favourite pasta dish for dinner. We eat it on our laps in front of the blazing fire with a glass of red wine and I think that if life could always be like this, it would be perfect.

On Sunday Adam has work to do in his office so I leave him in peace and carry on with *Jane Eyre*. At this rate I'll have the book finished well before the next meeting of the book group. I'm finding it easier now that I've got past the first two chapters and Jane has been let out of the red room and sent away to boarding school. Even the death of her best friend, although obviously tragic, doesn't affect me as much as the opening chapters did. I find I can breathe easier now.

CHAPTER 10

Adam leaves early on Monday morning as usual and I have the cottage to myself again. I change the sheets on the bed and put the laundry on. Then I get ready to go to the weekly market in town. It's very cold again, so I muffle up warm in my coat and hat. I wrap a scarf around my neck and pull on some thick gloves. I'm just about to head into the village to catch the bus when the phone rings. I take my gloves off again to answer it.

'Hello?' I say, cautiously. Adam never rings me at this time of day, so I can't imagine who it is. Our number is unlisted, so we don't get unwanted calls. Nobody ever rings me except Adam. I wonder if something has happened to him. I suddenly have the idea that his plane might have crashed, and for a moment I am speechless, filled with terror. But it's only Bridget, wanting to know if I'm going to the market this morning. Of course, I gave my number to her when she arranged to collect me for the book group meeting, in case she had a problem.

'Oh,' I say, relieved. 'Yes, I was just going to catch the bus.'

'Don't be silly, Jane,' she says. 'I'll call in at the cottage and pick you up in ten minutes. I'm going to the market myself. You'll freeze waiting for the bus in this weather. Besides, I like the company.'

I hesitate, worried that by accepting her offer I am betraying my husband's wishes, but her voice sounds so warm that I push my concerns away. 'Thank you,' I say. 'You're very kind.'

She arrives soon after, just as she promised, and we travel to the market together. 'How are you?' she asks, as she drives. 'What did you do at the weekend?'

'Adam and I went for a long walk,' I tell her. 'Then he cooked for me on Saturday evening.'

'Wow,' says Bridget. 'I can't remember the last time Ben cooked a meal for me. I guess you could say that he's more spiritual than practical.' She laughs. 'Does Adam often cook?'

'Yes,' I say. 'When he's not in London.'

'He sounds like the perfect husband.'

'Yes,' I say. 'He is.'

'I bought myself a copy of *Jane Eyre*,' says Bridget. 'I've just read the first two chapters.'

'Oh,' I say. 'I bought a copy too. I've read quite a bit already.'

'How are you enjoying it?'

I'm cautious about what I should say to her. My thoughts about the book are still quite confused. 'I think it's affected me quite deeply,' I say, keeping my voice as neutral as I can.

'Why's that?' asks Bridget, her eyes on the road.

I could tell her about the scene with the red room, but she would want to know why that made such a deep impression. She would ask questions. She would say, *What happened to you in the red room?* I can't tell her the truth. I don't even know what the truth is.

I hardly know Bridget really. Like Adam said, I have to be more careful what I say to people. I have so little experience at talking to anyone other than Adam. I am too trusting.

'I'm not sure,' I say. 'But I found the opening chapters quite upsetting. I almost couldn't read any further.'

'Books can be like that,' says Bridget sympathetically.

~~~

I hurry around the market, buying everything I need for the week. I buy meat, cheese and fruit from the market stalls, and some fresh farmhouse bread from the baker on the corner of the market square. I finish my shopping long before Bridget has done hers, so I look around some of the other stalls, pretending that I still have things to buy. I don't want her to think that she needs to hurry on my account.

On the drive back from the market I'm unsettled. Talking to Bridget about *Jane Eyre* has left me in a state of confusion. I wonder if I should be more open with her, but I don't know if I'm ready yet to trust her with my innermost thoughts and feelings. When we reach the cottage I realise I should probably invite her in for a cup of tea or coffee, but I need to be on my own right now. I thank her for the lift, and hurry inside.

I make myself a quick lunch with the bread and cheese I bought from the market, and store the meat and other items in the fridge. I have bought enough food to last me all week. After washing my plate, I vacuum the floors upstairs and down. But really I'm just finding ways to distract myself. What I really want to do is get back to my book. *Jane Eyre* has got under my skin. I feel restless without it.

CHAPTER 11

Each day I read a little more of *Jane Eyre*. In fact, I am so eager to read the book that I force myself to ration it, reading just a few chapters each day, so as not to race through it all in one sitting. Jane's story is absorbing, and I'm finding that there's something compelling about being privy to her intimate thoughts and feelings, even though she is only a fictional character in a novel. Sometimes Jane Eyre feels more real to me than I do to myself.

It is too cold to go for walks, so between chapters I carry on with the housework. Today I decide to give Adam's office a thorough clean while he is away in London. I know he does not like me to disturb his things, so I am very careful, especially when cleaning his desk. I clean the computer screen first, and then dust each item on the desk, carefully replacing everything exactly where I found it. With luck, he won't even know that I have been in here.

Adam keeps his desk neat and organised, with a proper place for everything. Post-It notes, pens, pencils and scissors are arranged to the right of the computer screen. His letters and other correspondence are stacked in a metal in-tray on the left. The last time I was here, the letter from the bank was resting on top of the in-tray, but now it has gone. I wonder what has happened to it.

Normally when Adam finishes with his correspondence he files it away for safekeeping in the drawers below the desk. I expect that is what he has done with the letter from the bank.

I am suddenly gripped by an urge to read it again. I want to see the words on the page one more time, in case there was somehow a piece of information that I missed before, something crucial that would either verify or contradict Adam's explanation of where the money came from. I open the first drawer below the desk and search carefully through the papers and letters one by one, but they are just utility bills – telephone, gas, electricity, water, council tax. Everything is neatly ordered by subject and date, and all the bills have been paid on time.

The next drawer contains household items – insurance policies, receipts and guarantees for items purchased, and user manuals for kitchen appliances.

The final drawer is locked.

I tug at it, hoping it is just stuck, but it stays firm, unyielding. I hunt around the desk for a key, but I cannot find one. There is a small bunch of keys hanging on a hook near the window and I try to open the drawer with each key in turn. None of them fit.

Why does Adam have a locked drawer in his desk? What is he trying to hide? Perhaps he keeps all of his bank statements and other financial papers locked in the drawer for security. I have never looked in his desk drawers before, so I cannot say for sure. Adam always deals with money and bills and things like that. I hang the keys back on their hook, frustrated.

When he calls this evening, I could ask him about the locked drawer and about where he keeps the keys, but that would make him suspicious. He would want to know what I am looking for. He would think I do not trust him. I do not want that.

And if he really is hiding something from me, then alerting him to the fact that I am searching for it would be the worst possible thing I could do.

I dust around the rest of the office, cleaning the frame of an old map that hangs on the wall. The map shows the West Riding of Yorkshire. That's where the Brontë sisters lived, in the village of Haworth. It's not far from here, but I've never visited it. I've never been further than the market town on my own. I clean the skirting boards and wipe the dust from above the architrave of the door. Then I bring in the vacuum cleaner and give the wooden floor a thorough clean, lifting the rug and going right into the corners and under the desk. By the time I have finished, the office is spotless.

I try the desk drawer one last time, but it is still locked.

~~~

After cleaning the office I reward myself with another chapter of *Jane Eyre*. The book has reached an exciting point with Jane about to marry the dashing Mr Rochester. But at the wedding ceremony itself, two strange men arrive and reveal that Rochester already has a wife. Rochester is forced to admit to Jane that he is indeed married, but claims that his wife is insane and that therefore the marriage doesn't really count. Understandably, Jane is distraught and runs away from Thornfield Hall.

I have reached my daily quota for *Jane Eyre*, and reluctantly slip my bookmark between the pages and close the book. I can well imagine Jane's distress at discovering such an awful truth. It seems almost absurd that a man could have a secret wife, but then I think of Adam, living in London five days a week and only returning to me at the weekends. How much do I really know about what he does there? Only what he chooses to tell me. I have no idea if he sees other women whilst he is away from me. If he kept a mistress or even another wife in London, I would never know. A surge of violent emotion wells up in me.

I try to push the ridiculous notion out of my mind, but somehow it clings on, refusing to budge. I go into the kitchen to make some tea, and switch the radio on to distract myself. But now that this thought has occurred to me, I cannot settle to anything else.

The locked drawer is the cause of my anxiety, I realise. Although I am certain that Adam is hiding nothing from me, and that his explanation for the money is true, the locked drawer taunts me, making me think the worst. If I could just open the drawer, I would be able to see for myself that my husband keeps no secrets.

I wander back into Adam's office and try the drawer again. It rattles, but refuses to budge. Without really knowing what I am doing, I switch on Adam's computer. When it is ready I search online for *how to open a locked desk drawer without a key*. There are plenty of videos explaining how to do this. It seems like it may not be so difficult after all, if I can believe what I see in the videos. All I need is some paper clips, some patience and a bit of time.

I have plenty of time. I search for paper clips and find some in a small plastic box on the desk. Now it's just a question of patience. I take two of the paper clips and bend them the way I saw in the online videos. Then I insert them carefully into the lock. It is far harder than the videos suggest. I jiggle the clips around just so, but nothing happens. After a few minutes trying, my patience is exhausted and I tug furiously at the locked drawer, but it remains securely fastened.

In frustration I leave the office and go back into the front room. I pick up *Jane Eyre* and begin reading again, but the words swirl meaninglessly in my mind. I just can't concentrate. I close the book and leave the room. If I cannot open the locked drawer, I won't be able to think about anything else for the rest of the day. And my doubts about Adam will linger.

I return to the office and begin again. I fiddle with the paper clips again, but it still seems impossible. But after some more false starts I eventually feel something move inside the mechanism. Very carefully, I twist the bent pieces of metal and to my amazement the lock slowly turns. By trial and error I have finally succeeded. I withdraw the paper clips from the lock and hesitantly slide the drawer open, my hand trembling. I can scarcely believe what I am doing.

I am not spying, I tell myself. Adam has nothing to hide from me. He did not lock the drawer to keep me from prying into his personal affairs, but simply out of common sense security.

The drawer lies open before me. I'm expecting to see piles of documents and letters, but instead there is something completely different. A brown cardboard box, the size of a writing pad and about an inch thick. It is tied with a white ribbon. I regard the box uncertainly for a moment before removing it from the drawer and placing it carefully on the surface of the desk. Beneath the box is a manila folder and I remove that too.

The letter from the bank is most likely to be found inside the manila folder, but the box intrigues me more. I carefully take the ends of the white ribbon between my thumbs and forefingers and pull the knot apart. The ribbon unknots easily, leaving the box untied.

I lift the lid of the box and set it down on the desk.

The box is filled with cards. Sympathy cards. It feels slightly ghoulish to pry into them, but I carefully draw the first card out and examine it.

With Deepest Sympathy, the card reads. The image is tasteful – white and pink roses against a muted grey background. It is made from thick, quality card. I open it and read the handwritten message within.

To Adam,
So sorry for your loss. I can still hardly believe that Victoria is

dead. She will be much missed. My thoughts are with you at this sad time.

Carrie

Victoria? Adam's cousin? When he spoke about her he told me that they hardly ever saw each other. Yet this card suggests they were quite close. I don't recognise the name Carrie, but she is obviously a friend of Adam's from London, and someone who knew Victoria well too, by the sound of it.

I put the card down and lift out the next one. This one reads, *Sending our Condolences at this Difficult Time,* and seems to be from a group of people.

Dear Adam,

So sorry for your tragic loss. Victoria was an amazing person and a wonderful wife. We are all thinking of you at this difficult time.

From your colleagues at Lloyd's of London

A dozen or so people have scrawled their signatures beneath, some adding personal messages of sympathy themselves. I read them in growing disbelief before returning to the main message. *Victoria was an amazing person and a wonderful wife.* I re-read the words over and over, struggling to understand what they can mean.

Adam's wife? Victoria? I am in a kind of daze now. I lift out more cards. They are all different – pictures of flowers, of clouds, of sunsets and of autumn leaves – *So Sorry for your Loss, Sending Condolences, Thinking of you, With Deepest Sympathy* – yet they are also all the same. Each one pierces my heart like a poisoned blade.

I open the cards and study their personalised messages of condolence, each scribbled in different handwriting, yet every one containing the same fateful message.

Victoria.

Not a distant cousin, but a wife.

My husband's wife.

The words make no sense. Nothing makes sense any more.

I am too stunned to know how to react. I set the box of cards to one side and pick up the manila folder. The folder is marked *Insurance Claim*, in Adam's neat handwriting. Dazed, I peer inside.

On top is the letter from the bank. That is strange. Why is a letter about inheritance money in a folder labelled *Insurance Claim*? It is not like Adam to misfile anything, especially not something so important. I read the letter through once again in a kind of trance, just in case I have somehow missed a vital piece of information, something that could unravel the meaning of the sympathy cards, but the letter is as dry and opaque as before. I put it aside and examine the next piece of paper.

This is also a letter. It's from an insurance company, and from the date at the top I realise that it must be the letter that arrived on Saturday, the one Adam said was just a bill. I read the letter and feel a sharp pressure build in my chest. My eyes swim over the words and I can hardly take them in. My heart is racing away and a sense of terror overtakes me.

I breathe deeply, trying to slow my heart, and begin to read the letter again.

Dear Sir,
With reference to the claim for your late wife's life insurance…

I have to re-read these words about five times before I can continue. I double-check the address at the top to see whose wife the letter is referring to. It is addressed to Adam. Mr Adam Harvey. My husband. But that is impossible.

With a hammering heart, I read on:

With reference to the claim for your late wife's life insurance policy, we can inform you that payment of the sum of £250,000 has now been made to your bank account as detailed below.

'No!' I utter the word as if it has the power to protect me from what I am reading. But nothing changes.

I grab the letter from the bank again and compare the account details with the letter from the insurance company. They match. I re-check the numbers in disbelief, my finger shaking as I slide it across the paper, but there can be no doubt. The money was not from an inheritance. It was a life insurance claim. A claim for Adam's late wife. Victoria.

I drop the letter as if it were on fire and stand up suddenly, causing the chair to roll backwards on its castors and crash into the wall behind. I feel sick and dizzy, and for a moment I am sure I will faint again or throw up. I clutch the edge of the desk for support, my breath catching in my throat.

Adam had no cousin. He had another wife.

CHAPTER 12

It is not possible. It is simply not possible.

I stand upright by the desk, dazed, unable to think what to do next.

I study the letter from the insurance company again, convinced that I have somehow misunderstood. But its meaning is crystal clear. The two hundred and fifty thousand pounds was payment for a life insurance policy on Adam's late wife.

Late wife.

A thought comes to me and I cling to it like a lifeline. Adam must be involved in some kind of fraudulent insurance claim. He has somehow fabricated this Victoria in order to claim two hundred and fifty thousand pounds. I don't know why he would do such a thing. We already have plenty of money. Adam's investments amount to far more than two hundred and fifty thousand pounds. The house in London is worth millions itself.

But in any case, how can this explain the sympathy cards?

I lift them again and flip through them one by one.

Victoria was such a lovely person. Victoria will be so deeply missed. You and Victoria were made for each other.

I have never met any of Adam's work colleagues or friends from London, but I recognise some of the names written in the cards. He has talked about them to me. They are people he works with, or sometimes goes out for drinks with, people who know him well. And they obviously knew Victoria too. But how can that be so? How can she possibly have existed?

I am Adam's wife. A man cannot have two wives.

The letter from the insurance company offers no clues, but there is one more letter in the folder. It is from the same insurance company and is dated a couple of months earlier. The letter thanks Adam for sending all of the information they requested, and states that they are now able to authorise payment of the sum of two hundred and fifty thousand pounds. So she must have died quite recently, perhaps a few months ago. I think back, trying to recall Adam's behaviour over the past few months, seeking a clue that he might have been suffering from some shock or loss as a result of this bereavement.

There was a period at the end of the summer when he did seem a little distracted. He told me that he was very busy at the office and had to stay late several nights. Once he flew back on a Sunday to catch up with work. I thought nothing of it at the time, but now I wonder. Was he grieving for a dead wife?

The letter I hold in my hands includes two further pieces of information. The name of his deceased wife, and her address.

Her name was Victoria, and she lived at Adam's house in London.

I let out another involuntary cry. There is no room for any doubt. My legs are shaking so much I cannot stand anymore. I pull the chair back and collapse into it.

I do not faint, although I want nothing more than to block out all consciousness, all awareness of the truth. I sit at the desk with my head in my hands for I don't know how long.

I stare at the open drawer, the drawer whose lock I picked with the help of some bent paper clips and an online video. I wish that it was still locked, concealing its terrible secrets within. If I could undo my actions and start today all over again, I would. Not knowing would be better than knowing this. I don't know what to do with this knowledge. My mind simply cannot process it.

I sit in the chair, doing nothing but gazing out of the window at the bleak frosted landscape that stretches away, empty of all life and hope. I think of nothing. My life is as good as over.

Eventually, new thoughts begin to form out of the blankness that has swallowed me up. Feeling begins to animate my numb awareness.

I've been such a fool. All the time Adam has been living and working in London he has kept a second wife. He has not hidden her away in an attic like Mr Rochester. Instead, I have been hidden away up here, far from anywhere I might see them together and find out. He has taken advantage of my wish for a quiet life to keep me away from the truth. From Monday to Friday he lives his real life in the city. At weekends he comes to visit me, out here in the countryside, far from anywhere.

And I have played along with him unwittingly. Through my own weakness and fears, I have allowed him to keep me in this prison, as securely as if the door were padlocked and bolted from the outside.

Be careful what you say to people in the village, he has told me. *Keep away from strangers. Don't say anything about us.*

I have done exactly what he told me, thinking that it was for my own protection. Instead it was to protect him. To prevent me saying anything to anyone that might inadvertently reveal the truth. He has made me his fool.

A fresh shock hits me: I am not his true wife. This other woman, Victoria, was his real wife, the woman he lived with on weekdays. She was the woman who shared his daily life. I am his weekend wife, or perhaps not even a real wife at all.

But now she's dead.

I wonder what she died of, but the insurance letter gives no clues. Whatever it was, I feel no sympathy for her, only a black hate. I'm glad she's dead. My only regret is that I didn't get to kill her myself. If she were here now, alive, I would kill her without hesitation. I would kill them both.

I spring to my feet again and pace around the confined space of the office like a prowling tigress ready to pounce on its prey. My fingers are curled into tight fists.

What am I going to do?

CHAPTER 13

I shiver and realise that it's grown late. Outside it's dark. It has been dark for a long time, perhaps for several hours. The fields outside have vanished into blackness and all I can see through the window is the bright reflection of the office, my own pale face staring back at me from the glass. I don't know what I have been doing all this time. The pens, pencils and other stationery that were arranged so neatly on the desk are now scattered across the floor of the room, although I have no recollection of throwing them there. I remember shouting and screaming in rage at Adam. After that I was overcome by a dark thrill, knowing that this woman, Victoria, was dead. Then, for a while, I raged again at the injustice of it all. Eventually I calmed down, exhausted.

For a long while, time passed and I felt nothing, thought nothing, did nothing. My mind was frozen, like the dark, frost-covered landscape outside.

Now my mind is beginning to work again. I know what I must do.

First I close the curtains, blocking out the menacing darkness and the mocking reflections in the window. I gather together the sympathy cards and replace them in the box, tying the white ribbon carefully, just as it was tied before. I put the letters from the insurance company and the bank back into the manila folder where I found them, and return the folder and the box to the desk drawer. I close the drawer and lock it again with the paper clips. Fortunately my lock-picking exploits have not broken the lock. I tug at the drawer to check it is secure, and then I slip the bent paper clips into my pocket.

I kneel on the floor and carefully gather up all of the pens, pencils, and other items that have been hurled there. I straighten everything on the desk, so that it is exactly as I found it. I return the chair to its normal position under the desk and leave the room, switching off the light and closing the office door behind me. I go into the kitchen and drop the bent paper clips into the bin.

It is almost as if nothing has happened. The office is completely unchanged from how I first found it. But I have changed utterly.

Like Jane Eyre, part of me wants to flee from my home and lose myself on the moors. It would be a kind of freedom, to leave this cottage that is my prison, to turn my back on Adam, who is perhaps not even my real husband, and vanish into the darkness.

But where would I run to? Where would I go?

In these temperatures I wouldn't last the night in the open air. I could go to the vicarage and tell Bridget everything that has happened, and beg to spend the night there with her clanking heating system and her ghosts. Or I could throw myself at Diana and ask her if I could stay in the Corner House. She and Michael would surely welcome me into their home and look after me for as long as necessary. I could even go to Cath's flat above the shop, where there would be no space to stay but plenty of tea and sympathy.

But no. I am stronger than that. I have visited the blackest place inside my own mind and emerged again the other side. However much of a weak fool Adam may think

I am, I know that my inner core is resilient enough to overcome this. I will face this myself, and I will find my own solution.

I light the fire in the lounge and start to plan what I will say when Adam phones at nine o'clock.

~~~

Time passes. I do not do the things I normally do when I am alone in the cottage. I have no appetite for food. I cannot concentrate on a book. And I will certainly not do any of my usual household chores. Instead I sit and think. The fire beside me is hungry for wood, and I feed it while I wait.

When Adam calls at nine o'clock precisely, I am ready. I pick up the phone after the first ring and wait to hear his voice. I wonder if he will say anything different this time. Will he somehow know that my world has turned upside down? Or will he carry on as normal, as if nothing has changed and everything is exactly as it was before?

'How are you?' he asks, as always. 'Have you had a nice day?'

There are so many things I could say to him.

I'm in a state of shock, darling. You see, I just found out that my entire world is built on a lie.

Or, *I found the letters, Adam. Who was Victoria? How could you have done that to me?*

Or, *You are a lying, cheating, bastard, and I hate you, Adam.*

But I don't say any of those things.

'I'm fine,' I say. 'How about you?'

'Still very busy at work,' he says. 'There's some kind of bug going around the office, and several people are off sick. You know how it is at this time of year.'

He says it as if it matters. As if I am interested in his other life in London.

'Jane?' he says. 'Are you okay?'

I realise that I have lapsed into silence, that I have nothing to say to him anymore.

'Has something happened?' he asks.

I can hear the concern in his voice. It is almost as if he actually cares for me.

'Jane?'

I could remain silent and see what he says. Perhaps he would confess everything and beg for my forgiveness. But it's not very likely. 'Do you miss me when you're in London?' I ask.

He hesitates before answering. 'Of course I miss you. You know I'd rather be with you, but there aren't any jobs up in Yorkshire that would pay as well. We've talked about this before. I thought you understood.'

'I understand. What do you do at the house when you're all alone? It must be lonely there.'

'Jane, you know what I do here. Most evenings I work late so that I can get away early on a Friday and come back to you. I barely do anything in London except work, eat and sleep. If I'm lucky I'll get to microwave a TV dinner and watch a film or a box set.'

'On your own?' I ask.

'Of course. Who did you think I might see?'

Victoria. Her name is on the tip of my tongue, but instead I say, 'I wondered if maybe you see some friends sometimes.'

'I would tell you if I did,' he says. 'You know that most of my friends moved away years ago. Occasionally I see someone from work, that's all.'

Someone from work. Was that who Victoria was? A colleague, perhaps. Or a secretary. What a dreadful cliché. 'Who?' I say. 'Who do you see?'

'Oh, I don't know. David, perhaps. Sometimes Richard. We might grab a beer together once a month.'

'No one else?'

'No. Listen, what is this all about? What's happened? Have you been talking to someone?'

'No,' I say. 'I never speak to anyone. I would tell you if I did.'

'And are you certain you're okay?'

'Positive.'

'All right, then,' he says. 'I'll speak to you again tomorrow night. Same time. I love you, Jane.'

'Goodnight,' I say. If he wants me to say I love him too, he's going to be disappointed.

I put the phone down and tears run down my cheeks.

What did I expect? Did I really think he would spontaneously admit to seeing someone else, to having a second wife in London? I could have asked him straight out about her, but the truth is that I'd rather not know any details. Besides, I'm frightened about how he might react.

I cannot afford to lose my temper. One thing that frightens me is that if this woman, Victoria, was Adam's real wife, what does that make me? Is it possible that we are not legally married? Is Adam somehow like Mr Rochester in Jane Eyre? I don't understand how that can be true, but I know that a man cannot have two wives. If he was able to prove to the insurance company that Victoria was his wife, then is my own marriage invalid?

If that is the case, then I cannot risk Adam leaving me. If I accuse him openly and he decides to walk out on me, I would have nothing. No husband, no home, no job. I cannot imagine how I would begin to live on my own, with no one and nothing to help me.

And so, whoever this Victoria was, and however much she meant to Adam, I have to learn to live with her shadow over me, for the time being, at least. Whatever happened between Adam and Victoria, that's all over now. It's in the past. And although Adam has betrayed me, it is obvious from the way he behaves when he is with me that he still loves me. Even though he has wronged me, and however difficult it may be to fully trust him again, it is clear from what he says and what he does that he wants me to be his wife, even if only at weekends and holidays.

I will have to decide if that is enough for me, too.

And so, however much this Victoria has hurt me, I

have to let her go.

And anyway, she's dead.

The dead can't hurt us anymore, can they?

CHAPTER 14

By the time of the second book group meeting, I've regained my composure. Two days have passed since I discovered the insurance letter and I have not stepped foot outside the cottage, nor spoken to anyone other than Adam. When he phoned me last night I could tell that he was listening out for any hints that I was upset or angry, but I was careful to stick to my usual script and tell him that nothing of any consequence had taken place since we had spoken the previous evening. I did not accuse him of any misdemeanours, or demand to know who he spent his evenings with in London. In truth, I have decided to insulate myself from any knowledge about what he does when he is not with me. I will not grant him the power to hurt me again.

'How are you?' he asked cautiously, when I answered the phone to him. 'Have you had a nice day?'

'Oh yes,' I said. 'Very nice. How about you?'

'Good, thanks. What did you do today?'

I allowed just a second to pass before I answered him. 'Nothing,' I told him. 'Nothing at all.'

And that was the truth. I had not unpicked any more locked drawers, nor hurled any items onto the floor in a furious rage. I had not unearthed any devastating secrets that turned my entire life on its head. I had not contemplated running across the moors screaming in anger and pain. I had simply stayed at home, reading and listening to the radio. For once I decided not to do any housework. Instead I sat on the sofa with a warm blanket over my legs, drinking tea, finishing *Jane Eyre*, and then starting a new book. I listened to the news on the radio, and the afternoon play. I sat watching as dust motes danced in a shaft of sunlight that shone briefly through the window of the front room, and I did not worry about vacuuming the floor or dusting the furniture. I ate my lunch and dinner and left the dirty plates and dishes in the kitchen sink. But I did not tell Adam any of that. Instead I told him nothing.

In the aftermath of discovering the truth about Victoria, I had thought of phoning Diana or Bridget and cancelling the next book group meeting, giving them some made-up excuse. But I don't want to. I don't want to lie to my new friends. And in any case, Adam has caused me enough pain. I won't allow him to spoil this too. One thing I have learned for sure is that I cannot continue to build my life solely around Adam. I have to start to make new friends and get to know more people in the village. I have to find new interests that don't depend on Adam. And there is also a wicked thrill of deliberately going against his wishes and defying him. If Adam can keep secrets, then so can I, even if they are only small and harmless. So when Bridget calls to say that she'll pick me up at seven o'clock on Thursday evening, I accept gladly.

Now that I've finished the novel, I'm looking forward to hearing what the others thought of it, although I'm wary of sharing my reactions to some of the chapters. They might reveal too much. I'm not ready to talk about what's happened in my own life, and certainly not to some women who I've only known for a matter of weeks, even though I have come to like them immensely, especially

Bridget, who I have grown closest to, and perhaps has most in common with me. If I have learnt anything from my recent experience, it is that I am too trusting. I do not want to unwittingly grant anyone else the power to hurt me. I hope they do not want to spend too much time discussing the scene in the red room, and I would prefer not to mention Mr Rochester's first wife at all, although that is unlikely given what a major part she plays in the plot.

At least Victoria is dead, not like Rochester's madwoman in the attic, who almost kills him by setting his house on fire. Nothing like that can happen to me.

This time Bridget has offered to host us all at the vicarage. I wait for her by the window, and am glad when I see the headlights of her car lighting up the dark road. I am already wrapped up in my coat and scarf and so I go outside to meet her.

'Hop in,' she calls when I open the car door.

I slide into the passenger seat next to her, and feel like I am returning to sit in a favourite armchair. It has only been a few days since I saw her last, but I have missed her company enormously. She is starting to feel like a real friend, perhaps the only real friend I have ever known. I smile at her and wonder if I can trust her enough to tell her of my discovery.

I realise that she is the first person I have seen since I opened the locked drawer and came face to face with the truth about Adam and Victoria. I feel a sudden urge to tell her everything. Bridget has always been so kind to me. But something holds me back. I hardly know her, really. I hardly know anyone at all. I thought I knew Adam, but how well do I really understand him? The thought makes a tear well up in the corner of my eye, and I wipe it away quickly, hoping she will think it is just the cold.

'Hi, Jane,' she says, studying my face. 'How are you today?'

I wonder if she has noticed something in my

expression, or in my demeanour. I am trying to appear cheerful, but I don't know how well I am doing. I don't want her to worry about me.

'I'm fine,' I say, giving her another smile. 'I'm absolutely fine.'

Her eyes linger on my face for a while before she moves her attention back to the road. Then she turns the car and heads back towards the village.

The vicarage is an old Victorian house next to the church. Ivy climbs up its weathered stonework, threatening to block out the windows. Like Bridget said, the house is really much too big for just her and Ben. I wonder if they are planning to have children, and feel a pang for my own childless state. She and Ben would make good parents, I think.

She ushers me into a tiled entrance hall. Closed doors lead off the hallway, giving the impression of unused rooms. I wonder if the rooms are empty. I wonder if any of them are red. 'It's awfully chilly in here in this weather,' says Bridget. 'It's such a difficult house to heat.' She takes my coat and hangs it on a stand. 'Come into the sitting room where it's warmer.'

One of the closed doors opens and Ben appears, his hands cradled around a large mug of coffee. He offers me a smile. I haven't seen him since the party and I'd forgotten just how good-looking he is. Now I'm reminded what a kind face he has, youthful, almost boyish. His blonde hair is combed in a quiff, and the short stubble on his chin gives him a relaxed and carefree look. But there's an intensity to his eyes too, that suggests intelligence and insight. He's a good match for Bridget. I look at him shyly, not wanting to stare.

'Hello, Jane, how are you feeling now?' he asks me. 'No more fainting?'

'No,' I reply. 'I'm feeling much better, thank you.' I do my best to return his smile, but I feel it might be forced.

If he notices, he gives no sign of it. 'That's good,' he

says cheerfully. 'Don't mind me. I'm going into my study to write Sunday's sermon.'

I can't imagine he has many people in his congregation in a village this size. I feel a little guilty, never having been to one of his services. But neither Adam nor I are regular churchgoers.

He disappears into one of the other rooms off the hallway and Bridget shows me into the sitting room. 'Make yourself comfortable,' she says. 'I'm going to boil the kettle.'

The sitting room is large, with a high corniced ceiling, but warm and inviting. The décor reflects Bridget and Ben's easy-going personalities. There's a comfy sofa covered in colourful scatter cushions, a coffee table littered with old copies of the *Sunday Times* and a sunny modern painting of an Italian landscape on the wall. I take a seat on the sofa and get my copy of *Jane Eyre* out of my bag. The portrait of Charlotte Brontë stares back at me from the cover, as if she knows my secrets. Perhaps she does. It is uncanny how the story of Jane Eyre mirrors my own.

What would Jane do in my circumstances, I wonder. But the answer is plain, since I have read the book. *Run, run far away*. And yet here I am still. I refuse to run away from Adam.

But if not run from him, then what?

By the time Bridget has made the tea, Diana and Cath have arrived too. I hear her welcoming them into the house, and ushering them through into the sitting room.

'Hi, Jane,' says Cath, entering the room first. 'Are you well?'

'Very well,' I say, beaming at her. Since I have resolved not to tell them of my troubles, there is no reason to let them think I am unhappy.

Diana follows on Cath's heels, and the two sit on the sofa next to me. Bridget comes through from the kitchen with tea and a plate of chocolate biscuits. They all have their copies of *Jane Eyre* with them.

'I'm glad to see that everyone has brought their homework,' jokes Diana, a wry glint in her eye. 'Did you all finish reading it?'

'I had to stay up late last night to get it finished,' admits Cath. 'You know how it is, so much to do, I never find time for myself.'

The others all make noises of sympathy and agreement, and I realise with a start that I have the opposite problem. I have far too much time for myself. Bridget hands out cups of tea and then sits down in an armchair by the fireplace.

'We all finished it though, yes?' continues Diana. We murmur our assent. 'So what did everyone think?'

No one seems to want to be first to give their opinion, but then Cath says, 'Well, it was a bit different to the kind of book I normally read. It was a bit slow to get going, but I thought it was ever so good in the end.'

'I loved it,' says Bridget. 'I'm a big fan of Charlotte Brontë.'

Diana nods her agreement, then looks at me.

'Yes,' I say. 'I enjoyed it too.' I am nervous about saying any more, about how deeply it affected me, but thankfully Diana starts to speak again. I help myself to a chocolate biscuit to calm my nerves.

It's obvious that she has thought carefully about the kind of discussion she thinks we should have. I suppose it comes naturally to her, being a retired schoolteacher. She begins with some general questions about Jane's character and Mr Rochester's motives. We all chime in with our comments.

We very quickly get to the heart of the novel, namely Jane's discovery, on her wedding day of all days, that the man she is about to marry has another wife, a madwoman, hidden in the attic. It's on the tip of my tongue to say, never mind fiction, these things can actually happen in real life. It would be so easy to unburden myself and tell them about Victoria. They would be shocked, of course, and outraged on my behalf. There would be an outpouring of sympathy and support for me. But I know what would happen next. They would start to have ideas about what I should do. They would suggest possible courses of action for me to take. They would push me towards leaving Adam. They would try to control me, just like Adam has always done. That is the very last thing I want.

But then an even more chilling thought crosses my mind. They might not believe me. They may think that reading this novel has given me strange ideas. No doubt I'm already an oddity in their eyes, the woman who lives in the cottage outside the village, cut off from everyday life. Perhaps they already talk about me when I am not around. The woman who has no friends, no children, no job, and a husband who spends the week living as far away from her as possible. They will think I'm mad. I mustn't tell them anything.

The conversation has moved on and I haven't been paying attention. I focus on Diana who is speaking, and reach for another chocolate biscuit, cramming it into my mouth nervously.

'I'd kill Michael if I discovered he had another wife hidden away somewhere,' Diana says. Bridget and Cath laugh and I do my best to join in. Diana doesn't laugh though. For all her educated manner, there's something deadly behind her words, as if she really means them.

Kill him. A shiver runs down my spine at the thought. It's what I swore I would do to Adam when I first read the insurance letter. It's what I would have wanted to do to Victoria, if she were still alive. *Kill her. Kill them both.*

Cath is speaking now. 'My Ken wouldn't have the imagination to keep another woman hidden away in the attic,' she says. She chuckles at the thought of it.

I wonder though. *How well do you actually know your husband*, I think. *How do you know what he's really capable of? How can you be absolutely certain that he isn't seeing another woman?*

'The only things Ben keeps in the attic are boxes of old books,' says Bridget.

They all look at me and I realise they're expecting me to say something on the subject of husbands and their secrets, or what we keep in our attic. What can I tell them?

'Adam keeps nothing in the attic,' I tell them vehemently. 'Nothing.' They stare at me for a moment, and I realise that I'm at risk of losing control. I smile to take the sting out of my words. 'I know,' I add. 'Because I was looking in the attic just the other day.'

My comment seems to have released the tension, and the others smile, and the conversation moves on.

Diana says that people often brush over the opening chapters of the book, but she thinks they are significant for the development of Jane's character. I feel my stomach clenching. Any moment now she's going to mention Jane being locked in the red room. I wish I hadn't eaten two chocolate biscuits because I'm feeling slightly queasy.

'For instance,' says Diana, 'the scene in the red room would seem to be a very formative experience in the young Jane's life, don't you agree?'

I sit tight, hardly able to breathe.

Cath is the first to respond. 'Which bit was that?' she asks.

I can't believe she's forgotten the scene in the red room. She can't be a very attentive reader.

'Right at the start,' I say, turning to her. 'Jane has a fight with her cousin John and her aunt locks her in the red room.' I realise that I've raised my voice somewhat and I try to calm down again.

'You told me the other day you found that scene disturbing,' says Bridget gently, referring to our conversation in the car on the way to the market. 'Why was that do you think?'

Cath is thumbing through her copy of the novel, trying to find the relevant part.

I've said too much already and regret my outburst. 'I

don't really know,' I say. I can't tell them about my own red room. 'I suppose it's just terrible to think of a young girl locked in a room on her own. So frightening.'

'Books can trigger all sorts of deep-seated emotions,' says Diana, nodding her understanding. 'It is very distressing to think of a child being locked in a room like that. Especially one where her uncle had died. You're probably just a very empathetic reader, Jane.'

'Maybe,' I say.

'Oh, yes, here it is,' says Cath. 'I remember now. Mind you, there were times when my two were young, I could have gladly locked them in a room. Not that I would have done, but these thoughts do go through your mind.'

I realise with a pang of guilt that Cath just has her plate full, what with running the shop and living in a cramped flat with two teenage boys under her feet the whole time. Why would she remember a scene right at the start of such a long novel? But Cath has experience of life that I don't have. I shouldn't be so quick to judge her.

She looks thoughtful for a moment, then adds, 'The difference between normal people and monsters like Jane's aunt is that we don't act on our fantasies and impulses.'

'That's very true,' says Diana.

I wonder whether Cath would regard me and Adam as 'normal' if she discovered the truth. I doubt it, and the thought makes me sad.

We leave the subject of the red room and discuss the ending of the book, where Jane returns to Rochester, but only after his wife is dead and he's lost a hand and his eyesight in the fire that engulfed his house.

'It's not exactly a happy ending, is it?' says Cath, sounding disappointed. 'I mean, I know they get married and all that, but he's blind and poor now.'

'I think the point is that Jane accepts him on her own terms,' says Bridget thoughtfully. 'They are now equals. I think you could say that Charlotte Brontë was quite a feminist.'

'I agree,' says Diana.

We've exhausted the topic of Jane Eyre and move on to chatting about general matters. Then Diana raises the question of where to hold the next meeting.

'I'd love to have you all over to my place,' says Cath, 'but it would be such a squash, and the boys will be home watching the telly.'

I remember that we agreed to host the book group at a different house each time, and I realise with a jolt that I need to invite everyone over to my place. Diana hosted the first meeting, Bridget the second, and there simply isn't enough room at Cath's. My immediate instinct is to invent a reason why they can't come to the cottage, but then it occurs to me that I would like them to come. I want to open my home to my new friends. And besides, it would be a small act of rebellion against Adam. The idea of these women sitting in the front room of the cottage, one of them perhaps even occupying Adam's place on the sofa, unbeknown to him, fills me with glee.

'You're very welcome to come to my place,' I say, 'if you don't mind traipsing all the way out of the village.'

'I can give you both a lift,' says Bridget to Diana and Cath.

'All right then,' I say. 'Same time next week?'

'We don't have to read another book by then, do we?' asks Cath, sounding alarmed.

'No,' says Diana. 'We can decide next week what we'd like to read next. This is meant to be fun, not stressful.'

I help Bridget to clear up and carry the cups and plates back to the kitchen.

Ben is in the hallway again when I go to leave. 'All done?' he inquires. '*Jane Eyre*, wasn't it?' He grins. 'Mr Rochester and the madwoman in the attic.'

I smile weakly at him. 'Thanks for your hospitality,' I say.

'No problem. I hope to see you again soon.'

Bridget drives me back home.

'You're lucky to have Ben, you know,' I tell her on the way back. 'He's so easy-going.'

'Yes,' she says. 'I am lucky. And you're lucky to have Adam. He's a very attentive husband, isn't he? He was ever so concerned about you when you fainted at the party. He seemed to think it was his fault. Sorry, I probably shouldn't be telling you this.'

'No, no,' I say, 'it's fine.' I'm curious to know what Adam said whilst I was out for the count. I can't imagine he revealed anything too startling because he's too controlled for that. Too good at keeping secrets. 'What did he say?' I ask casually.

'Oh, I can't remember exactly, something about the pair of you not intending to stay so late because late nights don't agree with you, I think. He was clearly very worried though. He picked you up and carried you through to the other room.'

I imagine myself as a lifeless doll in Adam's arms and a shiver runs through me.

We've arrived at the cottage and Bridget signals and pulls over. I thank her for the lift and open the door, letting in a blast of cold air.

'Take care, Jane,' she says as she waves me goodbye.

I watch her car heading back towards the village. The red lights grow smaller as the car disappears down the narrow road. Eventually they vanish completely. When the car has gone, the darkness here is almost complete.

I haven't been paying close attention to the time, and I realise that it's almost nine o'clock. As I walk into the cottage and begin to take off my coat, the phone rings. It's Adam. The idea that I almost missed his call ought to alarm me, but I find to my surprise that I don't really care. I pick the phone up, my coat only half-unbuttoned.

'How are you?' he asks. 'Have you had a nice day?'

I feel a sense of freedom, of courage bordering on recklessness. I could say anything to him. Anything at all.

I have a secret to tell you, Adam. I joined the ladies book group without telling you. What do you think of that? They're coming here next week, and there's nothing you can do to stop them.

What might he say in response? A sense of abandon seizes me, and I start to think what else I might say to him.

I'm leaving you, Adam. I found out about Victoria and I'm filing for divorce. Don't ever come here again.

But a sense of dread grips me. I still don't know what I really want. I don't even know for sure if I am legally married to him. And I have no idea what he might do if I ever defied him openly.

And so I tame my wild thoughts before they can escape and betray me.

'I'm fine,' I say. 'How about you?'

CHAPTER 15

The next morning I see a flash of bright red through the windows of the front room. It's the postman's red van. He parks it outside the cottage and I hear the sound of his van door opening, followed by the scrunch of boots walking up the path. He drops some letters through the door and retreats back to his van. I wait inside, peeping out at him as he goes. The van door slams shut and the van roars away again along the road. It is only then that I find the courage to creep into the hallway and see what he has delivered.

More letters have arrived, and all of them are addressed to Adam, or else consist of marketing material addressed simply to 'The Homeowner'. There is nothing addressed to me, Jane Harvey. There is never anything addressed in my name. The letters from the bank, the electricity company, the phone bills, and the local council are always addressed to Adam, and now I begin to understand why.

I am tempted to rip up the letters and throw them onto the fire. But what would that achieve? Nothing.

Instead, an idea begins to take shape in my mind. I place the letters on Adam's desk ready for when he returns home from London, and I fetch my coat. To get at the truth, I am going to have to be as cunning as he has been.

He will be home this evening and I have work to do.

Hours later there's a coq au vin simmering on the stove. Even though it wasn't market day, I took the bus into the town and bought all the ingredients I needed from the local shops that line the market square: a butcher's, a greengrocer's and an off-licence. Thankfully I didn't run into Bridget this time. I don't know what I would have told her if she'd asked how I was. I'm getting tired of lying, or of not being open with her and the other women. I would like nothing more than to tell them everything, from the very beginning. But I'm half afraid of what they might say. I'm scared that they might not believe my version of events, and think that I've made it up, or imagined it. When I think about what Adam has done, it does seem almost unbelievable.

Although I thought that I didn't want to know anything about Victoria, or about how Adam spends his time in London, I realise now that I need to find out. The only way I can decide what to do next is if I understand what's really happened. There are so many questions I don't know the answer to. Was Victoria really Adam's legal wife? How long had they been married? How did they meet? What was she like? And did he love her? I'm not sure I really want to know the answer to that last question, but if I'm going to decide what to do next, I need to face up to even the hardest questions.

Unfortunately, the only way I'm going to discover more is through Adam. The insurance documents only hold the bare facts that I already know. If I'm going to find out more, I'll need Adam to let something slip.

I have this idea that if the way to a man's heart is through his stomach, then maybe I can take the same route to the truth. And so I've prepared a special meal for him tonight. I've taken care over my appearance too and made sure that everything is just how he likes it. I haven't poisoned the chicken, although the idea did fleetingly cross my mind.

I hear his car pulling up outside and my stomach lurches. I don't know if I've got the courage to see this through. But I do my best to compose myself.

'Something smells good,' he says as he walks in. He drops his briefcase by the front door and takes me in his arms. I let myself be pulled into his embrace. He kisses me warmly on the lips and says, 'You've been busy.'

'I felt like cooking something a bit special tonight,' I say. 'I thought we could have a nice meal together.'

'That's good,' he says. 'I've missed you.'

'I've missed you too,' I say. It feels like an age since I said goodbye to him on Monday morning. Since then, everything has changed. We are no longer the same two people, although Adam knows nothing of what has happened. To him, I am still the same Jane he left behind to catch an early morning flight to London. 'The food will be ready in ten minutes,' I tell him.

'I'll just run upstairs and get changed.'

He disappears into the bedroom and I light the candles on the dining table.

Ten minutes later we're sitting down to coq au vin with steamed vegetables and a bottle of red wine.

'What's all this?' asks Adam, indicating the candles. Soft music is playing in the background. He's looking approvingly at the low-cut dress I'm wearing, and I'm pleased that he's noticed. After so many years of marriage, some husbands no longer see what their wives are wearing. Whatever has happened, he must still love me. He must still find me attractive.

The corners of his mouth twitch into a smile. 'I haven't forgotten our anniversary have I?' he asks. He knows he hasn't forgotten our anniversary. He's watching me intently, trying to gauge the meaning of this unexpected romantic dinner.

'I was thinking of the time we first met,' I say. I take a sip of wine and wait for him to take up the thread.

'You mean the day at Oxford when you and your

friends had punted into the river bank and got stuck?'

I nod. We both know how the story goes, but I want him to tell me everything again. I want to see if there are any inconsistencies that somehow allow room for Victoria to exist in his life. I have already racked my brain to think if he has ever mentioned a woman called Victoria – a work colleague, an old acquaintance, the wife of a friend – but I'm certain that he hasn't. But Adam is always careful. He would not simply let something like that slip. It will not be easy to catch him out.

I can see him thinking back. 'You were stuck in the weeds and Charles and I pulled you clear. You were so grateful, you agreed to come for a drink with me afterwards.'

'I did. But it wasn't really gratitude that made me agree to spend the evening with you, was it?'

'No? Then it must have been love at first sight.'

That is the story we always tell each other. And looking at photographs of Adam in his student days, it is easy to believe that I could have been swept off my feet by such a handsome man coming to my rescue. Even now, I still find him incredibly attractive. And Adam has always had a charm, and a natural affinity with women. I remember the way that Bridget looked at him during the party. I could tell that she was also captivated by his looks and his manner.

But Adam never flirted with other women. He was always true to me. Until he met Victoria.

'Charles was very jealous because he fancied you too.' Adam is smiling to himself, remembering his moment of triumph. 'He couldn't understand why you preferred me to him. I teased him and told him that it was because of his ridiculous moustache and he actually shaved it off. But of course that made no difference at all.'

'I couldn't believe that someone as good-looking as you didn't already have a girlfriend. It didn't seem possible.' I watch him closely to gauge his reaction.

He shrugs. 'I'd never met the right person, until I met you.'

'Was there really never anyone else? Before we met?'

'Of course not,' he says. 'I would have told you.'

'What about before Oxford?'

'Nothing serious. You were my first love. You know that.'

And your only love? It's on the tip of my tongue to ask, *When did you first meet Victoria?* But I refrain from mentioning her. I mustn't say her name before Adam does. I have to see if he will trip himself up and reveal something about his other life. His other wife. There must be some cracks in this carefully-constructed façade that is Adam's life, something that will hint at Victoria. I have to find those cracks.

I top up his glass but am careful not to drink too much wine myself. I must keep a clear head. But with a little alcohol inside him, he's likely to become more talkative. I glance across at our wedding photo on the sideboard and Adam takes the bait.

'You looked so beautiful that day, walking down the aisle,' he says. 'I couldn't believe my good fortune. Part of me was sure you weren't going to turn up. But when Charles nudged me on the arm and said, "She's here," I was the happiest man on earth.' He leans across the table and takes hold of my hand. The way he talks, the expression that animates his face, he seems so sincere. I force myself not to pull away.

'Do you ever think we should have waited?' I ask. 'We were so young when we got married. Did you ever have any doubts that I was the person you wanted to spend the rest of your life with?'

He frowns. 'No, never.' He rubs his forefinger against my palm. 'You were the only one for me. I always knew that.'

He's utterly convincing. If I hadn't seen the letter from the insurance company and the condolence cards with my own eyes, I would find it impossible to believe he was lying. I feel certain that he couldn't already have been married when we met at Oxford because he was still a student then. And he couldn't possibly have met Victoria between then and our wedding day, because we got married as soon as we could after we'd graduated from Oxford. So he must have met her later, maybe through work. If there is a gap or an inconsistency in his story, that's where I'll find it.

Adam is still looking concerned. 'You don't have any doubts about spending the rest of your life with me, do you?' he asks.

My heart leaps into my throat. A part of me would like nothing more than to do that, to sweep away all knowledge of Victoria and continue just as we were. But I cannot go back in time. Victoria will always be between us now. If I am to stay with Adam, I will have to find a way to deal with her.

'I just wish I could be with you more,' I say. 'I miss you so much when you're away in London all week.'

A sad look passes across his face. 'I miss you too, Jane. But we've talked about this before. You know how much you dislike being in crowded places. You couldn't possibly live in London.'

'I know,' I say. 'I wasn't like that at Oxford, though.'

'No,' he says quietly. 'You were different, then.' He can tell where I am leading him. He doesn't want the conversation to go this way. But it must.

'It's all because of the red room, isn't it?' I say.

Everything always comes back to this. The red room was when my life lurched uncontrollably off course. But had he already met and married Victoria before then, or did it happen afterwards?

'I don't want to talk about that now, Jane,' he says. 'Let's not spoil this lovely evening.'

I persist. 'If it hadn't happened, maybe I could have come to live with you in London.'

'Perhaps. But there's no point thinking about what might have happened. We should be glad for what we have. You like it here, don't you?'

'Yes,' I say quickly. But then I wonder. Do I like it here? Am I happy the way my life has turned out? Before I found out about Victoria, I was. Before the letter from the bank arrived and filled my head with doubt. At least I thought I was happy. I didn't know any different. But I'm beginning to suspect that I wasn't really happy, that I've never been truly happy since I came to the village. I'm starting to see that I've been desperately lonely and that my life has been a shadow of what it might have been.

'Why did we never try harder to have children?' I ask him. 'After we found out that I couldn't have a baby, why didn't we try fertility treatment?' It's a fact that I've always just accepted. But now I wonder why I didn't question it before.

Adam gives a deep sigh. 'You know that I would have loved to have children,' he says. 'But it just wasn't meant to be. We spoke to the fertility clinic, but the doctor didn't recommend it for us.'

'But why didn't we try anyway? Why didn't we insist on trying?'

'The treatment can be expensive, you know that. But that wasn't the main reason. There was such a small chance of success. The doctor strongly advised us against proceeding. He said it would be highly traumatic and upsetting.'

'Yes. But we could have tried, couldn't we?'

'I guess so,' he concedes. 'But it's too late now.'

He's probably right about that. I'm already thirty-eight. Old to be trying for a pregnancy even if everything was normal. But the idea that motherhood has been snatched away from me makes my anger flare up. And then I think – how old was Victoria? Was she much younger than me? Might Adam have married her because I couldn't give him a baby? Is it even possible that she and Adam had a child together?

The idea is shocking. But surely he and Victoria didn't have a baby. What would happen to a child now that Victoria is dead? Adam couldn't possibly abandon a child in London to come and see me every weekend. And yet, this is a man who has kept two wives. He's capable of anything.

I pull my hand away from him.

'It was your decision not to proceed with the treatment,' he says, and it's like a slap to my face. I know that he is right though. I didn't want to risk the possible upset of repeated failure. I won't take all the blame though. 'It was a joint decision, wasn't it?' I say. 'We agreed not to proceed.'

He nods. 'We decided together. You, me and the consultant. We all agreed not to go ahead.' I know he is right. We have talked about this so many times before. I don't know why I have allowed it to upset me so much now. And besides, I have deviated from my goal of tripping Adam up and revealing the cracks in his story. I was hoping for a glimpse of Victoria, but instead I have seen a piece of my own tragic past staring back at me.

Suddenly I don't want to talk about the past anymore. 'Hold me,' I say, and he pushes his chair back from the table and comes to me. I let him take me in his arms and he pulls me tight against him. I can feel tenderness as well as strength in his arms, and it is impossible for me to think badly of him. Whenever I have needed Adam, he has always been there for me. We have been together for such a long time, I cannot imagine a life without him.

Victoria is dead. Whatever happened between her and Adam is well and truly over. I should leave her buried. It is foolish to want to disturb the dead. What possible good may come of it?

We finish our meal. I've even bought desserts: tiramisu from the bakery in town. Adam helps me clear up and then we curl up on the sofa whilst he finishes off the bottle of red. I've only had a glass, he's drunk the rest himself. Then we go to bed and make love. He is tender, and again, I cannot reconcile the Adam I know with the Adam I discovered when I broke into the locked drawer.

With the food, wine and sex, he's fast asleep and snoring within seconds. It is as if he doesn't have a single care in the world. But I lie awake staring into the darkness.

It is tempting to think that Victoria never existed, that he never betrayed me. I wonder if the insurance company might have made a mistake. Could Victoria be nothing more than an administrative error? But the letter thanked Adam for sending them the relevant documents. It can't simply have been a computer glitch. And the money in the bank confirms it.

Victoria was real.

I eventually fall into a dream-filled sleep in the early hours of the morning. I dream that there's a madwoman in the attic and that she wants to kill me. I try to run away but the door is locked and I can't get out. The walls of the attic are painted red.

CHAPTER 16

Saturday is wet so we stay indoors. Adam is still in a good mood from Friday evening but I'm nervous and tense, not having slept well. I tell him that I think I might be going down with a cold and he should keep his distance if he doesn't want to catch it. He takes the hint and disappears into his office saying that he needs to catch up on email anyway. He offers to cook dinner so that I can take it easy.

Taking it easy doesn't help. I roam the cottage restlessly, unable to settle to anything. I gaze out of the window, wishing that it wasn't so cold and wet. I listen to the drumming of the rain against the window and watch the raindrops as they strike the glass. I sleep badly once again.

On Sunday the clouds have cleared so we go for a brisk walk across the moors. The fresh air and exercise do me good, and this time I sleep like a log all night. I don't wake up until I hear the front door closing early on Monday morning and Adam driving off to the airport. He is so considerate that he didn't even disturb me to say goodbye. Or did he sneak away because he had something to hide? I no longer know what to think about anything.

I have slept well, so I slide out of bed and take a

shower. The hot water invigorates me. I feel much better than I did, but I am still no further forward in my quest to find out more about Victoria. She is nothing more than a name to me, although my imagination has already begun to fill in some details.

I see her as being younger than I am; as more attractive. I picture her as an outgoing, carefree person, at ease in the city and amongst crowds. In a strange way, she is the person I would like to be myself. I can almost understand why Adam took her as his second wife.

But I cannot forgive him.

The cottage feels very empty now that Adam has gone back to London. I have never really felt its emptiness before. I have never felt quite so restless. I walk from one room to another, unsure what I am looking for. I know I won't find any more clues to Victoria here. So what is it that I am searching for? I do not know.

Normally on a Monday morning I would do the laundry before going to the weekly market. But today I decide not to do any household chores. It seems a petty act of rebelliousness, but I no longer care if Adam has clean sheets. Would Victoria have spent her days washing and ironing for him at the house in London? My imagined version of Victoria would not. She probably had an exciting career, otherwise how else could she have met Adam in the first place? I picture her in a business suit, a powerful woman who knows what she wants.

Instead of doing the laundry, I go upstairs and change my clothes. I pull on a skirt and blouse and a smart woollen jacket, and I wait for Bridget to come and pick me up as we'd agreed.

Her car appears in the road outside, and I go straight out to meet her. 'Hi!' I say to her.

'Hello, Jane. You look happy this morning. Have you had good news?'

'No. Nothing special,' I say. 'Just feeling good.' It's ironic that I should be in a good mood after all that's happened. It's partly that I realise how lucky I am to have Adam, despite what he's done. But also, the shock of discovering Victoria has jolted me out of my old existence, and I feel that I am tasting life afresh again, as if I am seeing the world through new eyes. Through Victoria's eyes, perhaps.

I'm also enjoying being with Bridget. 'How about you?' I ask her. 'Did you have a good weekend?'

We set off along the narrow road in the direction of town. 'Yes, Sundays are always busy with Ben at church,' she says.

'Of course. It must be strange for Ben having his busiest day when everyone else is taking time off work.'

She laughs. 'We're used to that. In fact I can hardly remember what it was like before.'

'How long have you two been together?' I ask. 'If you don't mind me asking, that is.'

'Not at all. We've been married for just over two years now.'

Her answer surprises me. 'Is that all? I imagined you two had been together for ages.'

'Well, sometimes it seems like ages. But in a good way. But you and Adam have been married for a long time, haven't you? You said that you'd met as students at Oxford.'

'That's right. Seventeen years. I was only twenty-one when I married Adam. He was three years older.'

'Gosh,' says Bridget. 'You were lucky to find the right man at such a young age. And you've lived in the village for seven years. Where did you live before?'

'In Oxford. When Adam took the job in London, I didn't want to move house, so he commuted each day by train.'

'So he's used to commuting into London, then?'

'Yes,' I say. 'But of course he came home every evening in those days. It's only since we moved north to Yorkshire that he's needed to stay in London during the week.'

'That must be hard,' says Bridget. 'What made you move here?'

I can tell from the way she asks the question that she is desperately curious to find out. She has probably been wanting to ask for some time. It must seem very strange to everyone that we live so far from London, where Adam works. How many people take the plane to travel to the office each week? I can see that this must be a mystery to Bridget, whose husband lives right next door to the church where he preaches.

I am at a loss to explain it myself. 'It was...' I begin hesitantly. 'It was after...'

The red room.

We are back to this again. Every question somehow leads me back.

But I am not ready to confide in Bridget about this central event in my life, not yet. Instead I just say, 'Something horrible happened to me. We came here to get away. I'm sorry, I can't tell you anything more about it.'

Bridget's face is filled with sympathy. 'I'm so sorry, Jane,' she says. 'I didn't mean to pry.'

'No worries,' I tell her. 'You weren't to know.'

~~~

I buy more than I usually do at the Monday market. I am acutely aware that Diana, Bridget and Cath will be coming to the cottage for the next book group meeting this Thursday. I would like to make something special for them. My baking isn't as good as Adam would like it to be, but I'm sure that if I take my time and don't panic, I can produce some nice cakes ready for when they come round. I want to make a big effort to make them welcome.

Bridget examines my shopping bags with interest. 'You've bought a lot of food this week, Jane,' she says. She laughs. 'Sorry, that sounds awfully rude.'

I smile and nod, but I don't tell her what I've bought or

why. I'd like it to be a surprise.

After she drops me back at the cottage I transfer all my purchases to the fridge and the kitchen cupboard. The dirty breakfast dishes stare back at me accusingly from the sink. I feel foolish now that I did not wash them immediately after breakfast, like I normally do. My rebellion felt good at the time, but it is still me who has to wash them clean, not Adam.

I'm conscious that I also neglected to do my usual Monday morning laundry, and so now I am behind with my weekly chores, despite getting up early. I strip the sheets from the bed and bundle them into the washing machine. Then, after a quick lunch, I begin to vacuum and dust all of the rooms, moving the furniture out and going right into all of the corners and difficult-to-reach places that I don't always manage to do. Tomorrow I will give the kitchen and bathroom a thorough scrub, and then make sure that the windows are washed inside and out. That will leave all of Thursday for baking and last-minute preparations.

Although I am looking forward to hosting the book club, I am anxious too. Naturally I care what impression my home will make on my new friends. That's why I am so keen to make the cottage nice. I do not want to leave anything to chance. And besides, by keeping busy, I am able to push aside any lingering thoughts about Victoria.

I am also still worried that Adam might find out about the book club meeting somehow.

When Adam phones, I tell him that I have been having a spring-clean, although I don't tell him why. He sounds pleased to hear that I have been hard at work. It seems to be what he expects from a wife. I wonder if Victoria kept the house in London quite as neat and tidy. I can't imagine that she did, and I feel very pleased with myself.

But then I think, what if she didn't need to do any housework herself? What if the high-powered career that I have invented for her meant that she could easily afford to pay a cleaner to do it all? I have a vision of my imagined Victoria ordering a young girl around her London house, giving her a list of jobs to do. The notion leaves a bitter taste in my mouth, and I lie awake, tossing and turning until long after I have gone to bed.

CHAPTER 17

It's Thursday, and I wake up early, before it's light, thinking about the book group meeting. I feel a certain nervous excitement in the pit of my stomach at the thought that it's going to take place here, in the home I share with Adam. I still cannot believe that I volunteered to host it.

It seems ridiculous now I think about it, but we've never had visitors to the cottage before. It has always been our place, just mine and Adam's, a sanctuary, somewhere I have always felt safe. The outside world was not supposed to intrude. But now I wonder what I have been afraid of, all these years. Was I really afraid, or has Adam been afraid for me?

Now I've invited the outside world in. What would Adam say if he knew? He would hate it, for sure.

I'm not entirely relaxed about it myself. I try to imagine my home through other people's eyes and wonder what they will think of it. I have never even considered such a question before. What does my home say about me? The décor is neutral. The walls are white or cream, the carpets are beige, the Swedish-style furniture is all clean lines and no fuss. It's a stylish, contemporary look, I think. Some might say it has no character. Is it too bland? It's true that I avoid bright colours. Especially red. It's understandable under the circumstances, I think. On balance, I feel certain they will like it. The cottage still retains a lot of period charm, like the inglenook fireplace and the exposed beams in the ceilings.

I spend the morning baking and getting everything just right. We have agreed to meet in the afternoon, now that Cath's boys are back at school. I didn't want to risk the meeting over-running and the women still being here when Adam phones this evening. The chocolate brownies I've baked smell delicious, but I find that I'm too on edge to be hungry. I decide to skip lunch and instead spend some time pacing the cottage, nervously adjusting anything that I happen to chance upon. I plump up the cushions in the lounge and make tiny rearrangements to the ornaments on the sideboard – a couple of vases and some scented candles. I straighten the clock that hangs on the wall. It is quarter to two, and the others will be here on the hour.

The photograph of Adam and me on our wedding day snags my attention. I'm half-temped to hide it away. It seems too personal somehow, as if it reveals too much. I lift it up by its frame and examine it carefully for clues to the mystery of Victoria. Adam's face smiles happily and openly at the camera, and it is hard to imagine that he kept any secrets from me at that time in our lives.

Did you already know her, Adam, on the day we got married? The idea appals me, and I shake my head, resisting the thought. *But if not then, when?*

The red room is the obvious answer. The red room drove us away from Oxford. Did it also drive Adam into the arms of Victoria? Is it possible that he betrayed me when I needed him most? I don't know how he could have done it, though. He has always come home to me every weekend. How could he have met and married a woman during that period? I simply cannot understand.

A car pulling up on the gravel outside pulls me back

from my dark thoughts. I glance at my watch. It's two o'clock. The sound of the car is familiar, even without me going to look. It's Bridget's. She said she would give the other two a lift. I peer out of the window as they get out of the car. Cath stands there for a moment, looking the cottage up and down as if she were a potential buyer. She looks faintly bemused, as if she's wondering why Adam and I have chosen to live in such an isolated place. The cottage wouldn't suit Cath at all, I'm certain of it. She likes to chat to people too much. Despite her complaints about her flat being so cramped, I know that really she loves being constantly surrounded by her family.

I go to the door and let them in. Diana hands me a homemade lemon drizzle cake. 'Just a little something to have with our tea,' she says.

'What a lovely home,' says Cath, as they take off their coats and hang them up. 'It's so tidy here. I wish my place looked like this. The boys leave their clutter everywhere and my husband's no better.' She laughs, as if to say, what can you do?

I look at the cottage through her eyes then and realise that there is no clutter anywhere. Everything is precisely in its place. Except for the three women, of course. They are the ones who do not belong here. But it is Adam's voice saying that. They *do* belong here now. They are my friends. I invited them in.

I show them into the lounge and tell them I'll go and make the tea.

'I'll give you a hand,' says Bridget, following me into the kitchen. I realise that despite giving me a lift into town so often, this is actually the first time she's been inside the cottage. I should have asked her to come in sooner, but in the past I was always too nervous. I fill the kettle and switch it on.

'What a super kitchen,' says Bridget, admiring the granite worktop and the modern, fitted cupboards. 'The kitchen in the vicarage is ancient, but we can't afford to replace it, and the church certainly doesn't have the funds. Did you install this yourselves?'

'Yes,' I say. 'It was one of the first things we did to the cottage when we moved in.'

Those early days after we moved to the village are something of a blur to me. I spent a lot of time upstairs in bed, while the carpenters and other workmen installed the kitchen and bathroom and redecorated the downstairs rooms. Adam took some time off to supervise them, so that I wouldn't have to deal with them. In those days I was barely capable of meeting other people at all. So I suppose that the styling of the cottage reflects Adam's tastes more than mine. The strict aversion to bright colours was his decision. But perhaps he did it for me.

I open one of the cupboards and retrieve four white cups, saucers and plates. All of our crockery is pure white, to match our cotton sheets and bedding upstairs. Chic, I suppose. And also, not remotely dangerous. I drop a couple of tea bags into the teapot and wait for the water to boil.

'Does Adam have somewhere nice to live when he's in London?' asks Bridget.

'He has a house in Putney,' I say. The kettle boils and I start to pour the hot water into the teapot. 'Montserrat Road.' I put the kettle down, stunned at what I've just done. I haven't ever told anyone Adam's address before. He has coached me so well not to divulge any personal information that doing so makes me feel unaccountably ashamed of myself. But I must resist such thoughts. I have done nothing wrong, telling Bridget where he lives. Still, I worry that I've divulged too much.

I place the cups and saucers on a tray, my hand trembling ever so slightly. The cups rattle against the saucers, betraying my anxious state.

Bridget seems not to notice. 'Putney's nice,' she says. 'Near the river. Isn't that where the Oxford and Cambridge boat race starts? They row from Putney to

Mortlake, I think.'

'Yes,' I say. 'I think you're right.'

'Did you ever row at Oxford?' asks Bridget.

'Goodness me, no,' I say. 'Rowing is incredibly hard work. All those early morning training sessions and running down to the boat house and back to college afterwards, including in the middle of winter. I much preferred punting on a summer's afternoon.'

'I don't blame you,' says Bridget. 'Although I don't think I'd be able to keep the punt in a straight line. I'd probably end up in the bank.'

I'm suddenly reminded of last Friday's dinner conversation with Adam when he rescued me and my friends after we had, indeed, got stranded in the bank. I tell Bridget the story.

'How romantic,' she says.

But I am distracted by a sudden recollection. It wasn't Adam who pulled us to safety, but a man with a moustache. *Charles.* An image flashes in my mind. Me, wearing a thin floral-print dress, laughing as my two friends struggle to free our stranded craft from the shallow water weeds near the riverbank. Charles, wearing a straw boater, reaching out to grab at the stern of our craft. Adam standing tall, guiding the men's punt with the pole, a fiercely jealous look in his eyes, even though we have only just met for the first time. The image is so powerful I can smell the heady perfume of the wildflowers along the bank. I can feel the sun's rays warming my skin. A bee buzzes lazily past, and it almost feels like I have been transported back in time.

I try to lift the tray with all the tea things on it, but I am too distracted by the unexpected memory. I have forgotten where I am and what I am doing. The tray is heavy in my arms and tips over at an angle. Some tea escapes from the spout of the pot. The cups begin to rattle.

'Here, let me help you with that,' says Bridget, quickly taking the tray from me with two capable hands. 'You get the door.'

My hands are trembling from the intensity of the vision. 'Thank you,' I say to Bridget. 'I don't know what came over me.'

I grasp the edge of the granite worktop to steady myself. I must not faint, like I did at the Corner House. Not here, when everyone has come to my home. But after a moment my head clears and I feel normal again.

Bridget takes the tea things through to the lounge where Diana and Cath have made themselves comfortable on the sofa.

Cath is in full flow talking about her son, Diana listening and nodding her head. 'So I said to him, if you want to earn some money you can come and help me out in the shop, but of course, he's too lazy to get himself out of bed before midday at the weekend. Honestly, teenagers eh?'

She jumps up to help when she sees us coming in. 'I was just telling Diana all about my eldest, Jack,' she says with a sigh. 'He'll be off to university soon. We might have a bit more space then.'

'Yes,' I say distractedly. I cut into Diana's lemon drizzle cake and offer my own chocolate brownies.

'These are delicious,' says Cath, trying one of each type of cake. 'I'd have joined a book group sooner if I'd known it would involve such wonderful food.'

Everyone laughs and I feel myself more grounded. I'm in my own home eating cake and chatting with my new friends. What could be simpler than that?

Diana looks around the room. 'I can see why you love living here so much. It's so quiet, away from the village, isn't it?'

'Yes,' I say. 'In the spring you can hear the birds singing and the bleating of the lambs, but in the winter it's completely silent. Apart from when the wind blows across the moor. It can get quite wild in winter.'

'I can imagine.'

'What about when it snows?' asks Cath. 'It must be impossible to go anywhere.'

'I do get snowed in from time to time, but I don't really mind. As long as I have food in the cupboard I won't starve. It's only a problem if Adam can't get to the airport, but that's only happened once.'

'What did he do then?' asks Bridget.

'He just had to stay home for a couple of days. I think he quite enjoyed it.' I think back to last winter, when it happened. Adam really did seem to enjoy taking time away from work. He hardly seemed like a man desperate to get back to his second wife in London.

'So what are we going to do next?' asks Bridget. 'I suppose we should choose a new book to read.'

Cath is just about to take a bite of the cake, but she puts it back on her plate and says, 'I have to be honest. If we're going to read a book every week then I really won't be able to keep up. I got ever so behind with the laundry when we were reading *Jane Eyre* and no one had any clean socks for days. I did point out that they could learn to use the washing machine themselves, but you can imagine how that went down.' She chuckles and rolls her eyes.

Diana nods her head in understanding. 'I do understand what you mean about not taking on too many books. It's easy for me, now that I'm retired, but I couldn't have managed to read a book a week when I was working full time. And actually, I have a suggestion that I'd like to make. Something we might do instead of beginning another book straight away.'

We all look at her expectantly.

'Some friends of mine have offered me some tickets to go and see *The Mousetrap* in London. Four tickets, in fact.' She looks around meaningfully at me, Bridget and Cath. 'And I was already thinking that rather than reading books all the time, we might alternate books with going to see a film, or the occasional play. So this seems like an ideal opportunity. What do you all think?'

'That sounds like a fantastic idea,' says Bridget.

'Isn't *The Mousetrap* the really famous show that's been running for, like, decades?' asks Cath.

'Yes,' says Diana. 'It's not always easy to get tickets. These are for a matinée performance next Thursday. I thought we could take the train down to London in the morning. It only takes a couple of hours from Leeds to King's Cross.'

'Count me in,' says Cath. 'Hubby can look after the shop for a day. It won't kill him.'

'I'd love to go,' says Bridget. 'Ben won't mind. By Thursday he's always in his study thinking about Sunday's sermon.'

'What about you, Jane?' asks Diana, turning to me. 'Would you like to join us?'

I've been listening to this conversation with a growing sense of excitement tempered with fear. 'I've never been to London,' I say.

'Well then, you must,' says Diana, as if that settles the question.

But there's a reason I've never been. Crowds terrify me. We moved to the village so I could avoid crowds. And I've only just started to make these first tentative steps towards having friends in the village. To go to a West End theatre in the heart of London is too much.

And there's another reason why I can't possibly go. Adam. If I told him, not only would he dismiss it out of hand, but it would mean admitting to him that I have secretly been meeting the other women. I can't do it.

'I'm sorry,' I say. 'I just don't think I can. You three go without me. You can tell me all about it afterwards.'

The others try to persuade me to come to the show, but I won't change my mind. It's too much, too soon.

Seven years, a voice in my mind scolds me. *Seven years you've been hiding yourself away from the world. How long is it going to take?*

But the answer comes back to me immediately. *As long*

as it needs to.

It is a matter of self-preservation.

The women don't push me too hard once I have said no to them a second time. They obviously sense my distress. They have seen how fragile I can be. I demonstrated that well enough when I fainted at the New Year's Eve party. And I am grateful to them for their understanding.

The book group meeting fizzles out after some small talk, and the others leave, telling me that they will be in touch soon. Bridget places a reassuring hand on mine, as if to say that she understands how I feel.

But she doesn't. How can she?

I feel I have let them down. But I have to protect myself.

The voice in my head taunts me. *What would Victoria have done?*

I do my best to ignore the voice. I carry the tray with the tea cups and leftover cake back to the kitchen and wash up, scrubbing angrily at the white porcelain. But the voice continues to provoke me.

Victoria would have said yes.

It seems that she is a constant presence in my life now. So much for being dead and buried, it is like she is watching over me, comparing herself with me. Judging me.

I do not even know what she looked like.

I throw the tea towel into the sink in fury. It is enough. It is time I did something about her. It is time for me to confront Victoria head-on.

CHAPTER 18

I have the cottage to myself now that the women have left, and Adam isn't due to phone for hours yet. I have time. Time to find out the truth at last.

I abandon the washing up and creep hesitatingly into Adam's office. The neat expanse of his desk is just as I left it after I discovered the insurance letter in the locked drawer. I walk over to the desk and tug at the drawer, checking that it is still locked. It is.

I sit down at the desk and my finger hovers over the power button of the computer. I could easily have done this before. Everything is online these days. Even people who remain hidden in everyday life can be uncovered with a click of the mouse. People like Victoria Harvey. Deceased wife of my husband.

She might be only a search away.

I could have searched for her before, but there was a reason I didn't. Fear. There's no point denying it to myself. Fear of the unknown. But what am I really afraid of? That Victoria will turn out to have been much younger than me? Prettier? More successful? In my imagination, I have already painted a version of Victoria who is all of those things, and more. I have created a perfect wife for Adam. I

111

have imagined a monster, my nemesis.

I remind myself that she's dead. But that's irrelevant, because the one thing that truly terrifies me is finding out that Adam loved her. That he loved her more than he loves me. Is that something I can find out online? I don't think it is, but I have to find out as much as I can. It is the only way I can begin to exorcise her ghost.

I press the power button and it blinks on, a small blue light.

I wait for the computer to power up. My hands rest by the keyboard, anticipating the keystrokes I must enter. I'm excited and apprehensive in equal measure.

Victoria Harvey. Two words. Two very dangerous words. What secrets will they unveil?

The screen lights up and I begin to type into the search box. The keys click softly as I enter the letters, one by one. *Victoria Harvey*, they type. Still my finger hesitates on the mouse. This might be a big mistake. I won't be able to unlearn whatever I discover.

They say that ignorance is bliss. But it isn't. It's torment.

I click search.

The screen fills with results. Thousands of results are listed. Millions. A meaningless number.

They can't all be about Victoria. Not Adam's Victoria. I start to scan through the list. The first is from Facebook. I don't do social media myself – Adam would be furious if I did – but I think it might be a good place to start looking for someone. I click on the link, but the page that appears lists dozens of profiles of people called Victoria Harvey. Young, old. Some pictured on their own, others with partners or children. Some have chosen cartoon characters or even abstract images to represent themselves. This is hopeless. I just don't know what I'm looking for.

There is one key detail I know about her though. I know that she's dead. I go back to the search screen and key in *Victoria Harvey dead*. I click the search button a second time.

The screen fills with fresh results.

A shiver runs down my spine.

I am close. Closer than I have ever been to this dark secret. I am terrified by what I might find. But I look anyway.

The first few results are obituaries. They are for teenagers, or old people. Each one is a personal tragedy for someone, but they don't seem to relate to the Victoria I am looking for. This is morbid. Reading them makes me feel like a ghoul at a graveside. But I can't stop now.

The next is from an article on the *Daily Mail* website. *Missing Victoria Harvey Presumed Dead.*

Missing? Could this be her? With a pounding heart I click on the link and wait for the page to load.

The headline, in large bold type, fills most of the laptop's screen:

Advertising executive, Mrs Victoria Harvey, missing for seven years, now presumed dead.

A woman missing for seven years? This doesn't seem to fit, and yet something stops me from clicking the *back* button. The article is from three months ago, not long before the date of the letter that Adam received from the life insurance company. I scroll down and start reading:

A court has ruled that Victoria Harvey, who went missing in 2011 and whose body has never been found, may now be presumed dead.

Mrs Harvey, a high-flying executive with top London-based advertising agency Saatchi & Saatchi, has been missing since 2011. Her husband, Adam Harvey, has always maintained that his wife drowned whilst out sculling on the River Thames. A keen rower since her university days at Oxford, Mrs Harvey's empty boat was found washed up by the Thames flood barrier. According to her husband she had been rowing near their home in Putney. The Putney to Mortlake stretch of the river is famous for the annual Oxford and Cambridge Boat Race. Conditions on that part of the Thames are known to be treacherous on windy days.

After the court hearing, Mr Harvey commented that he was relieved at the judge's ruling. 'Victoria will always be missed by those who loved her, but now I can start to put the tragedy behind me and move on with my life.'

And suddenly everything fits.

Seven years. It is seven years since I left my home in Oxford and moved here to the village. It is seven years since Victoria Harvey went missing. My blood runs cold as I realise the implication.

No wonder I haven't noticed any recent changes in Adam's behaviour. Victoria Harvey has been missing for a long, long time.

I scroll further down the page and my heart almost stops. There's a photo of Victoria Harvey taken, so the caption says, at a party shortly before she went missing. I snap my eyes shut, but it is too late. I cannot forget what they have already seen. I open them again, taking in the image, drinking it in like water, allowing it to flow through me. The experience is almost overwhelming.

The caption describes her as *stunning and beautiful,* and I have to agree. Victoria is exactly like I pictured. She's elegant and confident-looking, wearing a strappy, sparkling dress with ample cleavage on display. Her hair is glossy and her make-up is flawless. She's holding a glass of champagne in one hand and smiling widely at the camera with crimson lips.

And just as I imagined, she had a successful career. A high-flying advertising executive. I think of my own daily routine of cooking and cleaning, with weekly shopping trips to the local market. Victoria's achievements make my life seem paltry and irrelevant by comparison. My hands are trembling visibly over the keyboard.

Victoria is the perfect version of me that I imagined.

But more than that.

She *is* me. I am looking at a photo of myself.

Victoria Harvey is me. I am Victoria.

I stare for a long time at the photograph, but there is absolutely no room for doubt. Even though the woman in the photograph is seven years younger than me, and even though I cannot remember ever dressing like that, I am Victoria Harvey.

Our lives have been entangled since the very beginning. Victoria went missing seven years ago, presumed dead. But she's not dead. She's very much alive. But now her name is Jane. Now she is me.

I continue to study the image on the screen for a long time, tracing the contours of her face, seeing the similarities to how I am now, and noting the subtle changes that time has wrought. I sit transfixed at my own younger face staring back at me.

And now, very slowly, I begin to understand the enormity of what Adam has done.

~~~

Seven years ago, my life ended.

Seven years ago, my life began.

I remember nothing about that day, apart from the red room, and barely anything about that. The few recollections I have are mainly emotions. Fear. Pain. Anger. Loss. Terror.

And some vague, fleeting images. Flashes of red. Red on the walls. Red on my clothes. And red on my hands and face.

Red for danger. Red for blood.

The red room was in our house in Oxford. Or at least that's what Adam has always told me. But now I realise that I must have been living in London.

Why I was in the red room, I don't remember. Nor what happened to me. Did I disturb an intruder in the house? Was I attacked? I simply don't know.

But something dreadful happened.

I just remember Adam finding me in there and opening the door and taking me in his arms. He rescued me from the red room. And he brought me here, to what was then our holiday cottage. We drove through the night, travelling for hours without stopping. When we arrived, he carried me from the car and into the cold, empty cottage. I remember sitting in the chair in the front room, shivering under a blanket that Adam had fetched for me, watching as he lit a fire in the grate. I was too numb to speak, too terrified to leave him, even for a moment.

I couldn't ever go back home. The holiday cottage became our new home. We had it redecorated under Adam's supervision, while I lay in bed upstairs, staring at the old wooden beams in the ceiling for long hours each day, tracing their lines and the shadows they made as morning turned to afternoon and then evening. Outside, the wind blew across the open moorland as I drifted in and out of sleep. After some while – I don't know how long – Adam returned to work, commuting to London from here and staying in the house in Putney during the week. More time passed and I began to heal. My injuries were not that serious, even though there had been so much blood on my hands. It was my mind that had been damaged and needed the longest time to recover. The scars still remain, inside my head.

Gradually, month by month, year by year, we settled into the life we have now. Looking back, not much has changed in seven years. But slowly I began to spend more time awake. Once the builders had finished their work and left, I began to venture out of my bedroom and spend time downstairs, reading. I learned to prepare simple meals for the first time. I began to care for the cottage, cleaning it ready for Adam's return at the end of each week. With Adam's support and encouragement, I built up the confidence to go to the village shop and buy food. When summer came I began to tend the garden and grow salad and vegetables. I eventually plucked up the courage to catch the bus to town and shop at the weekly market.

But there was a void in my life. I remembered nothing that had happened before Adam had rescued me from the red room.

Everything I remember, happened after that moment. What happened before, I do not know. My memories were wiped clean that day.

I don't know what took place in that room. I don't remember going in there. I don't recall anything of my life in Oxford. I can't even remember my wedding day. As for my childhood, it has all been erased from my mind.

Whatever took place inside that room was so terrible that it obliterated my entire life.

All I had left was Adam. And Adam cared for me so well in those early days. He has continued to care for me ever since.

In the immediate aftermath of the red room, I was almost speechless. I barely knew who I was, who anyone was. *Jane, Jane Harvey*, Adam told me, over and over again. *You are my wife, Jane Harvey. And I am your husband.*

That's what he said. He gave me back my identity. I clung to that knowledge like a lifeline, because it was all I had.

But it was a lie. I am not Jane. I am Victoria. And I do not understand why Adam lied to me.

In the days following our move here, Adam kept asking me what I remembered. Did I remember what happened in the red room? Was someone with me? Who? Did they attack me? Did I remember the day before? The week before? Anything? But I could remember nothing. I could not even remember my name.

It will come to you, Adam reassured me. *Just give it time.*

At first, I thought he was right. Tiny glimpses of my past came slowly back. I began to see flashes, fragments.

A garden, in summertime. Myself as a child, swinging high and low, as the ropes pull and creak, and the sun warms my bare arms.

A dusty library, filled with books. My head bowed low over a desk, studying hard.

Water flowing quietly past as I dip my fingers languidly into the River Cherwell, the sun setting as Adam guides the punt.

They were small scraps of a life lived. Clues to my past. But they were merely flashes in the dark. I could not make sense of them. I could not build a sense of who I was.

Adam assured me that more memories would come. But they never did.

Not until the night of the New Year's Eve party at Diana's house. That image of me surrounded by men in suits and women wearing party dresses. I didn't understand it at the time. It didn't fit with the stories that Adam had told me about myself. In his version of my life, I had never even been to a party. I had never been to London. I had certainly never been a high-flying business executive.

But it wasn't a hallucination. It was a flashback. It was a recollection of when I was Victoria. And it was nothing like anything Adam has ever told me.

~ ~ ~

In the days, weeks and months after the red room, Adam began to tell me all about myself. He told me stories about my life. About who I was, where I had come from, what I was like as a person. He told me about my life in Oxford, how I had met him while punting on the River Cherwell, how we had fallen in love at first sight. He told me of our wedding day, about saving up to buy our house together in Oxford. How we had been happy together.

I should start at the beginning. I was born Jane Reynolds, at least in Adam's version of my history. I have no brothers or sisters, and my parents were quite elderly, having married late. I lived an unremarkable life in a small town in Sussex, close to the coast. I attended the local girl's school before going to Oxford to study English Literature. At university I studied hard, spending long hours in the library. I think I remember that. I recall the smell of old books piled high on my desk, a bright shaft of sunlight streaming through a window, splashing light across the pages of text in front of me.

Although I don't recall the names or authors of any of the books I read, I have retained my love of reading. Sometimes I will open a book and find that the words are familiar, as if I have read them before and am returning to an old friend. I hope that re-reading the words will unlock my memories, but they never do.

Oxford is I where I met Adam. He and his friend Charles literally rescued me and my friends from our punting disaster. It was hardly a disaster, although the way Adam tells the story, it sounds like we were almost drowned at sea. It was in summer term, and my friends and I were discovering the joys of messing about on the river for the first time. Steering a punt is harder than it looks, by all accounts. Like many novice boaters we found ourselves floundering in the muddy shallows by the bank.

According to Adam, we fell in love at first sight. A whirlwind romance ensued and we spent all our spare time together that term, at least when we were not studying. From then on we were inseparable and we became engaged in our final year, when I had sat my exams and Adam had submitted his thesis. We continued to study hard however, despite making plans for our wedding. According to Adam I was shy and didn't really have any close friends apart from him. I don't even know the names of the girls I had been punting with when I first met Adam. Adam's best friend was Charles, and he was Adam's best man at our wedding.

The wedding was a small affair and took place at my college chapel in Oxford. That was during the summer after I graduated. We stayed on in Oxford, renting a small terraced house together. Adam took the job in London, commuting by train each morning. And I searched for work in Oxford itself. Being shy, and with a degree in English Literature, it wasn't surprising that I ended up working as a library assistant in one of the university libraries. I had no ambitions to do anything different.

But how much of this is true?

Every 'fact' I know about my life, Adam has told me. Every 'truth' I believed, was a reconstruction. Adam created my life for me. He created my identity.

But the newspaper article tells a different story.

Victoria Harvey didn't live in Oxford. She lived in London. She wasn't a library assistant, but a rising star at an advertising agency.

That was me. I did that.

If I am to believe what I have read online, then I can only come to the conclusion that Adam gave me a new identity. He took away my name and gave me a new one. He brought me to this place and he changed me from a confident, successful woman into a timid mouse, always afraid of other people.

He told me that it would be best if I lived a quiet life from now on, avoiding crowds, not talking to strangers. He warned me against making new friends in the village. He instructed me never to divulge any personal information to anyone, and to tell him if anyone started to ask questions or pried into our private life.

He told me that I hated parties and crowds.

He lied to me. He made me into someone else.

He changed my name and told the world that I was dead. He even went as far as having me declared legally dead and claiming the life insurance.

But why did he do those things?

CHAPTER 19

The magnitude of my discovery is too much for me to handle. I'm overwhelmed by so many thoughts that my mind threatens to burst. I feel a sudden urge to escape from this room and from this cottage where Adam has shut me away. If feels like a prison now. The bars are the lies he told me, the prison guards are my own doubts and fears. I cannot remain inside another second. I run out, into the freezing January air, leaving the door to the cottage open behind me.

It is already growing dim as the afternoon draws to a close. I am completely alone out here. The road stretches back towards the village and away in the opposite direction. It is empty of vehicles both ways and there are no lights visible, except the warm glow behind me from the cottage. There is no one out here except me. I run into the middle of the road and at the top of my voice I scream, 'I'm dead! I'm dead! I'm dead!'

The sheep in the field opposite the cottage raise their heads briefly, showing scant interest, before returning to their persistent grazing.

The cold brings me to my senses. I turn and go back indoors. I huddle by the fire in the lounge, but my teeth won't stop chattering. It isn't just the cold. I realise I must be in shock. People die of shock, I tell myself. But I can't die, because I'm already dead. I start to laugh hysterically and don't stop until my sides are hurting so badly that I think I might die after all. Afterwards I sit cradled in the chair, rocking gently, hugging my knees to my chest.

My mind has almost shut down as it resists the revelations that have flooded it. Just two thoughts persist in my dulled consciousness: *Adam lied to me*; and, *I am Victoria.*

Eventually I get to my feet and stagger into the kitchen. I'm surprised to see the kitchen unchanged, with the cups and saucers piled up by the sink exactly where I left them earlier. Since my whole world has been turned upside down, it seems odd that the dishes still need washing. I drain the sink and re-fill it with hot water and a squirt of washing-up liquid. I wash the crockery and lay it out on the draining board to dry. The security of this simple household chore helps me recover my equilibrium. I dry the crockery with a tea towel and put everything away in the cupboards. Once I've restored order I feel calmer.

I know what I need to do now. I make myself an extra-strong coffee and take it through to the office. I return to the search results and click on other articles, seeking further details, information that might help me understand. They all basically confirm what the *Daily Mail* article said. I used to be an executive at a big advertising agency and seven years ago I went missing. There was a big police hunt at the time, and although my empty boat was found, no body was ever discovered. I was officially missing, presumed dead.

Reading on, I learn that after seven years, Adam applied for me to be declared legally dead. A hearing took place at the High Court, but this seems to have been a formality. The judge accepted Adam's application, and a declaration of presumed death was made.

The police report from seven years ago confirmed that

I had been out sculling on the River Thames. I have to look up the word *sculling*. It means the sport of rowing in a small narrow boat. I didn't even know that, and yet it was apparently something I used to enjoy regularly.

It is hard to believe that I have forgotten so much. How can I begin to understand who I truly am if my past has been taken from me?

Adam has never mentioned sculling. The only boating story he has ever told me is the one where we first met. But now I am beginning to doubt even whether that story is true. It could be a fabrication, a humorous tale to make him look like the hero of the hour.

I realise that is how he must see himself. As a hero. He has recreated my past to suit himself. I've believed myself to be shy and timid, afraid of large crowds and better off living in a small village rather than in the centre of London. A woman who wants nothing more than to keep her little country cottage clean, and to please her husband. But when I look at the photograph of Victoria, of me, in the *Daily Mail* article, I see a woman who would never dream of swapping her *Jimmy Choos* for a pair of mud-splattered walking boots.

Jimmy Choos.

I don't know why I suddenly thought of *Jimmy Choos*. And then, in a flash, it hits me. I used to own a pair of bright red *Jimmy Choos* with heels like sky-scrapers.

Bright red. I never wear red. *But I used to.*

The memory is so vivid I catch my breath. Shiny, patent leather. If I close my eyes I can see the shoes in front of me. I can smell the leather. I could reach out and pick one up, hold it in my hand and caress it. I suddenly want those shoes so badly that a tear rolls down my face and lands on the desk. I blink open my eyes and the image vanishes.

To cry over a pair of lost shoes seems absurd. But I am not just mourning a pair of shoes. I am crying over an entire life that has been lost to me.

Once again, I can't bear to be inside. I feel as if the walls are closing in around me and I need to gain my freedom. I run into the hallway and pull on my muddy boots. Whatever happened to my red *Jimmy Choos*? I have no idea where they are now.

I grab my hat and coat and yank open the front door roughly, half expecting to find it locked. But it opens easily and I almost fall backwards with relief. Once outside I take a couple of deep breaths to steady myself, and set off in the direction of the village.

I trudge along the grass verge where the last remaining clumps of snow are stained black from passing cars. The wind is bitter and stings my face. I turn up the collar of my coat and plough on.

At the humpback bridge I pause and stare down into the stream as it rushes over the stony riverbed. The water level has risen, swollen by the melting snow. *A keen rower since her university days at Oxford.* That's what the article said. I try to imagine myself in one of those long, narrow boats. Eight rowers and a cox. Or in a single-person boat, out on the River Thames in the early morning. But I can't picture it. The clear water swirling beneath the bridge stirs no memories. I can't see myself as someone so energetic and competitive. Maybe if I saw a photograph it would come back to me, but for now my mind remains blank. I turn away from the stream and press on towards the village.

The village emerges from the dark, its warm yellow lights welcoming me into its fold. Yet when I reach the first houses I realise that I don't know where to go. It's not as if there are that many choices. I could pop into the shop and chat to Cath. I could call in at the Corner House, hoping to catch Diana. Or I could visit Bridget in the vicarage.

But what would I say to any of them?

My mind is running wild and I hardly know what I might say. If I start to talk, I feel sure that I will tell them everything, and I don't know if I want to do that. I cannot trust myself to speak to them right now.

Instead, I choose a different destination entirely. I turn right, away from the village square and up a narrow road that I have rarely used before. The lychgate stands here – the old wooden gate that leads to the church. The gate is closed and I hesitate, not knowing precisely why I have chosen this path. But there is no other way to go. The tiled roof above the gate offers little shelter from the elements, so this is not a place to linger. I push at the wooden gate. It opens with a creak, and I enter the churchyard, carefully closing the gate behind me. Darkness has descended fully now, and the path that leads to the church is shrouded in shadows. Only a few of the grey headstones are visible in the churchyard, and the thick yew trees that line the path stand almost black. But a faint light glimmers from within the church.

I stride along the path up to the church door. I don't know if the church will be open at this time of day, but when I try the handle, it turns. With a push the heavy door opens on its hinges.

The church is empty, but a light has been left on near the entrance. A lingering smell of candle wax and old books greets me. I inhale deeply, wondering if the smell might trigger a memory, but nothing comes. Behind me the door closes with a soft thud.

It is ages since I have visited the church. Adam and I are not normally churchgoers but we came here one Sunday afternoon in between services to look around. The church is an old one, a traditional village church, dating back many centuries. This connection with the past is perhaps what drew me here this evening.

There's a Nativity scene at the back of the church which looks as if it was created by the Sunday School children. The figures of Mary and Joseph are made out of papier mâché and pipe cleaners and dressed in outfits cut from coloured paper. In the manger lies a tiny baby Jesus. My own childhood is a blank. Adam has told me that my parents are dead, but now I wonder if that is true or if there is an elderly couple somewhere believing that I died in a rowing accident. I can't even be certain that I am an only child, like he said. But the idea that I might have brothers or sisters is too big to handle. The foundations of my life have been rocked, and if I am not careful everything will come tumbling down.

I wander a little way down the central aisle. An embroidered banner hanging on one of the stone pillars proclaims: *God created man in his own image, in the image of God he created him; male and female he created them.* It's decorated with a multitude of different faces: young, old, black, white, male and female, presumably to indicate that we are all children of God. But in whose image am I created?

My sense of dislocation from the world makes me feel dizzy and I sit down on one of the wooden pews.

Who am I?

It is the one burning question I have to answer. Perhaps I secretly believed that by coming to the church, God might offer an answer to my question. But there is no answer forthcoming, at least not for the moment. I must try to figure this out on my own. What caused Adam to lie to me and tell me that I'm Jane when really I'm Victoria? Why has he allowed the rest of the world to believe that I'm dead when I'm alive?

What dark secret is he hiding?

I jump at the sound of the door opening and closing behind me. Someone has entered the church and I hear footsteps approaching along the stone flagstones. I twist around sharply and am relieved to see Ben, the vicar, walking towards me.

I've never seen him on his own before, only in the company of Bridget. He's wearing his dog collar with a blue sweater and a pair of designer jeans. The effect is rather attractive, a combination of clerical authority and youthfulness.

'Hello,' he says, coming closer. 'I'm sorry, I hope I'm

not disturbing you.'

'Of course not,' I say quickly. 'This is your church. I'm not sure I should be here.'

'The church belongs to everyone,' he says. He stands with his hands in his pockets, watching my face. 'Mind if I join you?'

His question startles me, but I can hardly refuse him. I shuffle along the wooden pew to allow him room to sit next to me.

He slips into the space I have just vacated. The action seems curiously intimate. He rubs his hands together. 'I'm afraid it's not very warm in here today. We can only afford to heat the church during services.'

'I hadn't noticed the cold,' I say. There is such a tumult going on inside my head that I had been almost indifferent to my external surroundings. But now he mentions it, I shiver.

There's about a foot between us. I am very conscious of him sitting so close to me. I stare resolutely at the back of the pew in front of me.

'People come to the church for many different reasons,' he says, as if answering some unspoken question that I have asked. 'God welcomes them all, of course.'

'Yes,' I say.

'Some come to pray, some to sit in silence on their own and think things through.' He pauses. 'Some like to talk.' He leaves the invitation hanging in the air between us.

Would I like to talk? I don't know. If I start telling him about what has happened, I may never stop.

I glance sideways at him. His face is partly shadowed, but his strong brow and aquiline nose stand proud. His sandy hair is combed sideways across his forehead and there's a hint of a beard on his neck and chin. He has the kind of face that exudes trustworthiness. I sense that he is a good listener. He would listen to me for however long I spoke, and he would not judge.

'I don't know who I am,' I say to him.

He gives me a sympathetic look. 'You'd be surprised how often I hear that, Jane,' he says. 'It's all right to be confused, you know. None of us knows the answers. It's okay to ask questions. It's all right not to know.'

He doesn't understand, of course. He thinks I'm speaking metaphorically.

He clears his throat. 'Has something happened recently that has caused you to think that way?'

So much has happened. But the events that I have just uncovered took place many years ago. I am playing catch-up with my life. *I died, and was reborn.* If I say that, he'll think I've had a sudden religious conversion. It's on the tip of my tongue to say, *I'm not who you think I am*, but that would sound absurd and melodramatic.

He turns to face me and I am struck once again by the intensity of his eyes. He has rugged good looks, for a vicar. I feel a stir of desire.

He is looking at me in a concerned way, probably because I still haven't answered his question. His forehead creases with tiny furrows.

It would be good to open up to him, to tell him my secret. *I am not Jane. I am Victoria.* But it would be even nicer to touch him, to kiss him and lose myself in his embrace.

I cross my legs so that our knees are almost touching.

What would Victoria do? That's the question that rises to my mind. What would Victoria, the woman with the red lips, do right now? I am afraid of the answer.

Ben speaks again and the spell is broken. 'Jane? Are you all right?'

He's Bridget's husband, I remind myself. And I'm married to Adam, or at least I think I am.

And I'm not Victoria any more. I am Jane. Once I was the woman in that photograph. I was beautiful. I was confident. I was successful. But I'm not her now. I don't know her. I no longer know myself.

Adam has turned me into someone of his own making,

and I don't yet understand why. One thing's for sure. I'm going to find out.

But for now I must be Jane.

'I'm all right,' I say to Ben. It's a lie, one more lie piled on top of so many. But it's the only safe answer to give for the moment. I hope he doesn't ask me more.

Fortunately he seems to sense that I have said all I am willing to. 'I just popped in to clear away the Nativity scene,' he says brightly. 'It should have been taken down last week but the lady who normally sees to it has been in bed with the flu.'

'Would you like some help?' I ask. It's obvious that he doesn't need any help to clear away the Nativity scene, but I seize the opportunity to stay with him a little while longer.

'Thank you,' he says.

We lay the figures of Mary, Joseph, the baby Jesus, four shepherds, three wise men, a donkey, and assorted cows, sheep and goats into a cardboard box which he seals with some packing tape.

He picks up the box. 'That's a good job done.'

'You're welcome,' I say.

He looks at me. 'You know, if you ever want to talk about anything, you can always give me a call, Jane. If you feel afraid, or anxious, or depressed.'

'Thank you,' I tell him. 'But I should be heading back now.'

'Look after yourself,' he says as I head towards the door.

Back outside I feel much calmer than I did when I first arrived. I went into the church hoping to find answers, and maybe I didn't find the answer I was looking for, but I do see the way ahead more clearly now.

For the time being, I will carry on pretending to be Jane. But I will do everything I can to find out who I really am and what happened to me.

And then I will decide what to do about Adam.

CHAPTER 20

My life feels like it has had the scaffolding kicked out from under it, yet one thing remains certain. Adam will phone me this evening at nine o'clock precisely. I hurry home, walking quickly along the empty road. Seeing Ben in the church has given me a chance to gather my thoughts. I am in control of my feelings now, and I am ready for a fight. I am no longer afraid of how Adam may react to anything I say.

If I wanted to, I could go to the authorities right now and tell them everything I know. Adam would most likely be arrested for fraud over the fake insurance claim. He might have committed other crimes too by lying about my supposed death. At the very least he would be disgraced and lose his job.

All that gives me power over him.

But if I want to find out the truth, I will need to play my hand more subtly. Do I want him to go to jail for what he has done to me? To answer that question, I need to know why he did it. And to get to the root of that I will need to wait before I challenge him openly.

I return home in good time and make myself a cup of tea. I sit on the sofa drinking it while I wait for Adam to phone.

The call comes at nine o'clock precisely and I let the phone ring five times before I pick it up. 'Hello?' I say.

Adam sounds irritated that I didn't answer immediately. 'Is something the matter?' he asks. 'I was beginning to wonder if you were going to answer.'

'I'm fine,' I say. 'How about you? Have you had a nice day?'

'Yes, thanks. Are you sure that everything's all right?'

'Oh, yes. I feel great.'

He pauses. 'What have you been doing today?'

'I walked to the village church,' I say. 'It's very beautiful, you know. We should go there more often.'

'What were you doing there?' he asks suspiciously.

'Just thinking. I've been doing a lot of thinking today.'

'About what?' I can hear the nervousness in his voice.

'About the past.'

The line is silent for several seconds. When he speaks again it is with his 'concerned husband' voice, the voice he uses when he thinks I am feeling tired or worried. 'You sound strange, Jane. Have you remembered something?'

'About what?'

He is reluctant to answer, but I wait patiently for him to say the words. 'About the red room?'

'No,' I say. 'Nothing. Have you?'

I have caught him off guard. 'Have I what?' he asks.

'Remembered something. About the red room?'

'No. Of course not.'

'I just wondered if there was anything you'd like to tell me.'

I can hear his ragged breathing at the other end of the line. 'Jane, you're making me worried. Have you remembered anything at all?'

'No,' I say. 'But something occurred to me, and I can't really understand it.'

'What's that?'

'After what happened to me in the red room, why

didn't we go to the police? Why did you bring me here, to Yorkshire? If something bad happened, we should really have reported it to the police, shouldn't we?'

'You're right,' he says. 'You're right, as always. The thing was, I didn't really know what to do. My first thoughts when I found you were simply to protect you. I wanted to make certain you were safe and could come to no more harm. I guess I wasn't thinking clearly. I admit it. I panicked. You can't imagine how horrifying it was to see you in that state.'

I persist. 'But afterwards, once you knew I was safe. Why not report it then?'

'I could have done, I suppose. But what would I have told them? I didn't even know if you'd been attacked. I suppose they could have investigated and discovered some clues to what had happened. But you were in no fit state to answer questions.' He pauses. 'I'm sorry. I feel like I let you down. We could report the incident now, if you like. It's been a long time, I know. But if you'd like me to, I'll call the police now and make a statement. Tell me what to do, Jane.'

He's good. His words sound so sincere. I almost believe that he would do it if I asked. But there's no point pushing him. 'It's okay,' I tell him. 'I agree. There's nothing to be gained by reporting it so many years later. We don't even know what happened, do we?'

'No,' he says. 'We don't.'

There's nothing more I can say to him over the phone. He'll be home tomorrow, on Friday evening. I can try to find out more then.

I keep the rest of the conversation short and we both seem relieved to say goodbye.

'I'll see you tomorrow, Jane,' he says. 'At the weekend.'

'Okay.'

'I love you.'

CHAPTER 21

Adam arrives home on Friday evening as usual. This time I haven't gone to so much trouble to cook a special meal for him. After what he's done to me, he doesn't deserve to be looked after so well. *Liar*, I think, as I hear his door key turning in the lock. I stay in the kitchen, and begin to boil a saucepan of water to cook some pasta.

'Hello, darling,' he says, as he comes through to find me. 'Everything all right? I brought you something.'

He's carrying a large cardboard box wrapped up with tape. From the way he's standing with both arms under it, whatever's inside the box must be heavy.

'What's that?' I ask.

He smiles, as if he knew the box would arouse my curiosity. 'You sounded strange on the phone yesterday,' he says. 'I wondered if you were feeling a bit down. So I brought you something you might find interesting.'

Well he's certainly got me intrigued. 'What is it?' I ask.

'Let me put the box down in the other room. It's rather heavy. I can show you what's inside after we've eaten dinner. First tell me all about your week.'

I have already decided not to tell him anything about the secrets I've uncovered. I'm not even going to let him know that anything is amiss. I was rather reckless when I spoke to him on the phone yesterday, and I don't want to arouse his suspicions further. I'm much more likely to coax information out of him if he's relaxed and not on his guard. I pass him a bottle of red wine. 'Why don't you open this while I cook? We can have a glass before the meal if you like.'

He takes the bottle from me and goes to fetch some wine glasses.

'I've had a quiet week, really,' I tell him, heating some ragù sauce. The pan of water comes to the boil and I add the spaghetti. 'I went to the weekly market on Monday. On Tuesday I spoke to Cath in the village shop – she's happy that her boys are back at school after the holidays. And I bumped into Diana too. She's planning to go into London to visit the theatre.'

He frowns at that. 'You weren't thinking of going with her, were you?'

'No. She did invite me, but I told her I didn't want to.' That much is honest, at least. I find that by mixing truths in with my lies and omissions I can be quite convincing. That's probably what Adam has been doing all these years, telling me stories of my life. How am I ever going to sift fact from fiction in what he's told me?

He hands me a glass of wine and takes a large mouthful himself. 'Good. That's very sensible of you. You know how badly that New Year's party affected you.'

'Yes.' Adam doesn't even know just how much it did affect me. It was at the party that I had the very first flashback, even though I didn't know what it was at the time. I still don't fully understand what I saw that night.

The pasta is ready and Adam helps me serve it. We take it through to the other room, where he has left the cardboard box on the coffee table in front of the sofa. My eyes flit over it, but I don't question him about it now. He obviously wants to show me later.

'And you went to visit the church?' he says, tucking

into the meal.

'That's right. We should go there together one day. It's quite pretty.'

Adam sniffs. 'As long as we don't have to go and listen to that vicar preaching a sermon.'

I can tell from the way that he mentions Ben that he's suspicious. Adam is always suspicious, I realise. It hadn't struck me quite so obviously before, mainly because I almost never speak to other men. But ever since we were introduced to Ben at the party, Adam has been asking questions about the handsome young vicar. What does he imagine might have happened in the church?

Then again, what exactly was *I* imagining that afternoon?

If Adam knew just how strongly attracted I was to Ben, he would be furious. Perhaps he is right to feel so protective of me. Perhaps his jealousy is rational.

We finish the meal and still he's said nothing further about the box. It sits before us on the coffee table, wrapped in tape and shrouded in mystery. Is it here just for his amusement? Is he deliberately tormenting me with it? I can't imagine what it might be. The box is old, so I don't think he's bought me a present. At last I can't stand it any longer. 'So what's in the box?' I say, trying not to sound too eager.

'Why don't you take a look?' he says.

The box is bound up tightly, so I fetch some scissors from the kitchen and carefully cut away the tape. A faint musty smell emerges from the box. I unfold the top of the box to reveal a stack of tightly-packed books. They are a mix of hardbacks and paperbacks, all well-read. I draw out a few and scan their titles. *Selected Poems* – Alfred Lord Tennyson, *Tess of the D'Urbervilles* by Thomas Hardy; *Jane Eyre* by Charlotte Brontë. I look at Adam, startled by the find.

He chuckles. 'They're all yours. From your undergraduate days at Oxford. I found them in a cupboard in the house in London.'

I turn the books over in my hands, studying the covers. The tops of the books are covered in a thin film of dust. I wipe the copy of *Jane Eyre* clean with my palm. It's a different edition to the one I bought recently, an older one with a plain cover. I open it and begin to thumb through. The book falls open at the scene where Jane runs from Rochester on discovering that he is already married. Someone has written in the margin.

The madwoman in the attic represents Jane's own repressed passions and desires.

It is my own handwriting. I have read the book before. And I had completely forgotten.

It seems impossible that I could have forgotten so much. I forgot my own name. I forgot who I was.

I wonder why Adam has brought these books to me now. 'Was there anything else?' I ask him. 'Anything else that belongs to me?'

'No,' he says, but I sense a slight unease behind his words. He is lying. I am sure of it.

What else might he be hiding from me in the house in London? Suddenly the answer is obvious. Everything. My whole life is probably stacked away in dusty boxes. My *Jimmy Choos*. Where are they now? Unless Adam has disposed of them, London is the only place they can be.

I flick through the copy of *Jane Eyre*, reading the copious notes that I have scrawled all over the book. And suddenly it hits me.

I am back in Oxford, in the Examination Schools. It's Finals, and I'm sitting at my desk, one student among so many bright young things. The oak-panelled walls and leaded windows of the building are quintessentially Oxford. Huge oil paintings of the great and the good from times past gaze sternly down at me from their gilded frames. Sunlight falls across the examination paper before me, and I open it nervously and start reading. Questions one and two are as bad as I feared – authors I didn't find time to revise. I should have studied harder and spent less time out on the river. Then my eyes alight on question three. *Discuss ambiguities in the representation of gender and social class in the work of nineteenth-century novelists.* The gods have been kind on me, after all. I pick up my fountain pen and begin to write about the work of the Brontë sisters.

Afterwards, I am back in college and Adam is waiting for me in the quad with a bottle of champagne. 'Don't tell me anything about it,' he says when he sees me. 'Not until you're at least fifty percent of the way to being drunk.' He gives the bottle a quick shake and pops the cork. A fountain of alcohol and foam begins to spray all over me. I shriek and hug him close.

A tear wells up in my eye at the recollection from all those years ago. So vivid, so clear. So much has been lost. So many happy moments. But they are beginning to return, very slowly. Perhaps more will come if I open my mind to them. And if I can find objects like these books to help unlock my memories, perhaps they will begin to flow like the champagne.

Adam regards me with concern. 'You're crying, Jane,' he says softly.

The copy of *Jane Eyre* closes in my lap. The memory it unlocked was bittersweet. Bitter because it reminded me of what I've lost. But sweet because it confirmed just how good Adam always used to be, and how happy we were together. 'I've lost so much, Adam. My whole life has gone. You're all I have left.'

He gathers me to him and hugs me close. 'I'll never let you go, Jane. After all that's happened, you can be certain of that.'

CHAPTER 22

Adam and I made love last night with a passion that is new. After discovering my old books and the memory they unlocked, my emotions reached a new height of intensity, and I gave myself to Adam fully.

It is almost as if the lies he has told me have been wiped clean by my recollection of how happy we were together as students. Blissfully happy. There are no other words to describe it. Recovering that lost knowledge has stabilised my feelings again.

We have sex again this morning, as if we are still young students in love for the first time.

I must admit, I am surprised by my rollercoaster emotions. I haven't forgiven Adam, but I am willing to put aside my doubts until I discover more about why he did what he did. Is it possible that everything he has done has somehow been with my best interests at heart?

I'm also feeling guilty about what happened between me and Ben at church on Thursday. Or what nearly happened. Fortunately very little actually took place, but that was only because he showed so much self-restraint. I fear that if he had encouraged me more I might have thrown myself at him. The idea of having an affair with

Ben makes me feel ill. He is a married man. And I would despise myself if I caused Bridget any pain. I must be more careful as I come to terms with the fact that I am Victoria. My emotions are unstable, and I must make allowances for that.

Meanwhile, I am enjoying having Adam home for the weekend. In the past I have always been content with my own company. But now I am beginning to feel lonely when he is away in London. I wish I could be with him more.

After making love, he cooks breakfast for me in bed. Farmhouse eggs and toast made from fresh local bread. It makes me wish I'd made more of an effort to cook for him yesterday evening.

In the afternoon we go for a walk together.

'Let's go and take a look at this church we've been missing,' he says.

We walk together down the country road to the village, following my footsteps of the other day, holding hands. In the daylight the churchyard and its lychgate seem plain and grey. The church itself is empty. The table where the Nativity Scene had been is stacked with pamphlets advertising various good causes. I pick some up. 'Perhaps we could make a donation to one of these,' I suggest to Adam.

'Of course.'

In the evening, as we return home to the cottage and as the light slips away, I begin to feel less secure. The doubts that assailed me when I first read the *Daily Mail* article begin to gather, like bats at dusk. Am I just being gullible? Adam has fooled me so easily these past seven years. I should not be so quick to forgive him. And I should not waste any opportunity to get closer to the truth.

'Jane?' We have taken off our raincoats and walking shoes and are warming ourselves by the fire. He is looking at me apprehensively. 'What is it?'

'Tell me about the red room,' I say.

He sighs and sits down in the chair by the fireplace. 'Tell you what? You know I don't know anything more than you.'

'Tell me. I want you to tell me again.'

He picks up the metal poker that hangs by the fireside and begins jabbing at the logs in the grate. 'I came home from work late that day. You know how it is with the trains from London. They are often delayed.' Sparks fly from the fire and the flames begin to swell and dance as he pokes at the charred logs.

'And this was at our house in Oxford?'

He frowns at me. 'Yes, of course. There was no sign of you anywhere in the house. I called but you didn't reply. But I knew you were home because the lights were on and your shoes were in the hallway.'

'My shoes? What kind of shoes?'

He gives me a funny look. 'I don't know. Just shoes. Everyday shoes. Anyway I began to search the house, moving through the rooms. There were signs that an intruder had been in the house. Cupboards had been opened, drawers pulled out. I was going to call the police, but I wanted to search the house for you first. I went to the bedroom, the bathroom, but there was no sign of you anywhere. And then I came to the red room.' He stops. 'Are you sure you want me to go on with this?'

I nod.

'The door was locked. I turned the key and pushed it open. And there you were.'

'What was I doing?'

'You were curled up on the floor. You didn't say anything, just lay there shivering. I had no idea what had happened. The room was a mess. The desk had been thrown onto its side, the chairs kicked over. The windows were wide open and rain was blowing in from outside. Some of the curtains had been torn down and almost shredded. And there were books and ornaments all over the floor. Do you remember that vase my father gave us

140

on our wedding day? No of course you don't. I'm sorry. Anyway, it was in pieces.'

'And me?'

'There was blood on your dress and on your face. It was all over your hands. At first I thought you'd been dreadfully injured, but there really wasn't that much blood when I looked more closely.'

What dress was I wearing?'

He looks puzzled. 'Your dress? I don't know. I think it was red.'

'Red?' He's never told me that before. 'Are you sure?'

'I don't know. I can't be certain.'

'I don't have a red dress. I never wear red.' But this was before I became Jane. I don't wear red now. But when I was Victoria I wore red all the time. My *Jimmy Choos* were bright red. I was wearing a crimson dress in the party I remembered on New Year's Eve. I even smeared scarlet on my lips. 'Where is that dress now?'

'I threw the dress away,' says Adam. 'It was ruined.'

I am hoping that Adam's description of events will stimulate another flashback, but nothing comes. 'What then?' I ask. 'What happened after you found me?'

'I brought you here.'

And that is it. He will tell me nothing more. Perhaps there is nothing more to tell. I don't know how much of what he is saying is the truth and how much is fiction. Some of it is true. I remember the red room. I remember the blood. And I recall the moment that Adam opened the door and found me there. Those things I cannot doubt.

But are there details that he's not telling me? I have no way of knowing. All I can be certain of is that something happened that night. And my life changed forever. 'I wonder how different things would have been if the red room had never happened,' I say to him.

My words seem to sadden him. 'Do you think I've never thought about that?' he asks. 'But we can never go back, Jane. We can't change the past. We have to move forward and take life as we find it. Wishing for things to be different will just make you depressed.'

Depressed. That's the word Ben used in the church. Do they think I'm depressed? I consider the idea. Maybe I am. A depressed and lonely woman. It wouldn't be surprising, the number of hours I spend alone here in the cottage. It would be a logical result of taking away all my memories, my identity, even my very name.

And if I am depressed, then one person is clearly to blame. Adam.

CHAPTER 23

The following day is Monday and Adam leaves early as usual to travel to London. I get up as soon as he has gone and get myself ready. Today is market day and I am eager to get out of the cottage. To escape from my solitude and see some people, even if they are mostly strangers to me.

Bridget phones to say she's going into town and do I want a lift?

I listen anxiously to her voice, worried that Ben might have said something to her about meeting me in the church. What might he have told her? That he is worried about me, about my mental health. Does he tell Bridget everything? I imagine them discussing me over dinner, Ben telling her earnestly of my strange behaviour.

'Jane? Are you still there?'

'Sorry, yes. I was just thinking about something.'

'Well, if you want a lift, there's one going, but I don't mean to intrude. Perhaps you've got other plans for the day.'

'No, a lift would be nice,' I say. 'I don't have other plans.' Except figuring out who the hell I am, I think.

'Great, see you in about half an hour.'

In the car Bridget is her usual cheerful self and there's no mention of me seeing Ben in the church. I hope he's too professional and discreet to discuss his parishioners, even with his wife.

'Look,' says Bridget, pointing out of the window. 'The river has burst its banks.'

It's true. What used to be a farmer's field is now completely under water. A stranded stone barn sits in the middle of the field. You would need a boat to reach it.

'It reminds me of Venice,' says Bridget. 'Ben and I went there for our honeymoon. Such a romantic city. Have you ever been there?'

'No, I don't think so.'

She shoots me a curious look and I realise that my strange choice of words must have inadvertently revealed something I didn't intend. But Bridget deftly avoids commenting on my reply and begins instead to tell me about her honeymoon. She talks fondly of canals and gondolas, of lapping water and young love, and an image begins to take form in my mind. I am also in a boat, but not in Venice. I am back in Oxford again, lying in a punt on a warm summer's day, trailing my fingertips in the cool green water.

A week has passed since I first met Adam. I haven't seen him since he rescued me and the girls from our punting disaster, but we have agreed to go out punting together again. Just the two of us, this time.

The dappled sun shines through the canopy of green leaves and sparkles on the surface of the river. When I look up I see Adam's tall, lean figure, standing on the end of the punt, expertly manoeuvring the pole so that we glide effortlessly through the water, past less experienced punters who are going round in circles or crashing into the riverbank. He is wearing khaki shorts and a short-sleeved checked shirt. His skin is tanned from exposure to the sun. Every time he lifts the pole out of the water, his shirt rides up and I catch a glimpse of his belly button and the line of silky hair leading downwards below the waistband of his shorts.

'You've done this before, I see.'

He smiles at me. 'I few times.'

'How long have you been at Oxford?' I ask.

'Three years as an undergraduate, and one year as a postgrad,' he says. 'I've had plenty of time to practise punting. It's really not that difficult.'

I'm still in my first year at Oxford, and just beginning to explore the delights of boating. I think I could grow to like it, especially if Adam is willing to show me how it's done. 'I was thinking of trying rowing next year,' I tell him. 'I quite fancy myself as a rower.'

'Have you done it before?' he asks.

'No. But how hard can it be?'

He chuckles knowingly. 'Why don't you try punting first?' he asks.

'What, now?'

'Sure.'

'I thought you were going to do all the hard work,' I joke.

'Well, if you want to be a rower, hard work is part of the deal.' He stops punting and offers the pole to me. 'Come on. I'll show you how.'

We've left most of the crowds behind us as we passed the Victoria Arms. This is a quiet spot on the river. It's as good a place as any to try.

'Okay,' I say, standing up.

The punt rocks back and forth and some water slops over the side. 'Hey, careful,' says Adam. 'Move slowly.' He offers his hand to me.

I steady myself and move along the punt carefully, keeping my arms out for balance. The boat rocks a little with each step, but no more water spills inside. Adam reaches his arm out to me and I grasp it with both hands for support. He stands solidly on the wooden decking at the end of the boat as I steady myself.

I continue to hold onto his arm.

Adam is tall – a good few inches more than me – and I

look up at his face. His mouth and eyes crinkle into a smile. 'Think you can do it?' he asks.

'No question.' We're standing right next to each other now, and the punt has come to a halt in the middle of the river. The combined weight of the two of us is tipping it, and it feels a little unsteady in the water. I place one of my hands on Adam's shoulder.

'Here, take the pole,' says Adam. We shuffle around each other, swapping places until I hold the pole in my two hands and he stands next to me.

'Don't let go of me,' I say, and he rests his hands against me, gripping me gently but firmly. The feel of his fingers against my skin is exquisite. The sound of my blood in my temples is as noisy as the lapping of the water.

'Now push,' he commands.

I lower the pole into the water until it finds the muddy river bed. Then I push, gently at first, and then with more vigour as the punt begins to move forwards.

'Careful,' says Adam. The punt moves upriver, rocking as I push down on the pole. Adam stays at my side, holding me steady. The craft dips and a little water sloshes over my feet, making me start.

I lift the pole ready for a second stroke and water runs down the wet shaft, trickling over my arms. I start to giggle. 'Hey, you didn't tell me it was going to be so wet!' I tell him. The summer dress I'm wearing is starting to get soaked.

Adam keeps a hand on my waist. 'That's the trouble with water,' he says. 'It can be so wet at times.'

The punt begins to turn in the water and Adam guides my hand so that the pole steers it straight again like a rudder. 'That's it. You're doing fine. You're a natural, Victoria.'

And it's true. With each stroke I am gaining in confidence, pushing the punt upstream, keeping it away from the banks. It seems that I have found my natural environment. But Adam stays with me, and I let him keep his hands around my waist.

After a while we have sailed a good way up the river and my arms are growing tired. 'Why don't we stop and you can show me what you've brought in that picnic box,' I say. Adam has brought an old-fashioned wicker hamper with us.

'Okay,' he says. 'Pull over to the bank by that tree.'

We come to rest beneath a weeping willow. Adam ties the punt to a jutting tree root so that we don't drift away, then he sits down to open the hamper. He brings out a bottle of Pimm's and two glasses. 'Here, hold these and I'll pour.'

I hold the glasses while he tips the bottle, giving us both generous measures. 'To messing about on the river!' he says, raising his glass.

We drink the Pimm's, sitting side by side in the punt. We are a long way from the boathouse now, and there is absolutely no one else around. The sky above us is blue and hot, but we are shaded here beneath the trailing branches of the tree. I finish the drink and lie back on the cushions that line the punt. My dress is still wet, but it is starting to dry out in the warmth of the day. 'This is perfect,' I say. 'A perfect summer's day.'

Adam comes to lie down beside me, the punt rocking gently as he shifts his weight. I can feel the touch of his body against mine. 'It *is* perfect,' he says. 'And being here with you is what makes it so right.'

He puts his arm around me and our lips find each other's.

'Here we are,' says Bridget, jolting me out of my reverie.

For a moment I hardly know where I am. The weeping willow beside the meadow has vanished and I'm back in the cold north of England in a rainy market town on a cold January day. Bridget is driving around the edge of the market square, looking for a parking place.

'You were miles away,' she says, giving me a sideways

glance.

'Yes,' I say. Hundreds of miles away, and nearly twenty years in time. But even more significantly, I have crossed a divide into my past. 'Hearing you talking about Venice reminded me of a time when Adam and I went punting in Oxford,' I tell her.

'That's nice.'

But she doesn't understand the full significance of what happened. Another lost memory has come back to me, and I eagerly store it away with the others that I have snatched back from oblivion. Just a few brief snippets from a lost lifetime, but I am confident now that more will come.

I'm so excited that I almost blurt it out to Bridget, but of course she has no idea about me losing my memory and it would take too long to explain.

'There's a space,' says Bridget, signalling to pull over. She spends the next couple of minutes shunting the car backwards and forwards, trying to squeeze into a tight space between a van and a mud-splattered Land Rover that has probably come from one of the local farms. Eventually she's satisfied that she's close enough to the kerb. By the time she's finished, my excitement has subsided. Bridget reaches over to the back seat for her shopping bag and purse.

'I do wish there was a bigger town nearby, don't you?' she says as we get out of the car. 'It would be more convenient if we had a proper supermarket and somewhere decent to buy clothes.'

I'd never really thought about it before, but now Bridget mentions it, I can see that she's right. I'd thought that this market town was all I required. But now as we walk towards the stallholders I start to see the place in a new light. It's really very small and provincial, with its cobbled streets, its old stone houses and its handful of small shops. Many of the people who are doing their shopping here are old: women with tartan shopping trollies on wheels, and men in flat caps.

Bridget pulls a shopping list from her bag. 'Shall we meet at the café in half an hour when we've done our shopping?' she asks.

'Sounds like a good idea.'

She heads off in the direction of a fruit and vegetable stall. I don't actually have much to buy and I get my shopping done quite quickly. I wander around the edge of the market square, looking at the shop windows, trying to remember what happened after the punting trip, but my mind is a blank. The memories clearly need the right stimulus. They won't come on their own, or by me wanting them to return. I will have to be patient and give them time.

After Bridget's comment about the town, I can't help but feel more alert to my surroundings. I peer through the window of the small, independent pharmacy where the white-coated pharmacist is handing a prescription to an old lady. Next door is a charity shop with a display of china ornaments in the window. There's a handwritten sign asking for volunteers. *Time to spare?* reads the sign. *Get out more, meet new people and make a difference!*

I could volunteer, I suppose. I certainly have time to spare, and I'm ready to start getting out of the village more and making new friends. But until I discover more about who I really am, I don't feel inclined to take this step.

I carry on walking and come to an estate agent's. I pause to look at the properties for sale in the window. I realise I don't know which estate agent Adam and I used when we bought the cottage. Was it this one? The agent is selling a farm, various houses in the town and nearby villages, and a luxury barn conversion complete with a hot tub in the garden. I wonder what it would be like to live in a house with a hot tub. It's hard for me to imagine such decadence. It's not the kind of thing that Jane would be interested in, but what about Victoria? I suspect Victoria would love such a thing. The idea gives me a thrill, like I'm two separate people sharing the same body. It makes me think I could do almost anything if I could summon up enough courage.

I'm about to move on when a woman in the estate agent's gets up from her desk and walks over to a filing cabinet. She pulls out some brochures before going to sit back down. She's wearing a slim-fitting dark suit with a cream, silk blouse. Her hair is nicely styled in a layered bob and she's taken trouble to apply make-up, not too much but just enough to be sophisticated and professional.

I realise that what I really want to do is ask her about her job. I want to ask if she needs anyone to show people around the properties. I want to ask if I could come and work here. The thought makes me almost giddy. I could get a job. Not just working as a volunteer in a charity shop, but my own career. And why not?

I catch sight of my reflection in the window. I'm wearing old jeans, flat shoes and a parka. I hardly ever buy new clothes. I can't remember the last time I went to the hairdressers and my straggly locks blow around my face in the wind. I certainly don't bother with make-up. Adam never complains about the way I look, and so I have never really given it much consideration.

The woman in the estate agent's notices me staring at her and gives me a smile in case I'm a prospective client interested in buying a property. But it's not an entirely welcoming smile. She's probably thinking that I'm not a prospective house buyer after all, just a sad lonely woman who's let herself go.

The picture I saw of Victoria was a very different version of me. Styled hair, make-up, confident. Victoria wouldn't have allowed herself to look the way I do. What would she have thought of someone like me? The answer springs unbidden from my subconscious. Victoria would have scorned someone like Jane. I think back to what I read of her in the newspaper article. She (I still have trouble thinking of her as me, she seems like a different person entirely) had a high-flying career as an advertising executive. No one would employ me to work in an executive position, the way I look now.

'Seen anything you fancy?'

I jump at the sound of Bridget's voice behind me. She's done her shopping and is carrying two bags bulging with fruit and vegetables and other supplies.

'I was just browsing,' I say.

'Have you finished your shopping?' she asks, noting my single shopping bag.

'Actually, I didn't need very much.'

'No worries,' she says. 'Sometimes it's nice just to get out of the house isn't it? Shall we go and get that coffee or do you want to head back?'

'A coffee would be nice,' I say. I realise that I've grown cold, standing outside looking through windows.

CHAPTER 24

That evening when Adam phones and asks me what I've been doing, I tell him that I went to the market with Bridget.

'Again?' he asks. 'You really do seem to be spending a lot of time with the vicar's wife.'

I bristle at Adam's words. Why should he mind if I pop into town with a friend? Isn't that what normal people do? I think about the woman working in the estate agent's and say, 'Actually, I was thinking about getting a job in town. Maybe something part-time.'

'A job?' I can hear the incredulity in Adam's voice. 'You can't be serious. What on earth for?'

I think about what the sign in the charity shop said. 'To get out more,' I tell him. 'To meet new people. To do something useful with my time.'

'But Jane' – it's his cajoling voice – 'there's really no need for you to do that. I earn a good salary, more than enough for us to live comfortably. What sort of part-time work could you do in such a small town? Work in the café?' He laughs. 'You'd earn a pittance doing work like that. It wouldn't be worth the trouble.'

'That's not the point,' I say, keeping my voice level.

'And besides, there are other businesses in the town besides the café.'

'Such as?'

'Well, there's an estate agent's.' There aren't many other options, but I'm not going to admit that.

'An estate agent? But you don't have the right qualifications. You don't have a car. And you know how much you dislike meeting new people.'

'Do I?' I have raised my voice. 'Do I really know that?'

He ignores my question. 'You already have a job, Jane, looking after the house. Aren't you happy with that? Aren't you happy living in the cottage with me?'

I'm tempted to say no, I'm not happy. I'm not sure if I can even remember what happiness feels like. Instead I say, 'I just want to do more, Adam. Can't you understand that?'

It's almost like he hasn't heard me or has chosen not to listen. 'You'd find it very tiring going out to work,' he says. 'I really think it would be best if you...'

'Why do you always know what's best for me?' I shout.

There's silence on the other end of the line for a moment. Then Adam says, 'I think you need to calm down, Jane.'

'Stop telling me what to do.' I end the call and slam the phone down beside me.

A surge of anger wells up inside me. Red rage. I remember feeling like this once before. The feeling bubbles through my veins, and a memory hovers just out of view. And then it comes to me.

It's another memory from my Oxford days. I'm lying in a punt again, with Adam, underneath a willow tree, feeling the gentle sway of the water.

This is a different day, later in the summer term. This time we've brought the punt south from the boathouse at Magdalen Bridge and tied the punt beneath a tree on Christ Church Meadow.

The bright sunlight is dappled by the trailing leaves of

the willow, but I can feel its warmth against my bare arms. The silky-smooth river is flowing lazily past. Adam caresses my collarbone with the tips of his fingers. His fingers trace the curve of my lips and then move lower, caressing my neck. He kisses me and his fingers continue lower still. I return his kiss, parting my lips to let his tongue flick firmly against mine.

Suddenly we hear voices and laughter on the riverbank.

'What the —' Adam jerks upright, annoyed that this special moment has been interrupted.

I reach up to him. 'Ignore them,' I say, pulling him back towards me. 'They're not interested in us.' The voices are still some way off.

But Adam is sitting hunched in the punt, not looking at me, waiting for the people to pass. He can be so uptight sometimes.

I sit up and look around. The group is approaching and I recognise two of my friends from college, Carrie and Maddy, with a couple of boys in tow.

'Pretend you haven't seen them,' hisses Adam, but it's too late. They've already seen us.

'Hey, Vick,' calls Carrie. She has the room above mine on the same staircase. We first met in Fresher's Week and got blind drunk together in the college bar. The other girl is Maddy, my tutorial partner. We've been best friends all year. The two boys I know vaguely. They must be from a different college. Carrie's always picking up good-looking guys to bring back to her room.

I wave at them. 'Hi! Over here!'

'Don't encourage them,' says Adam petulantly, but I ignore him.

The four stroll over towards us, Carrie pulling her latest boyfriend with her. The girls haven't seen much of Adam previously. He prefers to keep me to himself.

'Hi, Vick,' says Maddy. 'We wondered where you'd gone. We knocked on your door, but you were out. Now we know what you were up to.' She giggles.

'You know Adam don't you?' I say. Maddy and Carrie were in the punt with me when Adam 'rescued' us.

'Sure,' says Maddy. 'This is Tom and Stuart.'

The guy that Carrie's clutching raises a broad palm and says, 'Hi!' in a strong American accent.

'Tom's a rower, aren't you?' says Carrie. He nods.

I take in his tanned, muscled arms, and I like what I see. 'I row too,' I tell him. 'I'm trialling for the college first eight.'

'Tom's hoping to qualify for the university team next year, aren't you, Tom?'

'Yep,' says Tom, flashing me a broad grin.

He's tall enough, at around six foot six, and strong too, even if he's a man of few words. I smile back.

Adam says nothing, but I know he's seen me. Let him see. There's no harm in looking at a handsome guy is there?

Maddy asks me, 'Are you coming to the party tonight?'

'What party?'

Maddy rolls her eyes. 'Carrie's party. Everyone's going to be there.'

'Who's everyone?' I ask.

'Well Tom and Stuart, for starters. Do say you'll come. You and Adam. You must!'

Adam's not big on parties, I know. But I love the idea of taking him along and showing him off. And if Tom and Stuart are going to be there too… I say, 'Yeah, we'd love to come to the party. See you there.'

'Later,' says Carrie, smiling at us both, and dragging Tom away along the tow path. Maddy and Stuart follow, arm in arm.

When they're out of earshot Adam turns to me and says, 'You could have asked.'

'Asked who what?' I say, lying back down in the punt.

'Asked me. If I wanted to go to the party.'

I tug at his arm, trying to pull him down next to me. 'Well do you?'

He resists my pull. 'I don't know. I thought we had plans for this evening?'

'What, going for a pizza?' I say. 'That hardly counts as *plans*.' The prospect of a party in Carrie's room is so much more exciting than just going out for a pizza, I don't know what his problem is. 'We can get a pizza anytime.'

'But I thought we were going to spend the evening on our own, just the two of us.'

'We're spending the afternoon on our own,' I point out.

'Well, we were until your friends turned up.'

'They've gone now. And anyway, I didn't know they were going to be here.'

'You didn't arrange for them to just walk past?'

'What? Why would I do such a thing?' Suddenly I'm really cross. Adam is being totally unreasonable. I sit up in the punt and scrabble to my feet. 'Move aside,' I say, starting to climb past him.

'What are you doing?' he demands.

'I'm getting out of the punt.' I lunge for the tree root on the bank.

He tries to grab my arm. 'Don't be stupid, you'll make us capsize.'

I shake him off. 'Let go of me!' I shout. The punt tips sideways and water sloshes over the side. I've got one hand on the tree root now and I'm determined not to let go. I scrabble onto the bank, soaking one foot in the process.

'I can walk back from here,' I say, stomping off. 'And don't bother coming to the party. I'll go by myself. You obviously don't want to.'

'Suit yourself,' he shouts after me.

CHAPTER 25

Last night's row with Adam on the phone and the memory it triggered have left me a little shaken. Anger isn't an emotion I'm comfortable with. I'm hardly ever angry or upset about anything. My days in the cottage are calm, and the fiery emotions I relived when remembering that afternoon out on the river with Adam have left me fearful of what else I may uncover.

But I'm determined to explore the possibility of finding a job. Adam doesn't own me. He can't always tell me what to do.

He might be right about getting a job at the estate agent's however. I don't have any suitable qualifications. But they might still be willing to take someone on and train them. I shouldn't give up without even trying.

What I really need to do is buy a copy of the local newspaper and see if there are any jobs advertised. There might be opportunities in the other nearby towns and villages. I won't know unless I look.

So after putting the laundry on and clearing away the breakfast things, I wrap up warm and set off towards the village. A light drizzle fills the air, but I'm used to worse. I pull my hood up and concentrate on avoiding the water-filled potholes at the edge of the road.

When I reach the village I head straight to the shop. As always, Cath is behind the counter. A smile lights up her face as soon as she sees me. 'Jane!'

'Hi!' I say. I'm really glad to see her again. Arguing with Adam has left me with a slightly sick feeling, and it's good to see a friendly face.

'I haven't seen you since last week,' she says. 'What did you do at the weekend? Something nice? We never get any time off on Saturday. The boys have to fend for themselves, but of course they're used to that. Sunday's the day I get to put my feet up. But someone always seems to need me even on my day off. Boys, eh?'

I'm happy to listen to Cath's chatter. It helps to distract me from my own concerns, and she doesn't seem to need me to make much of a response.

'It's nice seeing you in the shop,' she says. 'And I've been enjoying the book group meetings very much too. Have you?'

'Oh yes,' I say. 'Absolutely.'

'Our trip to *The Mousetrap* is this Thursday,' she says. 'Are you quite sure you won't come?'

'I'm sorry,' I say. 'Thanks for asking, but no. I meant what I said.'

'Oh.' She looks crestfallen, but I won't change my mind just because Cath asked me a second time. I have to start being stronger than that, otherwise how am I ever going to stand up to Adam?

'There is one thing you can help me with though. Could I have a copy of the local newspaper?'

'Of course,' she says. 'Are you looking for something in particular? You don't normally read the local news, do you?'

'Actually...' I can't think of any reason not to tell her the truth, so I say, 'I was interested in looking at listings for jobs.'

Cath looks astonished. 'For yourself? I mean... no

reason why you shouldn't get a job. I just didn't think you needed one, with Adam having such a good job in London.'

'I don't really need a job for the money,' I admit. 'But I think, perhaps, I might like one. It would help to get me out of the house and meeting people.'

'Well good for you,' says Cath. She picks up the local paper and turns to the pages near the back. 'Most of the jobs are advertised online these days,' she says. 'But there might be some part-time ones listed here.'

I try to see what she's reading, but the newspaper is upside-down.

'What kind of thing are you interested in?' she asks. 'What job did you do when you worked in Oxford?'

'I worked as a librarian in one of the libraries,' I say. It's an automatic response, based on what Adam's always told me. But as soon as I say it, I realise that it's not true. I didn't work in a library. I didn't even have a job in Oxford. I lived and worked in London. I was an advertising executive.

Cath looks doubtful. 'Librarian? I don't think there are many openings for a librarian. The nearest library's miles away. But maybe you could use your skills to do some office work or something?'

'Yes,' I say. 'I'm sure I could do something like that.'

We chat for a little longer and I pay her for the newspaper. I fold it and tuck it under my coat so it doesn't get wet on the way home, and then I trudge back along the road towards the cottage.

The drizzle has started to turn into steady rain and by the time I reach the edge of the village, my hair is already soaking wet. I wish I had worn a hat. I quicken my pace, but then another idea occurs to me. Instead of going home, I could pop into the church again. At least it will be dry in there. I can wait inside to see if the rain eases off. And it will give me a chance to read the newspaper and think about my options. After all, I am in no hurry to get

159

home.

I turn back and head up the narrow path that leads to the lychgate. The wooden gate creaks open as I push it, and I head up the path between the dark yews. The headstones that line the path are already streaked grey by the rain, and I hurry inside the church in search of shelter.

CHAPTER 26

The heavy door creaks open and I duck into the dim interior, letting the door close softly behind me. I shake the worst of the rain from my hair and walk towards the central aisle, leaving a trail of wet footprints on the stone floor.

The church is deserted and I experience a moment's disappointment that Ben isn't there, in his jeans and blue sweater, to brighten the place up and keep me company. I wonder what he wears on Sundays when he's taking a service. Does he don a cassock, or is he a trendy vicar who leads worship in a pair of Levi's?

My eye is drawn to a stunning flower arrangement on one side of the altar. I walk down the aisle to take a closer look. Perhaps they are left over from a wedding at the weekend, or perhaps they are just from Sunday's service. I will have to ask Bridget about it.

The flowers are small, delicate blooms – nothing showy – the kind that are in season at this time of year. Snowdrops, primroses, lemon-coloured winter sweet. Someone with an expert eye for design has cleverly mixed them in with evergreen leaves, bright yellow catkins and late holly berries.

I bend over to sniff them and the muted scent of the winter blossom triggers a sudden flashback. The sense of being transported so suddenly to another place and time is so powerful that I find myself shaking, my legs unable to carry my weight. I clutch at the altar rail for support, but I am already falling. I'm in another world entirely, and it is too late to do a thing.

I'm back in Oxford again, this time in Carrie's room in college. It's the party she and Maddy were talking about earlier. Carrie has one of the best rooms in college – in front quad overlooking the porter's lodge and the college chapel. It's practically a small suite, with a large sitting room and a small bedroom attached. The sitting room has oak-panelled walls and creaky wooden floorboards covered by a threadbare Persian rug. Her bookcases are filled with obscure French novels, textbooks on existentialism and Jean-Paul Sartre, and CDs by Nirvana, Blur and Garbage. Right now, Courtney Love is playing, her sweet, throaty vocals and twanging guitar chords jumping off the walls. The leaded casement windows of the sitting room have been thrown wide open, letting the music escape into the quad outside, like the soundtrack to a psychotic rendition of a *Midsummer Night's Dream*. It's only a matter of time before the porter will come banging on the door, demanding quiet. But until then, the party rages on.

I'm dancing with Carrie in the middle of the room. I don't know how much we've drunk. A lot, I guess. Her rowing hunk, Tom is here, slouching in the corner. He and Carrie have had a bust-up since the afternoon, and she's ignoring him like he's a piece of dirt on the carpet. Maddy and Stuart are snogging by the record player, hands all over each other. All around us, other students dance frenetically, or gaze sullenly from the sidelines.

'Where's Adam?' asks Carrie over the sound of the music.

I roll my eyes. 'Nowhere. I think we might have split up.'

'You too, huh?' she says.

'He can be so dull, sometimes. Possessive too. A real creep.'

'Yeah?' Carrie hardly knows Adam. That's another sign of how Adam behaves with me. He wants to keep me all to himself. I've been neglecting the girls in recent weeks, spending all my time with Adam. Well, that's changed now. The mournful way he looked at me this afternoon when I abandoned him in the punt, it was like I'd stabbed him through the heart. I don't think I'll be seeing him again anytime soon.

'Why don't you try your luck with Tom?' suggests Carrie. She casts a quick glance over her shoulder to where the tall, tanned rower is gazing back with the lovesick eyes of a kicked puppy-dog. 'On second thoughts, don't bother. Stick with me.'

'Just us girls, together,' I shout, and we dance together in the middle of the crush.

A tap on my shoulder makes me turn around. It's Adam.

'What?' I demand. I'm amazed to see him here after all. I didn't think he'd have the balls to come back, after the way I treated him.

'Here,' he says. 'These are for you.' He's holding out a bouquet of flowers. An *enormous* bouquet. He thrusts it towards me. 'Take them,' he says.

I'm so surprised, that I take them without thinking. 'They're beautiful, Adam,' I say. Suddenly the music has faded into the background, and all I'm aware of is me, Adam and the flowers. The perfume fills the summer air like honey.

He smiles cautiously. 'I came to say I'm sorry,' he says. 'I was stupid today. Stupid and petty. I should have said yes to the party. I know how much you like to have fun. I was just... over-protective.'

'You were jealous,' I say.

'Yes. Absolutely. How could I not be, when you're so

beautiful?'

'Come on,' I say to him, taking him by the hand.

'Where?'

'To my room.'

'But you said you wanted to spend the evening with friends. You didn't want it to be just you and me.'

'Yes,' I say. 'But I've changed my mind. Come on.'

I wave goodbye to Carrie and lead Adam out of the party and down the stairs. My own room is below Carrie's, but is about half the size. I open the door and draw Adam inside.

The room is dark, but the music from Carrie's room is almost as loud in here as it was upstairs. I turn on the bedside light and sit down on the bed, laying the flowers on the pillow.

'Come and sit next to me,' I tell Adam, patting the bed sheets.

He stands nervously for a moment, then slides onto the bed next to me. He takes my hands in his and lifts them to his lips, kissing them gently. 'You know that I'd do anything for you, don't you, Victoria?' he says softly.

I giggle. 'You are such a romantic, Adam,' I tease. 'Flowers, grand gestures... you treat me like I'm a princess from a fairy tale.'

'You are a princess,' he says earnestly. 'You are my princess.' He touches his palm to my cheek, stroking it gently. His touch is soft and strong and I push my face into his hand. He begins to caress me with his fingers.

It is almost possible to believe that I am a princess.

Suddenly I want him, desperately. I kiss his palm, then take his finger in my mouth.

His other hand is on my knee, advancing cautiously.

Caution isn't on my mind at all. I move my lips to his and then we are kissing, passionately. Above us the music thumps through the ceiling. I begin to undo the buttons of his shirt, and then he is pulling at my top, easing the straps down over my shoulders, revealing bare skin beneath.

I pull his shirt from his broad shoulders, revealing strong arms. His chest is covered with fine dark hairs. I smooth them with my fingers, feeling the throbbing beat of his heart through my fingertips.

He lifts my top and I raise my arms so that he can pull it over my head. He casts it aside. He says nothing. There is no longer any need to speak. I watch his eyes as he wraps his arms around me and unhooks my bra to reveal my nakedness.

We kiss again.

The smell of the bouquet on the pillow fills my nostrils as we lie down on the bed. I push the bouquet aside and the roses and peonies, dahlias and irises begin to tumble to the floor, one by one. Now they are gone, and only Adam and I remain.

It is our first time, and he is exquisitely gentle.

'Jane? Jane? Are you okay?'

Flowers are tumbling again, but they are pale winter blooms this time, and the air is cold and bright. I'm lying on the stone floor of the church, covered in flowers and water from the floral arrangement. A face gazes down on me and anxious hands come to my aid.

Ben. The vicar.

'Can you hear me Jane? Are you hurt?'

I must have fainted. I don't think I'm hurt. Just wet, and dazed. 'I'm fine,' I hear myself telling Ben. 'I think I must have tripped on something.'

'Just stay where you are for the moment,' he says. 'Don't try to get up just yet.'

My head is clearing quickly and the memory that the smell of the flowers dislodged is already receding. I mustn't let it go completely though. It is a treasure to be kept and placed with the slowly building library of memories I am collecting.

I push myself up into a sitting position.

'Careful,' says Ben.

'Oh dear,' I say. 'I'm very sorry. I seem to be making a

habit of this.'

'Not at all,' he says. 'Are you sure you're not injured in any way?'

'I'm fine. Really.' With his help I lift myself to my feet and stand uncertainly, regaining my composure.

'What is it that you tripped on?' he asks, scanning the debris of flowers on the floor.

'I'm not sure. I'm terribly sorry about the flowers,' I say. 'I'll be sure to pay for them.'

'Don't be silly,' he says. 'I'm just relieved that you're okay.'

I nod. I am all right. More than all right. My memory has answered one of the burning questions that has been haunting me for so long.

Adam does love me. And I love him.

'Come back to the vicarage with me,' says Ben, offering me his arm. 'I can make you some tea and then drive you home.'

I wonder what Adam would make of his offer. It's not hard to imagine his reaction. But what Adam thinks isn't my main concern. The fact is that I don't need Ben's assistance, however kindly it is meant. 'Thank you,' I say. 'But I'm absolutely okay now. I can walk home myself.'

CHAPTER 27

The rain has stopped by the time I leave the church, although it is starting to turn dark under the low grey clouds. I pull the collar of my coat around my neck and set off away from the village, along the country road that leads to the cottage.

The memory of making love to Adam for the very first time is still fresh in my mind. I replay the image slowly, recalling the sensations, the emotions that I felt. Almost miraculously, the details are still crystal clear, as if they happened yesterday. They have been preserved in my mind, like the scent of roses in a jar of perfume.

I realise now that I have been unfair to Adam. Yes, he has deceived me, but until I truly understand why he gave me this new identity, I should not be quick to judge him. I cannot doubt any more that he loves me. His love is present always. I should never have doubted it.

And now I am beginning to have doubts about myself. Adam has made it clear that he disapproves of me getting a job. Perhaps he is right. Look at how I fainted in the church. And I know that he only has my welfare at heart. Perhaps a job would be too tiring.

But it would do no harm to look in the newspaper.

When I return home I light the fire in the front room, change out of my damp clothes and make myself a nice hot mug of tea. Then I sit by the fireside and open the newspaper to look.

The front pages of the newspaper are filled with local articles featuring events at schools and churches, and other human-interest stories. Photographs of children and animals feature prominently. I skip through them until I find a page dedicated to job adverts. Like Cath said, there are not many openings advertised here. Mostly they are part-time jobs, but that isn't a problem. A part-time position would be a good way for me to begin to get back into the workplace after so many years spent at home. Mostly they don't require too many qualifications, which is good since I – or at least *Jane* – possess no paper qualifications whatsoever. I hope that won't restrict my options too much.

I flip through the positions advertised. As I expected, they are all in nearby towns. How would I get there? The bus service is hopeless in this area. I don't have a car. I can't even drive.

Or can I?

All I know is what Adam has told me. He has lied to me about so many things, I can't really trust anything I think I know.

One thing I have discovered is that my memories can be unlocked by a suitable stimulus. Perhaps if I could look at photographs of cars, I could trigger some kind of recollection? It sounds ridiculous, but it can't hurt to try. I certainly can't get a proper job unless I have a means of transport, and I could hardly ask Bridget to chauffeur me back and forth to work. So really, if I am to get a job, being able to drive is essential.

I make myself a fresh mug of tea and take it through to the office. I always used to think of it as Adam's office, but I am spending more time here myself these days. I switch on the computer and when it's powered up, I type 'cars' into the search box. It seems vaguely futile, but what do I have to lose?

Some pictures of cars appear on the screen, all different makes and models and colours. I have no idea what I might be looking for. A car is a car, surely? Of all the online searches I have made recently, this one seems like the most stupid.

I click on a website that lists cars for sale and begin to click through the photographs. Sensible family cars, compact hatchbacks, executive saloons, SUVs and even electric cars clamour for my attention. Mostly they come in dull colours – silver, grey, black, white. If I owned a car I would want something a little more interesting. I sip my tea and keep clicking. Car after car appears on the screen. None of them triggers any kind of memory. After all, I see cars nearly every day in the village, or in the town. I have travelled to the market with Bridget in her car, and nothing happened then. And if I had learned how to drive a car, I would surely know without having to be told.

I keep clicking and then I see it.

It's a red car. A bright red sports car.

I know the make and model without needing to read the details. That's *my* car. I drove a car like that once, I'm certain of it.

Is it really conceivable that I could have forgotten how to drive a car? I had forgotten that I once read *Jane Eyre*, so I guess that it's possible. Maybe if I sat in the driver's seat, my hands and feet would begin to remember. One hand gripping the leather steering wheel, the other resting on the gear stick, my foot pressing the accelerator pedal…

And suddenly I am there, the wheel in my hands, my toes pressing hard to the floor as the engine shifts from a deep hum to a throaty roar. I engage the clutch and snap the gearstick up a gear. The whine of the engine drops an octave and begins to climb higher once more.

The car is mine. I bought it with the money from my annual bonus. It is my toy, my treat, my luxury. I love this car.

Adam sits in the passenger seat beside me. He hates the car. He hates its speed. He hates how much I spent buying it. More than anything, he hates what it represents – my independence. My freedom.

'Victoria,' he warns. 'Slow down.'

But I continue to press down with my foot. The more Adam dislikes it, the more I will do it. 'I bought a sports car so that I could drive it fast,' I tell him. 'If I'd wanted to drive slowly, I'd have bought something dull. Like your car.'

'You don't need a car at all living in London. Especially not this ridiculous sports car. We could have used that money from your bonus to pay off some of the mortgage.'

'Remind me. Whose bonus was it?' I ask.

'That's not the point. We're married. We're supposed to share everything.'

'We can share it. You're welcome to drive the car if you like.'

'I don't want to,' he says. 'It's not practical. This car just isn't practical.'

'That's the point. It's meant to be fun, Adam. Have you forgotten what fun is? Perhaps you never really knew. Sometimes I wonder why I ever married you.'

I continue to drive fast, laughing, the wind making my hair flap. The car rounds a bend, tyres gripping the road hard. A slower vehicle appears before me and I pull out into the other lane, overtaking it seamlessly, leaving it far, far behind.

Adam is clutching at the door grip, his knuckles white. 'Sometimes I think you just do these things to torment me,' he says petulantly.

I shouldn't tease him so, but he's such an easy target. So square. So predictable. 'I'm sorry, Adam,' I say. 'I don't do these things to spite you. But you know that I have to be free. I'm not a bird that you can keep locked in a cage. You knew that right from the start.'

'Yes.' He sounds contrite, or perhaps just resigned. 'I know.'

I slow the car to a speed that's less terrifying, for both of us. 'So you'll allow me this one indulgence?'

'It's your money, Victoria. You work hard. You deserve it. And you can spend it how you like.'

'That's right. I can. And if you want me to love you, you have to indulge me sometimes and let me be the person I am. You have to allow me to be happy, Adam.'

'Yes. I know,' says Adam. 'But you have to let me be happy too, Victoria.'

The memory comes to a halt, like a newsreel that has played out. I sit, cradling my mug of tea, gazing at the blank office wall, turning the details over in my mind. It was all so vivid – the feel of the leather under my fingers, the exhilaration of the speed, and the plunging and soaring emotions of my relationship with Adam.

I have lost so much.

Not just a car, or a job. Not merely a name or a collection of memories. An identity. It has been stolen from me.

I look again at the job adverts in front of me. I had a career, and like so many other things it is over. It ended long ago. I could start again, applying for a part-time local job that doesn't need a degree, or any kind of qualification – after all, Jane Harvey has no paper certificates to show anyone, not even a driving licence – but I know that I'm capable of so much more. I screw up the newspaper and hurl it against the wall in rage.

It's no use just getting mad. Raging at the injustice of it all will get me nowhere. I need to find out the truth. And then I'll be able to put things right.

~~~

When Adam phones in the evening I casually mention that I'm thinking of getting a car.

'What?' He is almost speechless at my suggestion. 'A car?'

I help him out. 'To get around more easily. You know how unreliable the bus service is around the villages. That's why I've been catching a lift with Bridget to the market every Monday.'

That pacifies him a little. I knew that the idea of pushing Bridget out of my life would appeal to him. He's still nervous about the prospect, however. 'It's a nice idea, darling,' he says hesitatingly, 'but you don't know how to drive.'

I play along with him. 'I could get lessons. I'm sure I could master it if I had a good driving instructor.'

'We'll need to think about it carefully,' he says. 'It's a big step to take. We shouldn't make any decision in a hurry. Let's talk about it again at the weekend.'

'Okay,' I say. I can guess how that conversation is likely to turn out. There's no way that Adam will allow me to take driving lessons. To do that, I'd need to apply for a provisional driving licence, and that would really let his secret out of the bag.

This is why he was so keen to dissuade me from getting a job, I realise. Not just because he wants me to stay home and avoid meeting other people. If I started applying for a job, I'd need to show proof of identity, get issued with a tax code, and make myself official in innumerable ways.

Jane Harvey can't do any of those things. Jane Harvey doesn't officially exist.

'I'll call you again tomorrow,' he says. 'Goodnight, Jane.'

The sound of his voice stirs my emotions into a complex swirl. Now that I have begun to remember how happy we were together during our student days, I have grown to love him more deeply than I ever did before. He is undeniably tender and sensitive in those recovered memories. I don't know if I could go on living without him.

172

And yet he is the man who committed the most appalling crime against me. He continues to perpetrate that crime every time he calls me Jane. I still cannot imagine why he did it.

But I am on the brink of discovering the truth. And when I find out, I won't hold back from whatever actions are necessary to right that terrible wrong.

CHAPTER 28

I awake early on Wednesday morning, and I already know what must be done. My memories have begun to come thick and fast. More will follow, I'm sure of it, but I have already discovered enough about myself, about the woman I used to be, to know what I must do next.

Adam has hidden so much from me, and lied outright about so many other things, that I have been in a state of confusion and uncertainty. But now the essentials are clear. I know that deep down, despite everything he has done to deceive and coerce me, he loves me. And I still love him. I hate him too, and I don't yet know whether the love or the hate is stronger.

I can see clearly now what I have lost – my career, my self-confidence, my independence – and I know that Adam can't be blamed for all those things. He took away my identity, but I still don't understand why. To complete the picture of my past, I need to find out what really happened to me in the red room.

Was I attacked, perhaps by an opportunistic burglar coming in through that open window? Or did something more sinister take place in that room? Why didn't Adam call the police? And why, instead, did he whisk me away to this village in Yorkshire and pretend to the whole world that I was dead? What would make a man like Adam do such an outrageous thing?

There is only one way to find out. I have already discovered that I can recover my lost memories with the right stimulus. The event that precipitated my memory loss took place in the red room, and that is buried deepest of all within my mind. To uncover that event, I must go back to where it happened. I must return to the red room.

I had always believed what Adam told me – that the red room was in our house in Oxford. But I realise now that this was a lie. I don't think we ever owned a house in Oxford. We lived in London, in the house where Adam now lives during his working week. The house in Montserrat Road. That is where I will find the red room. And that is where I must go.

It is a daunting prospect, to return to the scene of my worst nightmare. I haven't been to London for seven years. I haven't travelled beyond the nearby towns and villages. And I don't know how I might respond to returning there. I fainted at the New Year's Eve party. I almost fainted again in the church. What might happen when I return to the red room?

And yet, now that I've uncovered so much, I can't go on living my life as Jane Harvey, not knowing that I was once Victoria, but without uncovering the rest of the mystery. I have to discover the truth.

This is not a journey I feel I can do on my own, but I have thought of a solution to that. Diana, Bridget and Cath are travelling to London in two days to see *The Mousetrap*. If I can travel with my friends, I'm sure that I will find the courage to see this through.

I will phone Diana first thing and ask her.

I get out of bed and check the time. It's only six o'clock. It's still pitch black outside. I can't phone her this early.

I shower and use the bathroom and make myself some

breakfast. I'm a bag of nerves though. I can barely pour the tea without my hand shaking and spilling hot liquid over the kitchen counter. I force myself to nibble at a piece of toast.

Eventually I can stand it no longer. I pick up the phone and dial Diana's number.

The phone rings. Twice, three times. The receiver is trembling in my hand. Four times, five.

A man answers. It's Michael, Diana's husband. 'Hello?' he says.

'Hello, is Diana there, please? It's Jane. Jane Harvey, from the book group.'

'Of course, Jane. How are you? It's been ages since I saw you. Keeping well?'

The last time I saw him, I was lying on his sofa after fainting at the party. 'I'm keeping very well, thank you. Please, is Diana in?'

'Of course. I'll put her on.'

Diana's voice comes over the line. 'Jane? Is something the matter?'

I hear the concern in her voice, and it's hardly surprising. It is far too early in the morning to be making a social phone call. And I haven't been myself recently. *Not for the past seven years.* 'Hello, Diana,' I say. 'Nothing's the matter. I was just calling about the trip to London tomorrow. I wondered – do you still have a spare ticket?'

As soon as I ask the question, I realise that I have probably made a big miscalculation. Diana offered me the ticket days ago, and I declined. Tickets for *The Mousetrap* don't come up very often. She has almost certainly offered it to one of her other friends – one of her many friends. I start to think what I might do if she says no. I could ask to come with them anyway, even if I don't have a ticket for the theatre. But that would look stupid. Perhaps I will have to travel to London alone. But I fear that if I don't go now, in the company of my friends, I will lose the courage to go at all.

My mind begins to run away, and I am almost in a state of panic when she says, 'Of course I still have your ticket, Jane. You didn't think I would give it to someone else, did you? I've been hoping that you'd change your mind about coming.'

'Oh, Diana, I'm so relieved.'

She laughs. 'So do I take it that you'd like to come with us after all?'

'Yes, absolutely.'

'Splendid,' says Diana. 'We'd be delighted to have you along. You'll need to set your alarm clock in that case, although I can tell that you're an early riser. I've ordered a taxi to pick us up and take us to the station first thing tomorrow morning. We'll collect you at eight o'clock. We'll be travelling down to London on an early train and going to the matinée performance.'

'That sounds perfect,' I say.

'We thought about staying overnight in a hotel,' continues Diana, 'but Cath wanted to get back home to be with her family, so we decided to do it in a day trip. We should be back in the evening. The trains between Leeds and London are very fast these days.'

'Thank you,' I say. 'I'm so grateful. I'll be ready for you at eight tomorrow morning.'

I put the phone down and breathe in and out deeply, steadying my nerves. I am both relieved and filled with trepidation. But it is done. I am committed. This time tomorrow I will be leaving to travel to London.

But I will be among friends, and I am sure that with their support I can do this.

~~~

I spend the rest of the day in an anxious state. To calm myself down, I throw myself into a fit of cleaning, washing and dusting, until by early afternoon I am quite exhausted. I still haven't really eaten anything, and I don't think that I can.

I sit down on the sofa in the front room and pick up my copy of *Jane Eyre*. It is the old copy of the book, from my university days, and my eyes scan not the printed text, but the handwritten notes that I have scrawled in the margins. My own notes are almost as extensive as the printed words, but I do not recall having written any of them.

I thumb idly through the book, before scanning back to the point near the beginning where Jane Eyre is locked in the red room by her aunt. I look to see what the young Victoria thought about that scene.

The red room is a pivotal event for Jane Eyre. Overcome by terror, she becomes hysterical after being locked in there. Later, her aunt sends her away, telling her that she is evil. Jane is a prisoner of how other people see her. She must fight to discover her true self and allow her own identity to be known.

Jane's red room is my own red room after all. And I must follow her path and find my inner strength too. Tomorrow I will test that strength to breaking point. And I will either overcome the horror of the red room as Jane Eyre did, or else be broken by it.

Right now, I feel the need to escape my emotional prison for a while. I need to marshal my inner strength. And I know the perfect place to do that.

I wrap up warm, this time making sure I have a hat to protect me from the rain. The weather is atrocious. A freezing rain lashes the windows, making it ill-advisable to go outside. Yet that is where I must go. I wrap a long scarf around my neck, and head out into the wet, my head bowed against the wind.

The walk to the village seems even longer than usual, yet eventually I arrive at its edge. My feet follow the right-hand turning back to the lychgate, and my hand pushes aside the creaking gate to allow me access to the churchyard. The wind seems to have grown even stronger here, and I hold onto my hat as I push along the narrow path past the cold gravestones to the church.

Inside, the old building is warm and still. I stand just inside the door, removing my sodden hat and shaking my hair out. Water is dripping from my coat. The church feels familiar, like an old friend. And although I am not sure if I believe in anything beyond this world, a comforting feeling takes hold of me as I walk down the aisle and find a seat close to the altar.

The church is silent, apart from the rain that patters against the coloured windows, and the wind howling around the stone tower. The sharp musty smell is strangely comforting, and I wonder how many hundreds of people have sat in this place over the centuries contemplating difficult decisions or worrying about the outcome of choices already made.

My own choice is made. To confront my ghosts. To allow the memories to unfurl from the darkest corners where my own mind has hidden them these past seven years. And when I see what they reveal, I must face more decisions, choices that I cannot even imagine right now.

But that is for tomorrow. For now, I simply sit, and allow my tensions to slip slowly away.

A door opens behind me, and shoes scuff the stone floor. I hear the door quietly close and footsteps approach, coming up the aisle towards the front of the nave, where I am sitting. I know these footsteps. I recognise their tread. And my heart begins to beat a little faster, air coming in shallower breaths as the steps approach and then stop before me.

'Jane.'

I look up. It's Ben.

He smiles. 'I'm seeing a lot of you here recently. Don't worry. I'm certainly not complaining. It's lovely to see you in the church again.'

'I just came in to shelter from the rain,' I blurt out. 'I was on my way to the village shop.' I don't know why I am lying to him. It seems easier than telling the truth somehow.

I came here to see you.

Is that the truth? There's no point in denying it. Wanting to see Ben again is a part of the truth, at least.

I came here to find myself, to gather my strength ready for a difficult task.

That's another part of the truth.

And to shelter from the rain and the wind.

That's also true. Truth can be complicated.

'It's not a good day to be outdoors,' agrees Ben.

'No.'

'I was worried about you after your fall,' he says. 'How have you been feeling since then? Any more faintness? Dizzy spells?'

'No, I'm fine now,' I say. 'Thank you for asking.'

He stands there, his face a mask of concern. 'And there was also that time at the party at Diana and Michael's house. Have you been to see a doctor about it?'

'It's nothing, really. I must have drunk too much wine that night. I'm not used to it. And I didn't really faint in the church. I just lost my balance.'

'Yes,' he says, although he doesn't sound the least bit convinced by my act. 'Bridget has been feeling faint recently too, you know.'

I'm disconcerted at the twist in the conversation. 'She has?'

'Yes, faint and sick too, from time to time. Especially in the mornings.'

'I see.' I understand what he is saying now.

'She hasn't said anything to you?' he continues. 'Then I won't say any more. She should tell you herself.'

I nod at the unexpected news. 'That isn't my problem, though. I'm not pregnant.'

'No? Then, may I sit down?' he asks, indicating the empty space on the pew next to me.

'Of course.'

I feel the wooden seat bend under his weight as he sits.

'Jane, is there anything you'd like to say to me?' he asks. 'Something that perhaps you feel you can't say to anyone else?'

'Like what?'

'Something close to your heart. Something spiritual, perhaps, or emotional.'

'I don't know,' I say.

I could tell him. I could tell him everything. About the red room, about Victoria, about Adam. I could tell him now, and he would understand, I know he would.

Yet that is not really why I came to the church today. That's not why I wanted to see him again so badly.

My desire is not to tell him my secrets. My desire is to touch him, to feel his arms around my waist, pulling my lips towards his.

But that would be wrong. I am a married woman.

My husband betrayed me, destroyed me. He is no true husband.

But that does not make it right to want another man. Ben is Bridget's husband. And she is my friend.

Ben reaches out a hand and closes it around mine.

I feel my own hand quivering under his touch. My lips part and I raise my gaze to his.

He holds it steadily for a few seconds. 'You don't need to be afraid of me, Jane,' he says.

'Afraid?' I say. 'I'm not afraid of you, Ben.' Although I am. I am terrified of being this close to him.

'Aren't you? Perhaps you are afraid of yourself,' he says. 'Of your own feelings. But you don't need to be afraid. You see, nothing could ever happen between the two of us.'

'It couldn't?'

'No. Because Bridget and I have no secrets, you see. I tell her everything. And she tells me everything. So there is no need to worry about you and me, because nothing could ever happen. It is impossible.'

'I see.' I try to pull my hand away from his, but he keeps hold of it.

'Jane, don't imagine that I am judging you, or criticising you in any way. I would never do that. And don't imagine that I don't feel the same desire that you so obviously feel. I do, very much. You are a very attractive woman.'

I want to look away from him and hide my face in shame. I did not imagine that my feelings could be so transparent. And yet I cannot look away, not yet.

'But no matter how we feel about each other, we have already made our choices in life. We should be thankful for that, I think. I love Bridget and she loves me. I can tell that you love Adam too. Does he love you back?'

'I... I think so.'

'That's good. I'm pleased. So don't worry about coming to see me here in the church. I'll always be ready to listen. And I hope that one day you'll be ready to tell me what's on your mind.'

I drag my eyes away from him at last and he releases my hand from his grip. My face is burning bright with embarrassment. I don't know if I can ever look at him again, or Bridget.

I tell her everything, he said.

Even this? But I already know the answer. I feel a sudden wave of nausea.

And yet I have a palpable sense of relief too. Ben has saved me from my own base desires. He has been strong when I was at my weakest and most vulnerable.

I will not be this weak again.

I raise my eyes back to his level. 'Thank you,' I say. 'Thank you for being so frank and honest with me. I wish everyone could always be so honest. And please give my congratulations to Bridget. I'm pleased for her, for both of you. You're so lucky to have each other.'

'Thanks,' he says. 'I'll tell her.'

I stand up, wrapping my coat around me, struggling to recover some dignity. 'I think that the rain has eased off a little now,' I say.

'Yes,' he says, making way for me to leave. 'I do believe

it has.'

CHAPTER 29

The meeting, or confrontation, or whatever it was with Ben in the church has left me more confused than ever. I hardly know who I am or how I'm supposed to behave anymore. What was I thinking of, coming on to Ben like that? The news that Bridget is pregnant has left me feeling mortified, both with shame that I tried to hit on Ben, and self-pity about my own inability to have a family.

It is more important than ever that I go to London and face my demons. If I don't discover who I really am, I feel that I might simply fall to pieces.

When Adam phones on Wednesday evening I'm worried that he'll notice my agitation. He'll sense that there's something different about me, that I've acquired some knowledge, no matter how small, about myself. But he's distracted by an idea that he's had.

'I've got a suggestion, Jane. Let me tell you all about it and then you can see how you feel.'

'Okay,' I say nervously. I wonder what on earth he has in mind. It isn't at all like Adam to be spontaneous.

'The thing is, it's not too busy in the office right now. The financial year end is still over a month away, so I was thinking that' – I hold my breath, wishing he'd hurry up and get to the point – 'maybe we could go away somewhere together.'

'Oh,' I say, taken aback. 'That sounds nice. Where were you thinking of?'

'There's a country house hotel in the Lake District, you know the sort of thing, roaring log fires, gourmet restaurant. It sounds perfect for a long weekend.'

'Well, yes,' I say. 'It does.'

'Oh, I'm so glad you think so too, Jane.' I can hear the relief in his voice. 'I was worried you wouldn't want to go. I'm looking at their website right now and they've got vacancies for tomorrow night and right through the weekend. I could catch an early flight home tomorrow and be with you by lunchtime. Then we could drive up to the Lakes and be there in time for dinner.'

'Tomorrow? You want to go tomorrow?'

'Well, if we want to have three nights there then that means Thursday, Friday and Saturday. We'll have to go home on Sunday because I'll need to be back at work on Monday.'

'But...' I can feel myself starting to shake. Much as I like the sound of this country house hotel, I can't go *tomorrow*. Not now that I've plucked up the courage to go to London and discover the truth about myself. And not now that I've asked Diana about the ticket and arranged for her and the others to pick me up at eight o'clock in the morning.

'What's the matter, Jane?'

I can hear the concern in Adam's voice, but it's also tinged with frustration. He's disappointed that I haven't jumped at the chance to go away with him for a romantic weekend. He thinks that I stay at home all the time with nothing to occupy myself except the housework and weekly trips to the local market.

'Don't you want to spend a long weekend together?' His voice sounds petulant.

'Of course I do,' I say. 'But the Lake District, at this

time of year? The weather will be atrocious. It rains all the time up there.'

'I wasn't planning on hiking up Scafell Pike. I thought we might spend more time in our luxury four-poster bed.'

My heart contracts. He's obviously thinking of last weekend when we made love with a renewed passion. And it's not that I don't want to rediscover that same excitement myself. But I'm caught in a dilemma. What do I want more? My husband or the truth? It's not something I have to think about too long. I need to find out the truth. The country house hotel will still be there next week, next month, next year. But the truth is something I must grasp now.

'I'm sorry,' I say. 'I don't think I'd be much fun this weekend. I've got a sore throat. I think I might be going down with something.' I'm glad he can't see me blushing at my own lie.

'You didn't say.'

'No, well, it wasn't worth mentioning before, but you won't want to spend the weekend kissing me in this state.'

'No, I suppose not.' He's really disappointed, I can tell. 'Well, it was just an idea.'

'Maybe another time.'

'Yes,' he says. 'Maybe another time.'

CHAPTER 30

On Wednesday night I can hardly sleep. What with my encounter with Ben in the church, the news of Bridget's pregnancy, and Adam's last-minute suggestion of a romantic break, my mind would already be spinning, even if I weren't about to set off on the trip to London.

London. The very name of it has been enough to strike fear into my heart these past seven years. The idea of a city filled with so many people is quite overwhelming after spending so long living in the wilds of Yorkshire, conditioned by Adam to believe that I am a shy, retiring person, terrified of meeting new people. If it weren't for the company of my friends, I don't think I would be able to make this journey.

And yet I know that I am capable of this. London was my home once.

I finally drift off into a kind of shallow half-sleep in the early hours of the morning, but my sleep is punctuated by disturbing dreams. Dreams of red rooms, of blood, and of being locked in a dark and terrible dungeon.

The alarm goes off at six thirty, sounding like the wail of a banshee, and I sit bolt upright in the bed, the sheets damp with sweat and twisted into a knot.

The day I have been dreading has finally come.

I shower and brush my teeth and begin to feel more human. Breakfast is too much of a challenge, and instead I spend time fretting about what to wear. My wardrobe does not contain many options. What would Victoria have made of my dowdy outfits and sensible shoes?

I choose something warm but smart, suitable for going to the theatre, even though *The Mousetrap* is the last thing on my mind. I haven't really given much thought to how I am going to slip away from the others. Should I tell them my plan, or secretly make a getaway? I just don't know. I must take today one step at a time. If I think too far ahead, I may lose my nerve entirely.

The taxi is due at eight, and I'm ready well before I need to be. I fill the time wandering around the cottage, the place that has been my home for the last seven years. Everything I know is here, the familiar and the comfortable. Does it matter that it's built on a lie? By going to London, I am risking everything I now have. You only have to watch the news on television to see that security is not something to be taken for granted in this world. I have security, here with Adam. But is security more important than the truth? I'm not entirely sure, but I don't think I have a choice any more. I cannot go on not understanding who I am.

I'm glad Diana's taking charge of the logistical arrangements because I couldn't possibly have managed to travel to London alone. With Diana in charge, I don't have to worry about any of the practicalities, as she is always so well organised. Sure enough, at eight o'clock precisely, I hear the sound of a car pulling up outside. I glance out of the window and see Diana getting out of the taxi. Bridget and Cath are already inside.

By the time I've grabbed my coat and bag, Diana is ringing the doorbell. I open the door, letting the cold early morning air inside. It's still not properly light.

'Good morning!' says Diana, beaming at me. 'I'm so

glad you changed your mind, Jane. All ready to go?'

'Yes, I think so.'

'Terrific. Let's get going then, shall we?'

I nod and follow her to the taxi. Diana sits in the front of the car and I squash into the back with Bridget and Cath. 'Hi,' I say.

I don't know if I can look Bridget in the eye after what happened yesterday between me and Ben. But I glance at her and she gives me a warm smile back. I'm sure she knows all about what Ben said to me. As he told me, they have no secrets. But their openness means that there is nothing to be afraid of. There is nothing for her to forgive.

A look of understanding passes between us, and I realise that I can trust Bridget implicitly. I wish now that I had told her my deepest, darkest secrets. It was foolish of me to doubt her. But it is too late to say anything, now that the others are present too.

'Isn't this fun,' says Cath as the driver sets off down the road. 'A day out with the girls! I can't remember when I last had a whole day away from the family. The boys will have to fend for themselves for once. No doubt I'll come home to a right old mess in the kitchen, but it will have been worth it just to have a bit of time away from them.'

'Get away with you,' teases Diana. 'You'll be desperate to get back to them before the day is over.'

'True,' admits Cath. 'But I mean to make the most of my freedom while it lasts!'

'Doing anything nice in London, ladies?' asks the taxi driver.

'We're going to the theatre to see *The Mousetrap*,' says Diana.

'Very nice,' says the driver. 'Took the wife to see the *X Factor Live Tour* at Leeds Arena before Christmas.'

'Ooh, I'd have loved to have seen that,' says Cath. 'Was it good?'

Whilst the others chat about shows they've been to see, I keep quiet about my own plans for today. I feel guilty about using this trip for something else, but I hope they will understand.

Gradually the conversation falls silent as the taxi driver navigates the country roads. It starts to get light and the number of cars on the road increases. By the time we're approaching Leeds we're sitting in a queue of traffic. The outskirts are a sprawl of post-industrial decay, warehouses and 1960s tower blocks, a world away from the village where I now live. Is this what London is going to be like? I shudder at the grimness of it. As we approach the centre, startlingly new apartment blocks and offices in architecturally interesting designs spring up, standing in stark contrast to the Victorian red brick heritage. The traffic is appalling, the multi-lane road junctions are complex to navigate and everywhere I look people are rushing to work, heads bowed against the cold weather. I've been living in such a sheltered environment for so long that the city fills me with a sense of dread.

The thought of driving to work here every day seems incomprehensible to me now, and I think that Adam was maybe right when he tried to dissuade me from applying for a job.

The taxi pulls up outside the train station and we all clamber out. 'Enjoy the show, ladies,' says the taxi driver as he pulls away.

Leeds station concourse is large and noisy. Smartly dressed men and women are hurrying towards the exit, on their way to work. I look at them, thinking, I used to be someone like that, but even more so. But that was Victoria, not Jane.

Diana has already bought our train tickets online and has reserved seats for us. 'We need platform eight,' she says, checking the travel details on her phone. 'The train leaves in ten minutes.'

We make our way to the platform, where the fast train to London is already waiting. The modern, high-speed train stretches down the length of the platform, its engines humming, waiting to transport us to the capital. Waiting to transport me back to my old life. To a different world which I've forgotten. I break out in a cold sweat. It's not too late to turn back now. I could make up some excuse about not feeling well. I could catch a bus to the market town and from there make my way back to our cottage in the village, my place of safety and security. Not for the first time, I wonder what I'm risking if I get on this train and follow through with my plan.

'We're in carriage F,' says Diana, striding along the platform, leading the way. I imagine her taking classes of schoolchildren on trips, organising them and making sure no one gets left behind. Suddenly I have a fear of getting lost in London. I can't do this. I stop, and a man wheeling a suitcase almost runs into me.

'What's wrong, Jane?' asks Bridget. The other two have gone on ahead, looking for carriage F.

'I don't know,' I say. 'London is such a big place.'

'Don't worry,' she says. 'We'll stick together.' She slips her arm through mine and we hurry to catch up with Diana and Cath who are waiting for us beside an open door.

'This is it,' says Diana. 'I booked four seats together.'

We board the train and find our seats.

'Does anyone mind if I travel forwards?' asks Cath. 'Going backwards always makes me feel queasy.'

I sit next to Cath in one of the forward-facing seats and Diana and Bridget sit opposite, facing us across a table. No sooner are we settled than the guard blows his whistle and the train starts to pull out of the station. I've done it, I think. I'm on my way. There's no going back now.

'We should be at London, King's Cross in just over two hours,' says Diana. 'From there we'll take the Piccadilly Line to Leicester Square. The theatre is just off Shaftesbury Avenue. We can have a bite to eat in Soho and then watch the show.'

She has planned the trip well. I'm only now allowing

myself to begin thinking about my own plans for the day.

My secret plans.

Yet more secrets. I still haven't decided what I'm going to tell the others. Or even if I should tell them anything. I haven't worked out any of the details of what I'm about to do.

I can probably afford to stay with them for lunch. If I sneak away immediately afterwards, I should have time to catch a train to Putney, although I haven't yet worked out a route. When I get to Putney I'm confident that I can find the house. And I've brought the spare door key that Adam keeps in the office, so getting into the house won't be a problem.

It's once I'm inside that my real problems will begin.

The train moves off from the station platform and Bridget leans across the table. 'There's something I'd like to share with you all,' she says. 'I've been keeping it to myself, but I think it's time to make an announcement. Jane already knows, I think.'

This is it. My stomach clenches tight in anticipation of hearing Bridget's news. But I nod at her, to tell her to continue.

'I'm pregnant,' she says.

'Ooh!' squeals Cath. 'How wonderful! I was saying to Ken just the other night that I hoped you and the vicar would be able to start a family now that you've settled in to the village.'

'Congratulations,' says Diana, looking pleased. 'I'm sure that you'll make a wonderful mother.'

'I hope so,' says Bridget. 'Thanks.'

Then they all turn to look at me.

When Ben first implied that Bridget was pregnant, my first thoughts were for my own inability to have children. But I've put that behind me now. Talking to Ben in the church helped me, I think. Realising just how open and honest Ben and Bridget are with each other made any jealous feelings seem trivial and petty. I am genuinely pleased for them both.

'Congratulations,' I say. 'You and Ben will be amazing parents, I know.'

'Thanks,' says Bridget. 'That means a lot to me, Jane.'

Bridget deserves a husband like Ben. They are both such good, caring people.

Then I wonder. Have I done something that makes me deserve a husband like Adam? Did I somehow bring the lies and deceit on myself? I can't imagine how.

'Would anyone like a tea or a coffee?' inquires Diana. 'I could use a shot of caffeine to keep me awake. I'm not used to these early morning starts.'

Cath laughs. 'Every morning starts early for me. But yes, I'd love a cup of tea. I'll come with you and fetch some. What would everyone else like?'

Bridget orders a tea and I ask for a latte.

As soon as Diana and Cath have gone to buy the drinks, Bridget leans across the table towards me and says softly, 'Is something wrong, Jane? You were awfully quiet in the taxi.'

'Yes, I'm fine,' I lie, not meeting her eye. 'I'm just tired from getting up so early.'

'I know what you mean,' she says. 'It is exciting though, isn't it? Going to London.'

'Yes,' I say. 'Look, about me and Ben...'

Bridget lifts her hand to stop me from speaking. 'Don't say anything,' she says. 'There's nothing you need to explain. Ben told me everything. You know, he often finds that he makes... connections with people in the parish. There's something about him that makes people trust him.'

I can feel the back of my neck flushing pink. The idea that other women have latched onto him before makes me feel foolish. Yet Bridget is regarding me so kindly that I find my embarrassment slipping away. 'Ben's a very good man,' I tell her. 'And you're a good person too. You and Ben are perfect for each other.'

'Thanks,' says Bridget. 'But are you sure that there's

nothing bothering you? You seem very distracted.'

Bridget's been such a good friend to me. If I could confide in anyone about my plans, she would be the one to tell. I begin to say, 'I...' but then the others join us again and I fall silent.

'Ah, that's better,' says Diana, taking a sip of her coffee. 'That'll keep me awake.'

'I haven't been to London for ages,' says Cath, cradling her tea. 'Never have a good enough reason to go. The last time I was there, I had a look round Harrods but everything cost a fortune.' She rolls her eyes. 'I just ended up buying a tin of shortbread so I could get a bag with Harrods printed on it. The shortbread didn't last long but I've still got the carrier bag.' She laughs.

An image of the iconic Harrods bag appears before me. But it's not just an image of a bag that I might have seen in a photograph. The bag I'm remembering is one that I held in my own two hands. In Victoria's hands. And now I remember what the bag contained.

'I once bought a dress in Harrods,' I say aloud.

'Really?' asks Cath, sounding impressed. 'That must have been expensive. What was it like? Was it for a special occasion?'

'Yes,' I say. 'It was an evening gown.'

Diana is studying me carefully. 'I thought you said you'd never been to London before, Jane,' she says.

I shrug. 'Yes, I did say that. But I was mistaken. I have been there before.'

Diana and Bridget exchange glances, and Cath has turned to stare in my direction. They must think that I've gone mad.

But my attention has switched to my inner eye. I am remembering more. 'It was a red dress,' I say. 'I wore it to a party.'

It was the party I first remembered in Diana and Michael's house on New Year's Eve. And now I'm back there. It's a New Year's Eve party at a top London night spot. In my red dress and matching Jimmy Choos, I'm looking rather stunning, even though I think so myself. But I don't need to rely on my own opinion – the heads that turn in my direction are proof enough.

'There you are, Victoria.' Adam appears behind me, holding two flutes of champagne.

I take one from him.

It's the office party. The company has hired the venue for all its managers and executives, and their partners too. The drinks are flowing and the music is pumping through the huge sound system. Some of the junior staff are already on the dance floor going wild. I'd be with them if it wasn't for Adam.

He takes my arm. 'Let's go outside for a moment.' He leads me across the room to the huge floor-to-ceiling windows that look out across the London skyline. He pushes open a door and we step out onto a roof terrace overlooking the River Thames. From here we have views over the Houses of Parliament at Westminster, and the London Eye opposite. The vast expanse of the capital is spread before us and I feel as if I'm on top of the world. I feel like opening my arms wide and embracing it all.

Adam puts an arm around my bare shoulders. 'Aren't you cold?'

'Not at all,' I say. I'm glowing with an inner fire.

He nuzzles his face in my hair. 'We should go home soon. I'll call for a taxi.'

'Oh, don't do that,' I say. 'The party's only just getting going.'

He pulls away from me. 'But let's not stay too late.'

I laugh. This is so like Adam. 'Well, we're staying until midnight, at least. I'm not going to turn into a pumpkin on the stroke of twelve!' I take hold of his hand. 'Come on, let's go back inside and dance.' Adam hates dancing but I'm not going to let him get away with standing on the side-lines all evening.

We head back inside and run straight into Julian, my

boss. He's wearing an expensive silk shirt and holding a glass of champagne in his right hand.

'Ah, there you are, Victoria!' He throws his arms around me in an effusive embrace. This is clearly not his first glass of champagne. 'I just wanted to say a million congratulations on your promotion.'

'Thank you,' I say. 'I'm thrilled by it. I promise I'll show everyone that they chose the right person.' I've just been promoted to executive level. It's a big step up, with a commensurate increase in salary and a lot more responsibility.

'You'll be fabulous in your new role,' says Julian. 'Won't she, Adam?' He turns to Adam, who is standing stiffly to one side, watching the exchange.

'Of course,' says Adam. 'She's worked hard for this. It's what she deserves.'

Yes it is, I think, and one day I'm going to be running the company, just see if I'm not.

My eyes bolt open. I'm back on the train.

They are all watching me, saying nothing.

'Are you feeling ill, Jane?' asks Diana.

'Sorry,' I say. 'I was just remembering something.'

'No need to apologise,' says Bridget.

There's an awkward silence which I don't know how to fill.

'The last time I was in London I went to an exhibition at the British Museum,' says Diana, deftly changing the subject. 'It was ever so interesting, all about ancient Mesopotamia.'

Whilst Diana tells us about the Sumerians and the Babylonians, I think about my memories which are flooding back now. Still not whole memories, but just snippets here and there, triggered by things like Cath mentioning Harrods. If I have a big enough trigger, will everything come back? And will I be able to cope with it if it does?

I look out of the window, watching the world fly by. In

what feels like no time at all we are coming into north London. The guard announces that the train will shortly be terminating at King's Cross station. *Please make sure you take all your belongings with you when leaving the train.* I feel an awakening in my breast. I'm back in London and it doesn't feel alien or strange, the way Leeds did. The approaching city feels more like home than I could have imagined.

But now my mind turns at last to what lies ahead of me. The red room. I will have to leave the others soon and make my way to Putney, to the house I lived in when I was Victoria.

Montserrat Road. I shiver at the thought of just turning up there, unannounced, like a stranger. But it is my house and I have every right to go there.

Adam will be out until at least six o'clock, probably later. The train back to Leeds leaves London at six in the evening. By the time Adam gets home from work, I'll be on my way home too. I'll be back in the cottage by nine o'clock, in time for his phone call. He'll never know that I've been to London unless I choose to tell him.

A sudden thought occurs to me. Does Adam ever work from home? The thought fills me with a sick dread, but no, I know that he doesn't. I'm confident that he will be at his office in the City all day.

The train pulls into King's Cross Station and comes to a stop. Doors hiss open and people start moving, gathering coats and bags, and pushing their way towards the exits.

'Be sure to stay together, ladies,' comments Diana. 'We don't want to lose anyone.'

But there's no chance of me getting lost here. My feet already know the way, and I let them lead me, not having to think about where they are taking me.

As we make our way along the busy platform, Cath says, 'I downloaded a map of the London Underground to my phone.' She's busy, trying to find the app.

'There's no need,' I say. 'I know where to go.'

For once in my life I'm leading the way. I haven't been

to King's Cross station for years, but I've done this journey so many times I could do it in my sleep. I weave around the crowds, heading straight for the entrance to the Underground. The others follow in my wake.

'Do we need tickets?' asks Cath.

'You can just use your debit card at the barriers,' says Diana.

King's Cross is a large station with lots of different Tube Lines passing through it. I lead the way along the tunnels and down the escalators to the Piccadilly Line which is buried deep underground, the way my memories have been buried deep inside me and are only now bubbling up to the surface.

'It's a long way down,' says Cath on the escalator behind me. 'I always find the Underground a bit claustrophobic.'

Before coming here I had thought that I would find London claustrophobic. I've been so used to the open spaces of the Yorkshire moors for the last seven years, I thought coming to the capital, with its crowds and traffic and pollution would make me feel trapped. But instead I feel liberated, as if I can breathe freely once more.

We board a crowded southbound train to Leicester Square and then make our way back up to ground level via the escalators.

'That's better,' says Cath. She looks relieved when we emerge in the heart of London's West End. 'Sorry, but I'm always a bit nervous underground. You hear about all these terrorist incidents and it makes you worry.'

'Statistically, London's a very safe city,' says Bridget.

'Even so,' says Cath.

I'm nervous too, but I'm not frightened of terrorists. I'm wary of the truth. Of Adam and myself.

'We've got time for a quick lunch before the play starts,' says Diana. 'Shall we look for a restaurant?'

'Sounds like a great idea,' says Bridget. 'Lead the way.'

I could slip away from them now and set off to

Montserrat Road. But I'm reluctant to leave. Besides, there's time for lunch. I have hours yet.

We set off in the direction of St Martin's Theatre and Diana soon spots an Italian bistro with red checked table cloths and a charming waiter in the doorway. 'What about this one?' she suggests.

'Looks good,' says Bridget.

The waiter ushers us inside and shows us to the table by the window. We order pasta dishes and side salads and, since none of us is driving, a bottle of Sauvignon Blanc to share. It seems like a luxury to be having such a meal in the middle of the day when normally I would just heat up a tin of soup or make a sandwich, and yet I have a feeling now that I used to lunch like this on a regular basis. Business lunches in expensive restaurants were no doubt a part of Victoria's life. What could possibly have happened to Victoria to turn her into the mousy, retiring creature that I have become? Soon I will know for certain, though as the time grows nearer, my nervousness grows. I sip my wine and try to relax, putting off the moment when I'll have to leave the others and head off alone.

Finally the meal is over and the waiter brings the bill. Diana pays for it with her credit card, saying that we can sort out the money later. She's very generous. We all get up to leave.

'Right,' says Diana. 'Time to go and see *The Mousetrap*. Everyone ready?'

I take a deep breath. I can't just slip away from them without telling them. They deserve better. Besides, if I simply vanish, they'll probably spend the rest of the day searching for me. They might even call the police.

'Actually, there's something I need to tell you,' I say. Three faces look at me expectantly. I almost change my mind. It would be easier just to go along with them, like they're expecting, and spend the afternoon in a darkened theatre watching a play that I don't want to see.

But I have no choice. I have to see this through.

'I'm really sorry,' I say, 'but I'm not coming to the theatre with you after all. There's something else I need to do.' For a moment no one says anything. They all look rather stunned, which is not surprising. 'But I'll give you the money for the ticket, Diana,' I add hastily, not wanting her to think that I'm taking advantage of her generosity.

'But you can't miss *The Mousetrap*,' says Cath. 'It's such a good opportunity to see it. And we won't be allowed to tell you who did it.'

'I have to go somewhere,' I say, trying to keep my nerve.

'Then I'll come with you,' says Diana, briskly. 'The play isn't important, but your welfare is. I don't mind missing it.' I suspect she's thinking back to New Year's Eve when I fainted at her party. She doesn't want the same thing happening to me on my own in the middle of London. Since the trip was her idea I suppose she feels responsible, like a teacher safeguarding her pupils.

'No, it's all right,' I assure her. 'I'm quite well. And this is something I have to do on my own.'

Bridget steps forward and lays a hand on my arm. 'Jane, you go and do whatever it is you have to do, but remember we're here for you if you need us.' She gives me a reassuring smile.

'Thank you,' I say. 'I promise I'll look after myself. And I will meet you all at King's Cross at five thirty.' That leaves me with hours to go to the house. 'Go on,' I tell them when they hesitate. 'You don't want to miss the show.'

Bridget gives me a quick hug. Then they make their way to St Martin's Theatre. I watch them leave, and then turn and set off alone in the opposite direction.

CHAPTER 31

I descend once more into the Underground and let myself be carried along by the tide of passengers, not giving myself chance to change my mind. More memories are filtering back. Or rather I have a feeling like a rising tide of awareness. A lifetime's worth of memories is slowly seeping back into my consciousness. Thousands of journeys made over many years, millions of steps walked, countless glimpses of the places I've been and the faces that I've seen. Sounds, smells, tastes, all percolating up from a lost part of my mind that has been walled off for so long. The underground station feels as familiar as the road from the cottage to the village – more familiar than the Monday market where I do my weekly shopping.

I take a Northern Line train and alight at Waterloo. The station is busier than in my memories. There seem to be more coffee outlets and more people rushing past, but its essence hasn't changed: the layout, the smell, the sense of urgency that people in London have. Living in the wilds of the Yorkshire moors has dulled my senses, made me into a shadow of myself. Back in the heart of the city I feel myself starting to come alive. I am beginning to find myself again.

From Waterloo, I catch a commuter train to Putney. I used to do this journey every day, I think, in the rush hour when it was often impossible to get a seat. It's not so crowded now in the middle of the day and I'm able to sit down as I watch suburban south London slip past the window. Adam will be making this same journey later today when he leaves his office to return to the house. I intend to be long gone by the time he comes home.

I exit the station at Putney and start to walk up the High Street. More memories come flooding back. There's the family-run Italian restaurant where Adam and I used to eat out when we were too tired from work to bother cooking at home. The smell of garlic wafting out of the door makes me pause in my tracks, remembering. My favourite was the tagliatelle with langoustine. Adam always tucked in to the lasagne.

But not everything is familiar. Coffee shops have changed hands. New shops have opened. The streets feel busier than I remember them, with more traffic and more people. Or maybe it's just the contrast with what I've been used to for the last seven years. I wonder if anyone will recognise me and call my name, but no one does. I'm not the same person I used to be.

I reach the corner of Montserrat Road where it joins the High Street and I come to an abrupt stop. I still don't know if I'm doing the right thing. Suddenly I'm filled with doubt. Coming back here might turn out to be sheer folly. What am I hoping to find here? To unlock my deepest, darkest memory? Some secrets are best left buried. Whatever I discover, it won't be anything good. And yet, if I don't go through with this, I'll continue to imagine the worst.

I take a step forward and then stop. It seems I'm incapable of making a conscious decision.

I stumble blindly into the nearest coffee shop and order an espresso. I drink it sitting in a window seat, watching people walk past. Most of them are glued to their mobile phones, oblivious of the world around them.

I wonder what Diana, Bridget and Cath are doing now. I check my watch. The curtain will have gone up nearly an hour ago. The afternoon is drawing on. When I walk out of this coffee shop I shall have to make a decision. Either I will turn left and go straight back to the train station, or I will turn right and go to Montserrat Road.

It would be easier if I had stayed with the others and was sitting in the theatre now, lost in the fictional world of a play. My life for the last seven years has been a fiction. There's something comforting about that. You can make up your own story and decide what to tell the world. The invented version of Jane can be whoever I want her to be.

And yet the fictional world I have inhabited is one of Adam's creation, not mine. I have been living a story that he concocted for me. I have been like a character in a story, reading lines that someone else has written. Or worse, like a puppet on a string, moving when the strings are jerked by the puppet master.

I finish my coffee and stand up. It's now or never. I open the door and turn right towards Montserrat Road.

It's as if the decision has been made for me by something more primeval than my conscious mind. I remember hearing a radio programme that talked about the amygdala, a tiny part of the brain that controls emotional responses. It's as if I can feel my own amygdala on hyper-alert, sending out signals to the rest of my body.

Feel. Remember. Beware.

My fingertips are tingling and my step quickens as my heart rate increases.

I walk down the familiar street with its Edwardian terraced houses. I stop outside Adam's house.

Our house.

The red brick house is well-proportioned and stands two stories tall next to its semi-detached neighbour. I can see that the loft space has been converted into a third floor of living accommodation. The house is set back from the road and shielded by a well-trimmed hedge of laurel. A black iron gate opens onto a paved path that leads past evergreen shrubs and bare rose bushes to the black-painted door. The door is glazed with the original coloured glass, and has a brass knocker and letterbox. Wooden slatted blinds shield the windows from prying eyes.

An expensive house in London in a good location. It was expensive enough when we bought it. It must be worth a fortune now.

I am seeing it as if for the first time. Yet I am seeing it in my memory too. I am Jane. But I am also Victoria.

I look up and down the street to see if anyone is watching me. On the opposite pavement an old woman is walking a small dog wearing a tiny tartan coat. Further down a young man in a suit gets into a car and starts the engine. No one pays me any attention. This is London, where people are anonymous, not a small village in Yorkshire where the shopkeeper knows everyone.

I push open the gate and walk the short distance up the path to the front door. In my pocket my hand is clenched around the spare door key that Adam keeps in his desk drawer at home in Yorkshire. I slot it into the lock, turn it, and push open the door.

A wide hallway beckons.

I slip inside, slamming the door closed behind me and leaning back against it, my breast rising and falling.

I've done it. I've entered the house.

CHAPTER 32

For a moment I stand with my back against the front door, my eyes tightly closed. My attention is focused on listening intently for any sound within the house. All I can hear is my own heart thumping and the blood rushing in my ears. Slowly I open my eyes and take in my surroundings.

The entrance hall is generously proportioned, with a wooden floor leading to a staircase up. Doors lead off the hall to other rooms. The hall is well-lit with natural light from the glazed door and side panels behind me. A strikingly modern mirror on the wall reflects more light into the further parts, and the cream and white walls and white-painted staircase make the space feel light and airy. I let my eyes drink in every detail, remembering. We repainted the hall when we first moved to the house. The stylish mirror was my own choice. Not much has changed since I lived here. It is almost as if I never left.

Adam's winter coat is hanging on a hook in the hallway. Its dark shape is framed by the white wall behind, as if Adam himself is lurking there, lying in wait for me. Is it possible that he might be at home? Could he have returned from work early, or taken the day off, like he suggested? But no sound comes from within. The house is still and empty.

After a minute or two I begin to creep forward stealthily towards the nearest door.

The open door on the right leads into the lounge. When we moved into the house we had such plans to make this the perfect home. We hired builders to knock down the wall between the front room and back room, creating a modern, open-plan space. We painted it white to reflect the light, and installed French windows at the back to open directly onto the garden. The curtains over the French windows are drawn now, making the room dim, but my eyes soon adjust and more details become visible.

An oil painting hangs above the fireplace. I'd completely forgotten about it, but I remember now. It's a stylised painting of a female nude, turned away from the viewer. It's evocative and seductive. We bought it from a gallery on Putney High Street. It was by an up-and-coming young artist and cost eight hundred pounds. Adam thought it would be a good investment. I fell in love with it at first sight.

I cast my eyes over the bookshelves in the alcoves either side of the fireplace. They are packed with books. My books. I go to the nearest bookshelf and look at the titles. Have I really read all of these books? There are so many of them. All read and forgotten.

There are photographs of me and Adam on the shelves too, and I pick them up one by one. How different I look in these pictures to the way I look now. Hair professionally styled, make-up expertly applied. Wearing clothes that look as if they cost a lot of money instead of the woolly jumpers and jeans that make up most of my wardrobe these days. The woman in these photographs isn't Jane. She's Victoria. Confident and outgoing, smiling at the camera with red-painted lips.

I replace the photographs and go back into the hallway. The house is still quiet, apart from the occasional creak of an old building. Before me, the staircase leads up.

CHAPTER 33

For a long time I stand at the foot of the stairs, one hand on the newel post, gazing upwards.

I recall now that when we first looked at the house as potential buyers, we fell in love with the high ceilings, the well-proportioned rooms, the traditional features like fireplaces and the elegant staircase with its gleaming handrail. My hand slides onto the handrail and I place a foot on the first stair.

Slowly, I start to climb the stairs. The third step creaks loudly under my foot and I remember that it always did that. I count the steps in my head. Thirteen to the turn in the stairs, then another five up to the landing. The décor here is the same as downstairs, with more paintings on the walls, but the upstairs doors are all closed, making the landing dark and gloomy, shutting me out. It is almost as if the old house is trying to repel me, trying to preserve its secrets for as long as it can.

I pause on the landing, listening carefully, but all is silent and still.

I try the first door and it swings open. It's the bathroom. I knew that. My gaze roams around the white-tiled space for a while, soaking up impressions, matching them against the memories they unlock.

The room is the same as I remember it, but different. Adam's shower gel and shampoo sit in the shower cubicle. On the sink are his razor, deodorant and toothpaste. A single white bath towel hangs on the chrome towel rail. The room feels empty and under-used. Just one lonely toothbrush. Where is my toothbrush? My body lotion, moisturiser, make-up, hairbrush, sanitary products and other paraphernalia?

I retreat and walk across the landing to the door that leads to the main bedroom. I hesitate, my hand hovering over the brass doorknob. Once I feared that this was the bedroom Adam shared with another wife. Victoria. But there is nothing to fear from Victoria. She is me. This is the bedroom I shared with my husband. I twist the handle and walk inside.

I realise I've been holding my breath. I let it out as I enter. The room is larger than the bedroom in the cottage, even though just one person sleeps here. A large double bed is covered by a white duvet, carefully made up.

I don't know what I had expected to find here, maybe evidence of another woman. But all I see are Adam's pyjamas laid neatly across his pillow, a pair of men's slippers on the floor and a paperback book on the bedside table.

The other side of the bed, the side where I once slept, is untouched, the pillow without a dent in it, as if no one has ever laid their head there.

I stand at the edge of the bed, waiting to see what memories it may stir, but nothing specific comes to me. Feelings, sensations, a warm touch in the dark, a moment of ecstasy. I do not recall anything more than that.

The room has built-in wardrobes. I go to Adam's side first and pull open the double doors. Ranks of professionally laundered and ironed shirts hang on the rail, still in their polythene wrappings. There are two spare suits and a collection of silk ties. It's the wardrobe of a busy executive, a man with a high-powered job.

I used to have a job like that.

With trembling hands I open the wardrobe doors on the other side. This is where I used to hang my work clothes and my evening wear. I saw from the photographs downstairs that Victoria always dressed well. I expect to find the wardrobe empty, so I am shocked when I open it. My old clothes are all still hanging there, as if my former life has been frozen in time. My wardrobe is much fuller and more varied than Adam's. I put out a hand and touch the beautiful fabrics: the silks, the cashmeres, the pure new wool. I work through them one by one, remembering each one and when I wore it. Here is the suit I wore to my job interview; here is the dress I wore on my thirtieth birthday.

I remember buying some of these outfits in department stores in London, shop assistants eager to please the woman with the credit card. Some of these individual garments probably cost more than the total I have spent on clothes in the last seven years.

There are older clothes here too – the thin cotton dress I wore that time I went punting with Adam, and other clothes left over from my student days. I work my way from left to right, touching, feeling, remembering. And then I see it.

I snatch my hand away as if it's been burned. On the last hanger is a crimson dress. It's out of place, not hanging with the other dresses. I was always very organised about my clothes: first blouses, then skirts, then suits, then dresses, and finally coats. This dress has been put back in the wrong place. It can't have been me who put it there. It's the dress I wore that night, the night of the New Year's Eve party.

Dark, hazy memories begin to crowd in around me. I'm at the party again, dancing till late. Midnight approaches and I join in with the others counting down to the New Year, then singing *Auld Lang Syne*. I was on top of the world that night. A new promotion had been offered to me, and I had jumped at the opportunity. Adam was happy for me too. Everyone was happy. And then something happened.

A voice shouts, *You can't do that!*

It's not a real voice, just the ghost of a memory. Whose voice was it? What were they talking about? I can't quite pull back the answers. All I can grasp is the voice itself and the feelings it unleashed – fear, anger and outrage. My head begins to spin and I feel like I might faint.

I push the wardrobe doors closed and turn away. I can't look at the dress any more. I shut it away like I have shut away my memories for so long. But I can't go on doing that. I have come here to confront the past, and so I open the door once more.

I grip hold of the clothes rail for support. Then tentatively, I reach for the hanger that holds the dress and pull it out of the wardrobe.

The dress slides off the hanger and falls in a silky, red puddle at my feet. My mind flashes on blood and I recoil, kicking the dress away with my foot. It lies curled in a tight knot on the carpet.

I stare at the twisted fabric for a minute, breathing ragged breaths, struggling to bring my racing heart under control. It's only a dress. It can't hurt me. I reach down for it and pick it up with shaking hands, holding it up to the light. A new shock takes me.

The dress has been violently torn apart. It's ripped from the neck almost to the waist. My blood runs cold. Was I wearing the dress when someone ripped it?

Then I see the blood.

It's not easy to make out against the red fabric, but now I look carefully, the lower part of the dress is covered in stains that have turned coppery brown with age. They can only be dried blood. My blood.

This is the dress I wore in the red room.

Adam told me that he burned it. Why would he lie about that? Why would he keep a ruined, torn dress?

I don't want to look at it anymore. It's too horrible. But I can't leave it lying on the floor, otherwise Adam will find it and will guess that I've been here.

I hurriedly pick the dress up and stuff it into the wardrobe, not caring where it goes.

I've been here too long. I've lost track of time. I look at my watch and am shocked to see how late it is. *The Mousetrap* will be finished by now. Diana, Bridget and Cath will have left the theatre and be making their way back to King's Cross. I'm going to have to be quick if I'm going to meet them as planned.

There's one more room in this house that I must visit before I leave.

Back on the landing I look up at the spiral staircase that leads to the loft conversion. With property prices in London so high, everyone was converting their lofts into extra rooms. It was one of the first things we did when we moved in to the house.

Adam's voice drifts back to me now. 'If we're going to start a family, we'll need as many rooms as we can afford.'

'Why?' I tease him. 'How many kids do you want? Three? Five? Ten?'

He smiles. 'As many as you like.'

It is obvious from the flashback that we both really wanted to have children. That feeling of longing for a family has an intensity that is almost painful, knowing now that I can never have children. Is that what drove a wedge between me and Adam?

The narrow staircase winds upwards. I take each step slowly, my heart thumping in my chest. This room would never have been suitable as a nursery, with its precarious winding steps. But I suppose that Adam and I could have made it our bedroom and converted the bedroom on the middle floor into a child's room. Perhaps that was our plan.

I remember that the attic room was my favourite room in the house. I would come up here to be alone, to read or to practise yoga. I wanted the room to have a warm, cosy feel to it, tucked away in the eaves of the house as it was. I was the one who insisted on painting the walls red.

I always loved the colour red. Red dresses. Red shoes. Red room. Red was an expression of my personality: strong and vibrant. It was the colour that defined me, when I was Victoria.

The stairs lead to a square upper landing and then to a door. The door is closed and a brass key protrudes from the lock. I try to picture the room that lies beyond, but my mind is a blank. I still cannot remember what happened in the red room that night. It's fighting me, trying to keep secret the memories that are struggling to rise to the surface.

I reach out to touch the door handle, and then I hear a sound from downstairs. A key is turning in the lock of the front door. My hand freezes in mid-air.

Downstairs, the front door opens and closes. I hear footsteps in the hallway and then on the stairs. It's Adam's slow, deliberate tread. The third stair creaks loudly.

I need to flee, or hide, but I cannot move.

The footsteps continue to ascend. Now he's on the middle floor landing. I hold my breath, keeping as still as possible.

The footsteps stop. Adam goes into the bathroom and closes the door behind him. I can hear him whistling.

I start to go back down the spiral stairs. I don't know if I have time to creep back along the landing, past the bathroom door without him hearing me, and down the stairs and out. If I'm too slow he will find me and catch me. I take one step down and then another until I'm standing on the landing again. I hesitate, not knowing what to do. The bathroom door is just yards away from me. The muffled whistling continues from within.

Then the toilet flushes and water splashes in the sink as Adam washes his hands. It's too late to escape. I creep as quickly as I can back up the spiral staircase to the upper landing. I crouch there, waiting to see what Adam will do next.

The bathroom door re-opens and I hear his tread along the middle landing, making his way towards the master bedroom. He stops at the foot of the stairs to the loft conversion.

I freeze every muscle in my body, trying to remain absolutely still and silent. And then I hear the sound I am dreading most.

He starts to climb the spiral staircase.

I grab hold of the door handle and turn it, but the door resists my attempts to open it. It is locked. I twist the key in the lock and try the door once again. This time it yields and I yank it open and flee inside, slamming the door shut behind me.

The walls of the room are painted a deep Moroccan red.

CHAPTER 34

I'm leaning against the door of the red room. My heart is thudding against my ribcage and the blood is pounding in my skull. Adam's tread continues on and up the stairs, slow and deliberate, like the hangman's step as he walks towards the scaffold. A thousand thoughts flutter through my mind. Why has he come home from work so early? How could I have spent so much time here? Is there still a way that I can escape? And if he finds me, what will I do? What will *he* do?

The footsteps stop outside the door. There is nothing but a piece of wood separating me from my husband. I can hear Adam breathing on the other side. He must have heard me slamming the door closed and I curse my stupidity.

I look down in horror as the door handle near my right hand starts to turn. He's coming in. I can't keep him out. He's so much stronger than me. I leap away from the door a second before he pushes it open. There's nowhere for me to hide. I'm standing in the middle of the room, like a madwoman, when Adam walks in. He stares at me. I can't read his face. Is he angry? Confused? Both?

More than anything he seems utterly shocked to find

me here. 'Jane,' he says after a moment's pause. 'What on earth are you doing here?'

I eye the heavy glass vase he is clutching in one hand, like a makeshift weapon. He shrugs. 'I thought you were a burglar.'

I get the impression he would rather have disturbed a burglar, than discovered his wife.

He takes a step towards me and I retreat from him. He stops.

'I'm not Jane,' I say. 'My name is Victoria.' I fling the name at him, challenging him to respond. There is no longer any point trying to conceal what I know.

'Victoria.' He turns the name over, as if it leaves a nasty taste in his mouth. 'I don't know what you think you know…'

'Stop,' I say, holding up my hand. 'Tell me the truth!'

'The truth is that I love you, Jane. I always have and I always will.'

'I don't know if I can trust you, Adam,' I tell him. 'You have to start telling me the truth. No more lies.'

The time for lies and deceit is well over. I must prise the truth out of him now, however dangerous it may be.

He shakes his head. The vase is still in his hand. 'I didn't ever lie to you, Jane,' he says. 'Not really. Or if I did, it was with your interests at heart. I told you what you needed to hear.'

'No,' I say. 'You told me what you wanted me to hear. You made up stories. And you lied to the police, to the insurance company, to everyone. You lied for seven years, Adam, and you're still lying now.'

He sighs. 'It was the insurance letter, wasn't it?' he says sadly. 'If it hadn't been for that, you would never have known. But I had to claim the insurance money. I didn't want to. We didn't need the money. We had enough. But if I hadn't made the claim, people might have got suspicious. I had no choice.'

No choice. Is that how he sees himself? As some kind

of victim of circumstances? Even now he won't admit that he's done anything wrong. 'Tell me what you did,' I say. 'Tell me everything.'

He seems to have recovered from the shock of finding me now. He seems perfectly calm. He says, 'Why don't we go downstairs and talk about this?'

But I don't want to be brushed off. 'No! Just tell me. Tell me everything, from the beginning.'

He sighs again. 'From the beginning,' he says. 'Who knows when it all started, really? Maybe it was the night of the New Year's Eve party. Perhaps much earlier than that. When we got married, or even the day we first met. Where do you want me to begin?'

I start to sift through the recollections that I have already recovered. I have remembered a lot. I remember the events he talks about – our first meeting, our early days together as students. I see now that our relationship was stormy from the very beginning. But there were moments of tenderness too, like the time we first made love. Adam is watching my face carefully as I try to make sense of it all.

What I need to know most was what happened in the red room. I look around at my surroundings properly for the first time since arriving. The room is long and narrow, stretching from the front of the house to the rear, but with a sloping ceiling making it feel smaller than its footprint. A single roof window lights the rear half, but the front has been opened up into a proper dormer window, giving it an open aspect.

The room is comfortably furnished, with a table, some chairs, and shelving on the walls with more books arranged along them. According to Adam, the furniture had been thrown around the room when he found me here. I look at the windows where he said the curtains had been torn down. There is a curtain rail above them, but no curtains. The details fit his version of events, and yet…

'This is the red room, isn't it?' I ask.

He nods.

'You told me you found me here when you returned home from work one evening,' I say. 'But that's not true, is it?'

'Jane...' he begins.

'Victoria! My name is Victoria.'

'All right. Victoria.'

'Tell me what really happened.'

He places the glass vase he's been carrying on the desk and sits down in one of the chairs. 'It was the night of your company's New Year's Eve office party,' he says. 'They hired the top floor of a swanky new skyscraper overlooking the Thames. There was champagne, dancing... you know the sort of thing.' The way he says it, I know that he must have hated that party. Adam always did hate crowds. Not me. I loved being the centre of attention.

'I remember it,' I say. 'I remember the party.'

'You do?' he says, surprised. Then a dark look crosses his face. 'What do you remember, exactly?'

I close my eyes and let the memory flow. The last strains of *Auld Lang Syne* come to a close, followed by a loud chorus of cheering. Adam takes my arm. 'Come on,' he says. 'Let's get out of here.'

I let him lead me out of the party, but not before saying goodbye to everyone. Adam is impatient to leave, but I can't just disappear into the night.

A taxi is waiting outside, its engine idling in the cold night. Adam arranged it earlier. We climb in together. 'That was fun,' I say.

'If you say so, darling. As long as you enjoyed it.'

I smile at him. 'I did. And thank you for coming. I know how you hate these things.'

'Well, there was certainly a reason to celebrate this year, with your new promotion,' he says.

'Are you pleased for me?' I ask. 'Really?'

'Of course,' he says. 'You know that all I want is for you to be happy. That's all I've ever wanted.' The sincerity in his voice and in his eyes is crystal clear.

I know in that moment that I can trust Adam after all. I open my eyes and look at him here and now in the red room, trying to trace the lines that have appeared around his eyes and across his forehead in the seven years that have passed since that moment. I can still see the man I married, the man I loved so much, and it is very hard for me to distrust him.

'I remember everything,' I tell him. 'I remember being on top of the world that night. I'd just been promoted, hadn't I?'

'Yes,' he confirms. His voice is tinged with sadness. 'It's what you'd always wanted. A glittering career. One of the things you wanted, at least. You always wanted so many things.'

'But what happened then, Adam? What happened after the party?'

'You don't remember?' he says.

I close my eyes, but the memory of leaving the party in the taxi with Adam won't come back. It has stopped at that moment, and I can't recall what happened next.

I open my eyes again and shake my head.

'The taxi brought us home,' he says. 'I went into the kitchen and you went upstairs. You came here, to the red room.'

'The red room? By myself? Why?'

'You often did,' he says. 'When you were feeling sad or needed time alone, you used to come here and lock yourself inside. This was always your room, never mine.'

'But why was I feeling sad, Adam? At the party, I was happy. We both were, weren't we?'

He won't meet my gaze. 'We had a disagreement in the taxi. An argument. You needed to cool off. Or so I thought.'

'What do you mean by that?' I ask him. I don't remember arguing with him that night, but I have remembered other occasions when we did. It's clear to me that though we were very much in love, our relationship didn't always run smoothly. Perhaps Adam had been jealous that my career was taking off in such a big way.

He still won't look at me. 'I was pouring myself a drink. Then I heard a noise from upstairs. Screams. The sound of some heavy object being thrown. Furniture being turned over. It was coming from the red room.'

I shudder at his description of events. 'What happened then?'

'I ran upstairs. And that's when I found you. Here, locked inside the red room.'

'Doing what? What had happened to me?'

He looks at me mournfully and shakes his head.

He has told me about this moment so many times before. About finding me in the red room. How he unlocked the door and discovered a scene of violence. I have imagined it so many times that I almost think I can remember it. The overturned desk. The ripped curtains. The books scattered over the floor. The key in the door.

My mouth feels suddenly dry.

I glance up at the door. There is no key on this side of the door. When I entered, the key was on the other side.

If Adam unlocked the door from outside that night, how could I have locked myself in?

He sees me looking at the lock. He sees what I have realised. His face hardens.

'Adam, you told me I was locked inside the red room.'

He nods.

'How could I have locked myself in if the key was on the outside?'

He doesn't answer my question.

'Adam,' I say at last. 'You locked me in the red room, didn't you?'

Eventually, slowly, he nods. 'Yes,' he admits. 'I did.'

My heart is racing now and cold beads of sweat form on my brow.

'There never was an intruder in the house, was there?' I

say. 'Everything you told me about discovering signs of a break-in was a lie, wasn't it?'

'Yes,' he concedes. 'It was a lie. It was only the two of us here that night, Jane. Just you and me.' He is sitting in the chair by the desk, the heavy vase at his hand. He is between me and the door. I could not escape, however quickly I moved. I search the room for an object I could use to defend myself from him. The only potential weapon I can see is the glass vase on the desk.

He sees what I am looking at and curls his fingers around the vase, holding it tight. 'Jane...' he begins.

Downstairs, the doorbell rings. Adam regards me uncertainly.

'Were you expecting a visitor?' I ask him.

A voice calls, perhaps through the letterbox. It's Diana. 'Jane!' she shouts. 'Jane, are you in there?'

'You brought them here!' Adam accuses, his eyes narrowing. 'You brought those women to my house.'

I can hardly believe my luck. But what on earth are they doing here?

'Wait here,' he says. 'I'll deal with this.' He slips back out through the door, taking the glass vase with him. Before I can follow him, the door bangs shut and I hear the key turn in the lock.

I run to the door and struggle with the handle, but it refuses to turn. He's locked me in. Again. I pound my fists against the door and kick it with my foot. 'Let me out!' I scream. But I hear his heavy tread descending the staircase.

Downstairs, the front door opens and I hear voices. I bang harder on the door and scream loudly. Surely they must hear the noise I'm making. I pause and listen carefully, but I can't hear anything.

I rush instead to the window that looks out onto the street and slap my hands against the glass. With a mounting sense of urgency I look for a way to open the window, but it is a modern double-glazed unit with a lock. I cannot see a key anywhere.

'Help!' I shout. 'Call the police! I am being held prisoner!'

It's no use. I turn and rush back towards the door. I pick up a chair, hoping to use it as a ram to batter the door, but I slip and fall. The leg of the chair catches my side and I crash onto the floor winded.

I touch my skin and my hand comes away red.

No! It is happening again, just as before.

I lie on the floor, staring at the blood on my hand. The metallic smell assaults my senses. With a rush I am transported back to that night long ago. The smell is the same. The room is the same. There is blood everywhere: on my hands, on my face, on my body. The very walls seem to be dripping with blood. Broken and splintered furniture lies all around me. Thrown books, the torn fabric of the curtains. And my red dress, ripped from the neckline to the waist.

The past and present have merged, and I can no longer tell them apart. I scream, and everything turns black.

CHAPTER 35

I feel hands pulling at me, turning me over. A voice mumbles something in my ear.

Cold daylight smarts my eyes. It's too bright to open them fully.

Hands touch me again and I cry out. My scream sounds muffled, like it's coming from another room. Or another person. Or another time.

But the pain is mine. My side burns, and I remember falling onto the upturned chair. I remember the blood on my hands.

'Jane.' The voice is distant and indistinct.

My eyes flicker open but I can't take in my surroundings. Everything is blurred.

'Jane. You're awake.' That voice again.

I am lying on my back staring up at the ceiling. Red walls close in around me and I feel hot and flustered. I wave my arms in front of me. 'Get away from me!' I shout. 'Leave me alone!'

'It's all right, Jane. No one is going to hurt you.'

The voice is not Adam's. It's a woman's voice.

My vision clears and I see Bridget kneeling beside me, a concerned look on her face. Cath is next to her.

'What happened?' I ask.

'We think that you must have fallen over a chair and fainted. There's a little bleeding, but nothing serious. Just lie still and you should be all right.'

I don't understand what's happening. 'What are you doing here?' I ask.

Diana's voice answers me from behind. 'We waited for you at King's Cross,' she says, stepping forward so I can see her. 'When you didn't show up at the agreed time, we came straight here.'

'But how did you know where to find me?'

'We guessed. We spent most of the afternoon thinking about you, to be honest. I don't think any of us was paying much attention to *The Mousetrap*. You'd told Bridget the street where Adam lived in London, so this seemed like the most obvious place. We had to knock on a few doors before we found the right house.'

'But Adam…' Fear clutches at me. If Adam is here, the women are in danger.

He looms into view, standing behind Bridget and Cath. 'I'm here, Jane.' He seems agitated, but that is understandable, I suppose. His hands are empty. Whatever he did with the glass vase, he no longer has it with him. He doesn't seem to be acting aggressively. He looks more frightened than anything.

'Adam let us in and brought us up here,' says Bridget.

'Although he still hasn't explained why he locked you in,' says Diana, and her tone suggests that he had better have a good reason.

I push myself up to see better.

Bridget tries to stop me. 'Just stay where you are for now, Jane.'

But I won't stay here on the floor. I need to see what is going on. With Bridget's help I manage to get up and sit on the other chair next to the desk.

'So why did you lock me in here, Adam?' I say.

He looks sheepish. 'I'm sorry. I shouldn't have done

that. I was just disconcerted by the doorbell ringing and I didn't want you to leave.'

Diana regards him sternly. 'I think you'd better tell us exactly what's going on here.'

Adam turns to me. 'Is that you want, Jane?' he asks. 'Do you want me to tell them?'

'My name isn't Jane. It's Victoria.' No one says anything to that, so I continue. 'Seven years ago, Adam faked my death and took me away from London to live in Yorkshire. He hid me away in a tiny village and told everyone there that my name was Jane. And I didn't know, because I had forgotten.'

Cath's hand flies to her mouth, stifling a gasp.

They all stare at me in shock and disbelief. My story must sound utterly crazy, I realise.

'He faked your death?' says Cath incredulously.

'And claimed the insurance money,' I add.

Cath looks to Diana for guidance. I can read the doubt on her face.

'Tell them!' I shout at Adam. 'Tell them that it's true!'

The three women turn to Adam. I can tell they don't know what to believe. It would be easy for them to think that I am completely mad after all. I have given them plenty of reason to doubt me, and this must look like yet another delusion. My behaviour today must seem completely inexplicable and irrational.

Adam remains mute and I can see the doubt and worry etched on the women's faces. They probably think I am having a nervous breakdown. I can see how this might end – with me being led away to the hospital by men in white coats.

'Tell them!' I shout at him again. I feel that I will hit him if he does not say something.

When he does eventually speak, his voice is quiet and subdued. It is little more than a whisper. 'It's true,' he says. 'Everything that Jane... that Victoria said. It's all true.'

I breathe a sigh of relief. They *have* to believe me now.

Diana says, 'We've heard enough. We have to go to the police. This is a serious matter.'

'No,' says Adam abruptly. 'You don't understand. You don't know why I did it. I was only acting in Jane's – Victoria's – best interests. You have to understand that.'

Bridget turns back to me, her face full of confusion. 'Buy why did he do that?' she asks. 'And how could you have forgotten who you really were?'

'Because of the red room,' I say. But that is not a reason. I still don't know what happened to me in here all those years ago. Adam still hasn't told me and I feel a kind of cold hatred towards him. 'What did you do to me in here?' My voice is like a growl. I push myself up out of the chair and throw myself at him with fists flying, pounding at his chest. A shriek falls from my lips. 'What did you do?'

He stands still, letting me pummel him and slap him. Bridget and Cath manage to pull me away from him and carry me back to the chair. I sit there panting, waiting for him to respond.

'I didn't do anything,' he says flatly. 'I didn't do anything to you.'

I scream. I stare at him, not believing what I am hearing. 'You are lying again!'

'No. It's the truth,' he says. 'We had an argument in the taxi on the way home from the party. We often did argue. It was part of our relationship, right from the very beginning. Perhaps we should never have married, I don't know. We loved each other passionately, but sometimes we hated each other too.' He shrugs. 'I didn't know what to do about it. Anyway, when we returned home that night, you came upstairs to the red room, like you often did after we fought. It was your refuge.'

He stops.

'What then?' I demand. 'What did you do to me then?'

'I didn't do anything, Jane. Victoria. Honestly. You became violent. You'd been violent once or twice before, but never anything like this. You turned over that desk.'

He indicates the desk where I am sitting now. 'You smashed chairs against the wall. You ripped the curtains into shreds. You even threw all of your books onto the floor.'

I am shaking my head at his words. 'No, you're lying. I didn't do any of those things.'

In response, a single tear runs down his cheek.

I get to my feet again. 'This is a lie!' I accuse. 'You locked me in here!'

'I was frightened, Jane. I locked you in because I was scared of you. When I came up the stairs you threw a vase at me. It was the vase my father gave us on our wedding day. You'd always loved that vase. You threw it straight at my head. The glass shattered and flew everywhere.'

I sit down again, my legs shaking. 'I didn't,' I say feebly.

'You did, Jane,' he insists. 'You hit me. Just like you did a moment ago. You scratched at my face until you drew blood. I locked you in here for my own protection. I hoped that you'd cool off after a minute.'

Now I am scared. I am scared he is telling the truth. I look uncertainly at the women for support, but they are frowning. I can tell that they don't know what to believe.

But I already know that Adam is telling the truth. I turn back to him, willing him to tell me something that will lessen the shock of what he is saying. 'But the blood? My hands were covered in blood. My hands, my face, my dress. It wasn't just from scratching your face. It was my own blood.'

Adam seems reluctant to say any more. But he has no choice. The truth must come out at last. 'You did that to yourself, Jane, after I locked you in. If I had known what you would do, I would never have locked the door.'

And now I remember. And it was exactly like he said.

I am in the red room. I am Victoria. And I am furious.

So mad I can hardly think. My mind is filled with hate. Hate for Adam, who has locked me in. A red rage has taken hold of me, and there is nothing else but that.

I pound my fists against the locked door, shrieking his name.

I kick the door as hard as I can, but it will not yield.

I scratch at the wooden panels, drawing blood from my own fingernails.

I can hear his breathing on the other side of the door. 'Victoria?'

'Let me out!' I scream.

'Not until you've calmed down.'

But I will not calm down. And if I cannot get at him to hurt him, then I will hurt myself instead.

My fingers take hold of my dress. The beautiful red dress that I love so much. My fingers flex and I pull as hard as I can.

The soft fabric rips, tearing from the neckline almost to the waist. The violent rending sound is like music to my ears. I scratch at my exposed skin with my red-painted nails. My flesh does not tear like the dress, but scarlet stripes appear on my body. Drops of blood begin to fly.

And now the fury consumes me utterly. I am about to do something so terrible that my mind has hidden it from me for seven years. I cannot face it, even now. The vision blacks out, saving me from seeing it unfold. My bloody fingers are frozen in time, as my eyes bulge in horror.

'Jane?' The voice brings me out of my nightmare. 'Jane? Do you remember?' It is Adam's voice, calm after the madness of my vision.

I nod, mutely. He told me the truth. I harmed myself because I could not hurt him. I can barely understand the feelings that animated me that dreadful night. I think I must have been truly mad.

Adam continues. 'When I heard the sounds and realised what you were doing, I unlocked the door immediately. But I was too late.'

Too late. Too late for what?

'I opened the door, and there you were,' he says. 'You were lying on the floor, curled into a ball. I don't know exactly how you'd done it, but there was blood everywhere. Your dress was ripped in half and soaked in blood. It was on your face, in your hair… and then I saw it.'

He stops.

'What?' I ask. 'What did you see?'

The tears are flowing down his cheeks now, unchecked. 'The baby,' he says, at last.

The baby.

I shake my head, not understanding.

What baby?

I do not want to understand.

My baby.

Adam looks at me with a mixture of pity and disgust. 'Don't you remember?' he asks. 'You were pregnant, Victoria. You were expecting a baby.'

'No,' I say weakly. 'It's not possible.' But deep down I know that it is the truth.

'You made yourself lose our baby,' continues Adam, hammering the horrible truth home. 'You gave yourself a miscarriage.'

A pitiful wail escapes from my mouth and suddenly I am back in the taxi with Adam. We are heading home after the party.

The sudden sense of happiness is almost overwhelming. This is the best night of my life, because it's not only the promotion I'm celebrating tonight. I have other news that I haven't yet shared with Adam.

I take hold of his hand in the back of the taxi. 'I have something else to tell you,' I say. 'It's even better news than my promotion.'

'What can that be?' he asks.

'Can't you guess?'

He looks at me quizzically. 'You surely don't mean…?'

'Yes,' I cry. 'I'm pregnant! We're going to have a baby, Adam!'

His reaction takes me unawares. I'm expecting him to

embrace me, maybe even shed some tears of joy. I know that this is something he's wanted for so long. But he doesn't respond in the way I'd anticipated. 'I don't understand,' he says flatly.

'What don't you understand? I'm having a baby and you're the father. It's what we always dreamed of.'

His lips break into a tentative smile at last, but his eyes still show confusion. 'But what about the promotion? You told your boss you were going to accept it.'

'I am,' I say. Now I'm the one who's confused. 'What's the problem? I thought you'd be happy.'

Adam's voice is cold now. 'But what about the baby? How can you continue with your career and have a baby too? What are you thinking, Victoria?'

'We can use professional childcare,' I say. 'There's a really good crèche close to the office. And we could hire a nanny. We can afford it. You know we can.'

Adam stares at me for a moment. Then he suddenly explodes in rage. 'You can't do that!' he shouts. 'Being a mother is a full-time job. I thought I'd made that perfectly clear!' He is frightening me with his anger.

'Don't be silly,' I say.

The cab driver looks up. 'Everything all right, back there?' he says.

'Yes,' growls Adam. 'We can talk about this at home.'

We spend the rest of the taxi ride in simmering silence.

The memory jumps ahead.

I try to stop it, but it is like a rollercoaster that I cannot escape from.

I am in the red room again, and the blood is flowing freely. Blood, blood and more blood. Far too much blood. It is coming mostly from between my legs.

The door bursts open and Adam rushes in. He sees me and stops. His eyes grow wide with horror. 'Victoria!' he says. 'Oh my darling, what have you done?'

I don't know what I've done.

I look at what he is looking at. On the floor beside me.

A bloody mess.

A bloody mess that was once my baby. That might have been a child.

It is too much. My mind cannot process the vision. It was too much before, and it is still too much seven years on.

I black it out before it kills me.

CHAPTER 36

It is all out in the open now, and I would do anything to undo the events of this day.

Once I was afraid that Adam was keeping a madwoman in his attic. Now I know that he really was. The madwoman was me.

I demanded the truth. Little did I know that Adam had hidden it from me in order to protect me.

He is explaining the rest of his actions now. 'I cleaned you up as best I could,' he says. I carried you to the bathroom and bathed you. You were barely conscious. You didn't seem to know where you were or what had happened. It was only later that I discovered that you really didn't know what you had done. You had forgotten everything. You didn't even know who you were.'

I am sitting in the lounge downstairs. Bridget has made me a cup of sweet tea. I hold it in my hands, not drinking, not saying anything. The others are watching me closely. I expect they think I might do something crazy. Maybe I will. I can't trust myself right now.

'I freely admit that I panicked,' continues Adam. 'What could I do? I had no one to ask for advice. You were almost incapable of speech, and certainly couldn't help me in any way. I wanted to get away from here as quickly as I could. So I bundled some things into the car and drove through the night. I didn't even stop at a service station. I drove until we arrived at the cottage. Then I carried you upstairs to the bedroom and left you sleeping. You slept for days, on and off. You wouldn't eat a thing. You hardly spoke a word. I had to make you drink water to keep you alive. And gradually I began to formulate a plan.'

His explanation makes perfect sense to me now. What else could he have done?

'Why didn't you take Jane – I mean, Victoria – to the hospital?' asks Bridget.

Adam shrugs. 'I don't really know. I suppose that I ought to have done. But the bleeding quickly stopped and she seemed all right.' His face pales at the memory. 'She wasn't all right. But neither was I. You must understand that. I was in a state of shock. My only thought was to get her away from here. It was only afterwards that I began to think clearly about the future.'

'But why did you decide to fake her death?' demands Diana.

'It was an extreme response,' admits Adam. 'I know that. I ran through all the options first. There were others that might seem more logical. But that was the one I kept returning to. You must understand, Victoria had forgotten everything. I had to explain that I was her husband, that this was our cottage. I couldn't bring myself to tell her what had happened. She was too fragile. And so I decided to draw a line under the past and to begin our relationship again. I told her what she needed to hear – that she was loved, that she didn't need to worry about anything, and that I would always look after her. I told her that she was a good person.'

He looks directly at me now. 'It was a kindness, you see, Jane. I erased your past so that you would never have to face up to what you'd done. I removed all the problems that had dogged our relationship, so that we could be happy together. You understand that, don't you?'

I gaze at him, barely understanding anything. My mind is still filled with the horror of discovery.

Adam continues telling the women what he did. 'After a few days, Jane seemed well enough to be left alone for a short while, and so I returned to London. It was fortunate that it was still the Christmas holiday and neither I nor Jane were expected back at work. So I cleaned the house, removing all the broken items and putting everything back as it should have been. I lifted the carpet in the red room and burned it. I was pretty confident that I'd removed all traces of blood. Then I went to the boathouse where she kept her boat, and I put it in the river. I left it a few hours, then phoned the police and reported her missing. They searched the river and found the boat. In the following days they dredged the river, but they didn't find anything.'

'So you lived a double life,' says Cath incredulously. 'In London and in the village.'

'Yes,' says Adam. 'It was incredibly hard at first. I couldn't leave Jane alone for any period of time, but I had to be in London to keep up appearances. Fortunately, the office was very understanding. They allowed me nearly two months of compassionate leave. It was enough for me to restore some kind of routine.'

'Didn't you worry that Jane would remember what had happened?' asks Bridget.

'Of course. I've spent every day for the past seven years worrying. But I don't regret a thing. After the accident she was a different person. Calmer. More contented. She's been happier these past seven years than she ever was before.'

No one seems to know what to say to that.

I hear my own voice break the silence. 'What happened to my baby?' My voice is hard and brittle, barely more than a whisper.

'It was a girl,' says Adam. 'A tiny baby girl. She was so small. You wouldn't believe how tiny she was. She wasn't even as big as a palm.'

My eyes sting as they fill with bitter tears for what was lost without me even knowing. 'Where is she?' I ask. 'What did you do with her?'

'I buried her in the garden at the cottage,' says Adam. 'I can show you where she is, if you like.'

CHAPTER 37

A month has passed since I discovered the truth about the red room. At first I was unable to process the information. I wished more than anything to turn back the clock and return to a state of ignorance. That's what I did in the aftermath of the red room seven years ago. My mind walled off the reality that it could not face and left me with a clean slate to start again. It wasn't Adam who erased my identity. His fault was only in giving me a new one, an identity of his choosing. But knowing what I now know, can I truly blame him for that?

My memories continue to return, slowly, one at a time. I am sitting quietly in a chair and I remember an event from my childhood, or from my university days. Yesterday I remembered my wedding day. I relived it again, seeing Charles, Adam's best man, and my two bridesmaids, Carrie and Maddy. That was the happiest day of my life. I wish I could rewind my life to that day and start over again, my whole future ahead of me.

I wonder where Carrie and Maddy and Charles are now. Adam says he doesn't know. He cut off all ties with friends and family the day that Victoria died. He couldn't risk any links with the past that might one day catch him out. I realise that he has made sacrifices too.

On a bright spring day in March, with the crocuses in full bloom and the daffodils just beginning to open, we gather in the garden at the cottage for a small ceremony of remembrance for our lost daughter. We have decided, Adam and I, to name her Rose. Ben says a few words about Rose being in the arms of God, and Diana reads a poem, *Do not stand at my grave and weep*, which has everyone reaching for their handkerchiefs and dabbing their eyes. Adam bows his head and I see a tear drop to the ground. I realise that Adam has shouldered this loss alone for the past seven years. I reach for his hand and hold it tight. At the end of the ceremony, Adam digs a hole and we plant a rose bush which will bloom with bright pink roses in the summer. Then we go back inside and tuck in to the chocolate cake that Cath made that morning.

Bridget's bump is just beginning to show. She says that she can't stop eating, she's so hungry all the time, and Cath says it's bound to be a boy in that case. Boys eat you out of house and home, apparently, even before they're born. And just wait until they're teenagers. Everyone laughs, and I join in too. Adam lays a protective hand on my shoulder and gives it a squeeze. We've decided to go for fertility treatment. I was pregnant once, so there's no reason to believe it can't happen again. He couldn't risk letting a gynaecologist examine me before in case the truth about my miscarriage was discovered. Now that fear is gone. And at thirty-eight I'm not yet too old to have children.

I've had a lot of processing to do over the last month. I know now, and not just because Adam has told me, that my parents really are dead and I never had any brothers or sisters.

But the biggest decision I've had to face has been about my future. At first the choice seemed to be binary. On the one hand, I could go to the police, tell them about Adam's fraudulent behaviour and reclaim my life as Victoria. I could even return to London and try to get back into advertising. And there were moments when this felt like the right thing to do. On the other hand, I could stay as Jane and continue the life I've led for the past seven years.

I spent many hours traipsing across the moors, or sitting in the solitude of the church, contemplating my decision.

In the end, I realised that there was a third way. Victoria was a temperamental, ambitious woman, obsessed with her own career and her own success. Jane was a timid, retiring creature who kept herself hidden away doing the household chores. But when I look at Diana, Bridget, and even Cath, I see women who are happy in their own skin, leading fulfilling lives, with happy marriages, and I want to be like them.

The village is my home now. Adam will always be the love of my life. But I will get a car and find a job in a nearby town. And we will open our home up to our friends. Adam is already talking about hosting a summer barbecue in the garden.

And my name?

I have grown to like the name Jane. Like my literary namesake I used to see myself as *poor, obscure, plain and little*. But I have come to realise that, like her, I am *a free human being, with an independent will*.

And I choose this life with Adam.

THANK YOU FOR READING

If you enjoyed this book, please leave a short review at
Amazon or Goodreads. Thank you!

ABOUT THE AUTHOR

M S Morris is the pseudonym of the writing
partnership of authors Margarita and Steve Morris. The
couple are married and live in Oxfordshire.

Find out more at msmorrisbooks.com where you can
join our mailing list.

Made in the USA
Las Vegas, NV
04 July 2023

74233249R00142